Habit of a Foreign Sky

Habit of a Foreign Sky

Published in Hong Kong by Haven Books Ltd

www.havenbooksonline.com

ISBN 978-988-18967-2-8

The author credits lyrics of the following songs, which are cited in part: "Fly Me to the Moon" (formerly, "In Other Words"), music and lyrics by Bart Howard, 1954; "Autumn in New York", music and lyrics by Vernon Duke, 1934; "The Song from Moulin Rouge" (*a.k.a.* "Where Is Your Heart?"), music by Georges Auric and lyrics (English version) by William Engvick, 1952.

Advance Praise for *Habit of a Foreign Sky*

"Xu Xi has a kaleidoscopic gaze and turns this to dazzling effect on each of the characters she explores. In part a sassy, fast-paced love story, in others a moving exploration of a Chinese/American daughter's relationship to her past; this accomplished, playful and graceful novel shows how swiftly life can change, or seem to, depending on where you stand."

—Jill Dawson, bestselling author of *The Great Lover*

"*Habit of a Foreign Sky* by Xu Xi is, in my opinion, an indispensable work of contemporary fiction by an important novelist at the height of her powers. A global narrative set against the background of financial upheaval in Asia, with a sophisticated female protagonist at the centre, the novel takes readers behind the scenes in a world that many of us have participated in only from the outside. It finely charts the shifting and ambiguous professional and emotional allegiances of a woman's journey through the high-flying world of international finance at a time of transition for Hong Kong. Personal loss and the shadows of the past compete with the momentum of moving forward. This gives the tale the Jamesian complexity of subtle moral and material conflicts and makes for a compelling, seductive reading experience.

Xu Xi writes lucidly and evocatively, from real knowledge and wisdom, and with a thrilling feel for the human drama at every turn. Her book is movingly intimate and exhilaratingly grand in ways that have strong appeal for me and for my colleagues on the Man Asia Prize jury."

—Nicholas Jose, Australian author and
Man Asian Literary Prize judge

"Xu Xi draws us into lives lived under more than one foreign sky, where we discover that the sorrows and satisfactions of family, of work and desire are similar no matter where they're lived out. At the center of her novel is a riveting character whose contradictions and longing to be her own woman make her fascinating to watch as she struggles for integrity. Whether she's transacting business or hoping for a love worth pursuing in Hong Kong or America, she's recognizable, daunting and beautifully drawn."

—Rosellen Brown, bestselling author
of *Before and After*

"In this smart, eloquent, cosmopolitan novel, Xu Xi breathtakingly traverses the globe to explore the intersections of love and desire, race and class, business and banking, and, above all, the haunting legacies of family and home. *Habit of a Foreign Sky* is a scintillating accomplishment."

—Don Lee, award-winning author
of *Yellow* and *Wrack and Ruin*

"Immersed in the trans-Pacific lives of those living in and between Hong Kong and New York, Xu Xi's new novel provides startling insights into their delicate yet hardened personae, flying alone and together."

—Alex Kuo, American Book Award winner
for *Lipstick and Other Stories*

Habit of a Foreign Sky

Xu Xi

For my mother "[illegible]" Kim, the flower of Tji[illegible],
and her sister Caroline Phoa (Auntie Auyin), who taught

For the women in my life, but especially,
Sanny Talbot Wood and Cheryl Welkley Wong

And for the "old girls" of MCS class of 1970

Away from Home are some and I—
An Emigrant to be
In a Metropolis of Homes
Is easy, possibly—

The Habit of a Foreign Sky
We—difficult—acquire
As Children, who remain in Face
The more their Feet retire

Emily Dickinson (1894)

Nor shall Death brag thou wander'st in his shade,
When in eternal lines to time thou grow'st

Sonnet No. 18
William Shakespeare

Part One

Hong Kong to New York New York Hong Kong

(or HKG–JFK RT)

1

Her maid, Conchita, told her.

The call from Hong Kong woke Gail in New York at three a.m. For once, she was silenced, unable to pass judgment.

"Ma'am?" For a second, Conchita wondered if her mistress had fainted, but decided that no, it was the shock. "The police said she probably died the moment the bus hit her." She paused. "She must have."

An image of her mother, flung into the air and slammed against a wall—*horrific*—yet even now, Gail's temper threatened to erupt. She checked herself, doing her best to stick to the facts. First unexplainable fact: her mother had crossed the harbor over to Kowloon which surely was an unnecessary journey. Taking a deep breath, she said in a quiet voice. "But why was she in Kowloon City, or even crossing Tokwawan Road? Everyone knows the traffic's dangerous around there with all the trucks."

Conchita heard the familiar intake of air. "I'm so sorry, ma'am." Then, she began to weep as the confession flowed. "It was all my fault because she said she wanted to go out when I was cleaning the bathroom. I told her to wait, said I'd accompany her. But when I came out of the bathroom, she was gone, and even though I ran out after her, she had disappeared already."

There was a silence.

Gail pressed her wrist against the back of her neck. The

persistent headache of the last two days was migrating downwards. She wanted to shout across the world—*How could you? Why didn't you …* but the words froze in her throat.

And then, Gail heard her maid's sobs. Wrenching. Unceasing. *Sincere,* and this touched her. The choked voice continued. "I'm very sorry, ma'am, very, very sorry. Please don't be angry with me. God will punish me forever. Forever. If you want me to leave right now I'll go. I'm so sorry, ma'am."

"It's okay, Conchita. It's not your fault," Gail said. The real responsibility was hers, she knew. "Thank you for calling. I'll be back Sunday on the usual flight," and hung up.

Clutching the receiver, Conchita, still crying, crossed herself.

Gail opened the curtains and leant her tall frame against the pane. Through the dark, there was a distinct outline of the World Financial Center, which housed her employer's headquarters across the West Highway. She wanted to cry but couldn't. Her thoughts skittered between life and work. Yesterday, at the end of an exhaustingly long day, nerves shot, she had started to call Gu Kwun and stopped herself abruptly. She had cried then, sobbed, because her late son was no longer her responsibility, sobbing because she knew that despite time and its assurance of healing, his loss would always burn her heart. Yesterday, when she should have been flying home, instead of sleeping at the Marriott, but hadn't because of yet another round of meetings.

And now this.

Yet right now, sitting on the king-sized bed, surrounded by the anonymity of her business travel life, she did not know how to feel about the death of a mother whose very existence often plagued her, this woman who still was a stranger. Happy? Of course not. How could she possibly be happy at her mother's horrible death! Relief? Gail did not allow even a whisper of this into her mind. She knew she should try to sleep but the very thought of sleep set her on edge. This mother, this foreign presence who always elicited such emotional turmoil, was gone, just like that. This woman whose life was so surreal, so unlike her own, a life that Gail tried to forget, to dismiss, to eradicate from her own reality.

Over the next few hours she sat, unmoving, trying to arrest the sensation—*was it panic, this frightening calm?*—that threatened to knock her off balance.

Eventually a pale orange light dissolved the dark to reveal a clear and pristine sky.

Promptly at six, Gail's wake-up call rang. She slammed the phone down so hard the receiver cracked.

Later, she offered to pay for the damage.

The front desk receptionist stopped his flurry of checkout activity. "I beg your pardon, Ms. Szeto?" The way he said it sounded like "Zedo".

"I broke your phone. Please charge the damage to my bill."

"Oh, I …"

"Please, just hurry. I'll sign an open receipt against my credit card if you want. I have to catch my flight." In the midst of her sorrow, she wondered about covering this unusual charge on expenses.

"But I don't know … I mean, we have to check …"

"Trust me, it's broken." Her voice sharp and a bit too loud.

He was miffed now, unrelenting. "I understand, but this is so unusual that …"

"Just do it, okay?" She shouted across the air at his smug countenance. The knuckles of her right hand, jammed against the counter, went white.

A supervisor hurried over. "What appears to be the problem here?"

Gail glared at the row of suited staff behind the counter. *Her last family in the world was gone.* They should understand and let her out of this city where she hadn't wanted to remain an extra night. She wanted to scream at their flustered incompetence, at their inability to handle anything slightly out of the ordinary.

Instead, she removed her sunglasses and looked the receptionist in the eye. "I was rude. I apologize." Then, she explained the charge problem to the supervisor, who made her wait another ten minutes before it was resolved.

In the executive lounge at JFK, Gail switched off her cell phone.

Surely this once she could be forgiven. The truth was, no one rang when she was in transit—not family, Conchita, office staff, her boss or New York—since she always thoroughly communicated her schedule. Gail's habit of remaining perpetually "on call" was perhaps to reassure herself that at forty-six, as the Asia-Pacific VP for Northeast Trust, an investment bank specializing in asset securitized corporate financing, she was indispensable. *You're worse than a doctor,* her mother often complained. *And people need doctors.*

Yet now, if only ... if only *she* could call someone. But whom?

Gordie's laughter resounded, raising her mother from the dead as their laughing voices merged. No, not him. Her half brother wasn't *real* family, so he could wait. Jason Chak, her ex ... a flash of anger whipped Gail. How angry she still was now, six years later, at his desertion, his betrayal, with a mere secretary at that! Her son's death photo filtered through memory. Why had everyone, all her family, deserted her?

Irrational demons! Irrational pain! Her head throbbed.

Gail directed her gaze at the row of planes, forcing her focus on their orderly formation at the gates. The pain subsided.

From immediately behind her, a voice snapped, "Kina, don't go running off now."

A girl ran into her vicinity and stopped. Her light brown hair was Caucasian curly, but her complexion and features Asian, most likely Chinese. Gail always found it easy to pick out others like herself, and in this girl the mixed blood was obvious.

"Hi," said the girl, who stared curiously. She waved at Gail with a shy smile.

Gail waved back. "Hi."

The child looked like a waif, hair uncombed, smudged face. Her old-fashioned frock, a pale pink cotton print with puffed sleeves, was too tight for her small frame. She gazed at Gail. "Are you blind?"

The girl's father hurried over and took the child's hand. "I apologize for her impolite behavior." Then, turning to his daughter, "Come away now and leave the lady alone." His girl could be tiresome. It had been lucky, running into the lounge manager, a friend from way back who let them in. Keeping Kina still, however, as he must here, wasn't easy.

Removing her sunglasses, Gail said, "It's quite alright. She was simply being very logical." She was grateful for the distraction.

"Too much so sometimes." He was looking down at Kina, frowning. Looking up, he was startled by this woman—this lady—who was, no, not beautiful, but striking, despite her exacting expression. Elegant demeanor. Her features, chiseled, prominent cheekbones, finely formed lips, the tapered, stylish haircut displayed a well shaped head. A sculptor's *rêve,* a lust-dream.

He held out his hand. "I'm Xavier Dopoulos, by the way." He pronounced his first name French style, the X a softened Z, instead of the English "savior."

She did not at first extend her hand, but did after a pause, and shook his hand. She did not give her name. Gesturing at the seat opposite, he asked, "May we join you?" His slight accent was vaguely European.

Oh yes, Gail wanted to say. Talking to other parents was one of the few pleasures of travel and such rare encounters gave her joy. She liked his manner, and the directness of the girl, although she felt a strange sympathy, almost pity, for her scruffy appearance which seemed out of place in this lounge. But today, Gail didn't trust herself not to break down, not now after the news about her mother. And could she really *not* say, "I once had a little boy," and then have to tell all, forcing him into embarrassed sympathy for a stranger?

Instead, she responded, "I have to board my flight, I'm afraid."

Xavier was disappointed. He would have liked adult company, especially a woman's. She *was* from Hong Kong, he was certain. Her slight awkwardness and appropriately fashionable dress suggested it. Also, despite her being obviously bi-racial, she struck him as very Hong Kong Chinese, sophistication masking a deep-rooted conservatism. With the women, especially, you were never sure of anything. In this case, he might have taken a chance. She wasn't wearing a wedding ring, or any rings, and women like her generally did, along with all the requisite carats.

Gail pulled a pale pink ribbon barrette out of her purse, a gift for her mother, who had liked girlish things. "Here," she held it out to the child. "Something to remember me by."

The girl reached for it greedily, excitedly, while her father demurred. It troubled him a little that Kina took so easily to strangers.

Gail reassured him. "Please, it's nothing. You have a very pretty child."

Kina held the gift up towards her. "Can you help me put it on?" Gail combed her long fingers through the girl's hair, and pinned it into a ponytail. She rubbed a kleenex over Kina's cheek, cleaning off the smudge. The ribbon looked slightly too large on her but matched the pink in her dress.

Xavier smiled. "Thank you, then. It's kind." Turning to the child. "What do you say to this nice lady?"

"*Merci.* Thank you. *Xie xie.*" She curtsied, flashing a charming smile, and pirouetted away, her ponytail bobbing as she turned.

Gail and Xavier laughed at her tri-lingual performance.

Gail awoke, startled, somewhere over the Pacific, from a dream of her half brother. He was an adult and not the boy, but it was without doubt a recurrence of *that* dream. Her watch was not on her wrist—where could it be?—but she guessed, correctly, that Tokyo was about three more hours away.

Years, decades since she'd had that secret dream. She had never told anyone about it, and hadn't had it since the night she met Gordon Ashberry, Gordie, when she was a teenager.

Why had it returned now?

The dream had begun the night of her eighth birthday and recurred, nightly at first, eventually slowing to a few times a week, and then weekly, until it locked in at once a month, for years, like clockwork, taking on a consistency she came to know by heart.

That night, Mom had told her as a "special birthday treat" about Gordie. *You have an American brother, Gay-lo, imagine! He's going to be a pilot just like your father.* Then she showed her a picture of father and son, a twelve-year-old who resembled Gail's Caucasian father—matching green eyes and the same angular jaw—although her brother had lighter hair, pale gold in contrast to their father's brown, and a fairer complexion. *You wait, Gay-lo, one day you'll meet him in your home in America.*

In that first dream, the boy Gordie crouched by her bed and took her hand. "Come fly with me, Gail," he invited. They flew to America, over Hawaii. "Do you have a plane?" she asked. "Somewhere," he replied, laughing. "Won't I fall?" "Hang on to me and you won't." Fearful, she clung tightly.

Eventually, they arrived at a little town next to the Atlantic. A full moon glimmered in the ocean over which they flew. From the sky, he pointed to a row of trees.

"There's our home. Can you see it?"

She peered at the ground below, but nightfall hid it from her. "It's too dark," she told him. "Can we come back in the morning?"

"No problem, Gail," he replied. "Anytime."

Then Gordie laughed, and turned into their father Mark.

No problem.

Now, she stared at the dark over the Pacific. Her eyes were damp, just as they always were as a teenager, whenever she awoke from the dream. She dried them, embarrassed to be crying in a public place. Absurd! Tears for a brother and a father, *chanyan,* these men she despised.

Against the engine's drone, the hours captured her, surrounding her like barbed wire that was safely distant but just close enough to seem like a threat. Gail pulled out her notes from the last meeting. Yet even work failed her and she could not concentrate. Instead, the dream nagged the way her mother's life did. And try as she would, she could not ignore the other nagging sensation, that this accidental death was all her fault because she had left her mother alone yesterday, as well as during those few crucial days before yesterday, when she knew she shouldn't have.

This was all because of the dream. That awful, illogical dream, recurring along some stuck memory loop, forcing remembrance of everything to do with Mom.

Ten days earlier, just days before Chinese New Year and the holidays ahead, New York had called. Another last minute meeting, very important, as they all were, articulated as usual with the hyperbolic urgency of life and death. *I'm really sorry to have to ask but can you go,* her boss had begged, because his own American family were already booked on holiday—a holiday cancelled twice before for work—to Koh Samui, *since the kids are also on break, you know how it is?* Of course she knew how it was, how could she not know how family life worked? She and Gu Kwun and Mom, wouldn't they have been booked also to go somewhere, taking advantage of the three public holidays and respect for family time during this most important time of the year?

But this year and the last, there had been no booking. She could no longer face a vacation without her son.

Her mother understood, wanting only a "crossing the year" dinner on New Year's Eve, perhaps with her old cronies, *could Gail arrange that and take her?* Gail had promised, reckoning it was the least she could do for Mom, though it troubled her to agree, not liking reminders of that life, and her mother was off like a shot, ringing up all those women and the restaurant, planning the menu down to the tiniest detail, but then the summons came, everything had to be cancelled and even though she knew her mother was upset, extremely upset, she had gone anyway. As she tried to tell Mom, *it's not a public holiday in New York; you can't expect them to care about Chinese New Year just because we do. You must understand. This is my job.* To which her mother had flung back that stinging rebuke, about Gail being worse than a doctor, adding, *and since when is your job your life?*

Why couldn't …? The protest cut itself short. She couldn't say no to management, could she? This unexpected trip wasn't her fault. There were no answers to this relentless travel, made worse since the middle of last year because of the economic crisis.

Last year, 1997, had been all about Hong Kong's handover. A pivotal year, said the world's media, because the British were leaving and the Chinese "taking over." Or so Wall Street feared. For Gail and her boss, it was tough enough persuading their investment bank's head office that Hong Kong *wouldn't* shut down on July 1. Instead, it was July 2 that proved pivotal, the day the Thai baht collapsed, followed rapidly by other Asian currencies, precipitating the regional economic crisis. Spreadsheets across the globe which once forecasted strong growth in Asia were shredded and recycled. Perplexed analysts, from Wall Street to Central with its views of the Hong Kong harbor, fell like dominoes, balanced in a game of synchronized collapse.

No more gold to be spun out of straw.

For Gail and her boss, it meant exhausting travel as New York panicked, summoning them both to countless, useless meetings at headquarters. Life turned upside down; twenty-four hours a day across two time zones. On top of her schedule of intra-Asian travel, she virtually lived in the air. Tightening belts and waiting for the inevitable turnaround was not the thing to say. Despite the fact that Hong Kong's currency was pegged to the U.S. dollar, its economy suffered, more perhaps from panic than from a true downturn. Meanwhile across the border on the Mainland, China preened as its economy continued to surge, robust, its currency also firmly linked to America's.

And now here she was again, shuttling, trapped onboard, insulated against the freezing sky. Why hadn't she simply said no, not this time; it's a family holiday, and New York will simply have to understand, because then at least Mom would be alive and Gail could still be part of a family, however small?

As the hours droned along with the engine—time elongated—teasing her mercilessly, there were moments her body felt ready to explode. Inured as she was to long flights and constant travel, this flight prickled every nerve, every muscle, sending impatient spasms to every part of her being. Not till her seat mate said, "Would you mind not moving around so much, I'm trying to sleep," his tone clearly irritated, did she finally settle down, embarrassed by her uncustomary behavior.

In Tokyo, Gail wandered in a daze through the transit relay at Narita, grateful to re-board right away. On the final leg, she picked at dinner, unable to enjoy the wine as she normally did, wanting only to land and dash home.

The flight attendants screwed up disembarkation, allowing several economy passengers off before all of business had exited. Gail fumed, annoyed at their incompetence. She saw Xavier and Kina leaving the economy cabin; why, she wondered, had they been in the business class lounge?

At Arrivals she raced towards Immigration and slid her identity card towards the officer. Toting only a carry-on, she headed straight for Customs and was waved through.

Her limo pick-up was nowhere in sight. It was the second time this had happened recently, she must tell the office to complain. Exasperated, she headed for the taxi stand outside Kai Tak. The queue was long, but it moved rapidly, unlike the slow lines at JFK. Someone jabbed her heel with a cart, propelling her forward. She turned and glared. They ignored her, unapologetic. Mainlanders. Typical. Not worth telling them off.

Climbing into her taxi, she caught a glimpse of the man and his girl at the end of the line. She waved but they didn't see her. Her taxi sped across the harbor tunnelinto the night, back to the safety of home.

2

At home, the eleven-hundred-foot flat felt cavernous. Six years ago, when Jason confessed to an affair with the woman who was now his wife, deserting her and Gu Kwun, this flat became the safe house where everything functioned perfectly. Now, in the middle of the compact living room, Gail wanted to scream. It was too large! She was afraid that this flat, with all its working parts, would also disappear. She knelt, the bag still on her shoulder. Lowering her weight onto her heels she wept, silently, for hours. At four, she pulled herself up. From the doorway of Gu Kwun's room, she gazed at the empty bed, the room long stripped bare of any sign of life. *It's okay, Mother. I know we're lucky you have a job.* Parroting her words, earnestly, wanting to please. He would have only been nine now. Unfair! Exhausted, she lay on the unmade bed and slept.

A knock woke her. "There's a call for you, ma'am." Conchita waited a few seconds for Gail to be conscious. "It's the police. I told them you'd be home this morning." She held out the portable phone.

Uncomprehending, Gail stared at Conchita. Her neck was stiff. She had fallen asleep at an awkward angle on the too-short bed, her long legs dangling against its side. A tingling seized the left half of her body as she sat up, momentarily paralyzed. Then, she snapped to and took the receiver from her maid.

openings and times were announced, thanks to numerous years of dealing with that government office. Otherwise, it might be *several* more days before she could get an opening. He nodded obsequiously, murmuring, *we know Madam Szeto understands about these things, doesn't she,* the expectation of a large tip abundantly clear.

The whole process disgusted Gail.

For a moment, she wondered whether or not to hold the funeral on the Island, in North Point for instance, since that was closer to her home on Stubbs Road. At least, that was where Gail wanted to live when she and Jason returned to Hong Kong. Yet Jason had gone "home" with his new wife to Kowloon where they both grew up, even moving to another hospital on that side of the harbor, just as her mother wanted to return home to Kowloon City. We belong to *dai luk,* the "big continent," her mother used to say, meaning Mainland China, the tiny slice of land at its tip comprising Kowloon peninsula and the New Territories where most of Hong Kong's population resided. In the end, Gail decided it didn't really matter—she too was a Kowloon girl after all—and this was the last thing she could ever do for her mother.

That afternoon, driving home in the underwater harbor tunnel towards the Island, Gail wanted, for one wild second, to crash through the curved metal wall into the sea. All her family, gone. There was no one, *not a single person,* to worry about any longer.

Daylight loomed near at the exit. She gripped the steering wheel, willing control.

Gail was thirteen. Evening darkened the skies over the South China Seas.

Her father was in their home, in the living room, talking to Mom. Straining to hear through closed doors—by now she knew enough to leave them alone when he visited—she heard choked sounds and her mother's voice. *She's touching him,* Gail thought, revolted.

Later, Mom looked in and said, *Uncle Mark is staying the night, so be quiet when you get up for school in the morning.* Why wasn't he leaving, she wanted to know, since he *never* stayed over, and would Mom *please* stop calling her father "uncle" since there wasn't anyone around to hear and this pretence was plain stupid. *Gay-lo,* as Gail cringed at her mother's pidgin, *don't argue with me tonight. There's a war on, don't you know?* As if she didn't know [illegible] *stop trying to speak English already,* she wanted to say but didn't dare, Mom being mean when her father flew in from Connecticut—but what did some dumb war have to do with them anyway? *Your brother Gordon, Gay-lo, he's burnt his draft card. He's made your father very unhappy.* She stared at her mother. What did she mean, what was she talking about? *Never mind, you'll understand when you're older. There's a war on for Americans, Gay-lo. Now, it's become our war too.*

When Gail returned, Conchita switched off the vacuum. Her eyes were red as if she'd been crying all morning. "Your office called. I informed them about what happened." Allowing this to register—her mistress must be very upset, because she obviously had forgotten to call work—she added, "They asked how long you would be out?"

Gail's mind whirled. Of course, she must tell people … it was expected. She must suppress feelings, put aside her selfish emotions. Too little time … only this afternoon and tomorrow before the cremation Wednesday morning. She glanced at her bare wrist. *Where* was her watch?

The blank silence worried Conchita. "Ma'am? Are you alright?"

"Of course I am. Why didn't you wait for me to inform my office?"

"But I thought … Ms. Szeto, are you *sure* you're alright? Would you like me to call Mrs. Leyland-Tang for you?" There, a reasonable offer. Surely a friend was needed right now? The Leyland-Tangs, Conchita's former employers, had originally recommended her to Gail when they had temporarily relocated to Singapore.

"I'll call *Mr.* Tang myself, thank you very much. You can go back to work, Conchita. I'll take charge now."

Stung, Conchita retorted, not quite under her breath, "No one's in charge of death." *This* was too much, *way* too much, inexcusable under *any* circumstances. God would forgive her this one mean utterance because she had confessed her own wrong doing, letting the old lady go off alone, and repented. Repentance mattered, whether or not you were a believer. Turning away abruptly, she switched the vacuum back on for several more minutes, even though dust was no longer evident on the blonde, unmarked parquet. The vacuum slid rapidly over the living room floor, sucking up air, its steady rhythm firmly in Conchita's control.

Gail, however, noticed neither her maid's manner nor the noise.

Take responsibility, she told herself. Pain could be anesthetized by the demands of ritual. She rang Tang Kwok Po. His secretary, recognizing Gail's voice, asked if the call was important because Mr. Leyland-Tang was in a meeting. Gail hesitated before replying, *yes,* although how silly, she decided, since their friendship went back—was it eighteen, no, *nineteen* years—to that Executive MBA at Harvard, pre-dating "Leyland".

He came on the line. "Yes?"

Kwok Po's curt tone unsettled her. "My mother," she blurted. "She's dead."

"What?"

"Killed." And then she stumbled through her narrative.

Kwok Po, attention still focused on his Singapore office's shrinking export sales, listened, half comprehending. He had never met Gail's mother. When Gail finished, all he could think to say was, "My condolences. Please, anything we can do, you can count on us. It was really fortunate to be able to schedule everything so soon," adding that she should call his wife for help. Later, back at his meeting, he thought his response insensitive—he should have taken time to console her—and resolved that he and Colleen would send a suitable wreath *and* attend the wake to make amends. It was not till much later that night in bed when his wife remarked how tragic this was, coming only a little more than a year after the son's death, did he remember.

Replacing the receiver, Gail glimpsed Conchita headed for Gu Kwun's room. *What* was that woman doing? Surely the room didn't need cleaning. Everyone was being obtuse. Why was Kwok Po so indifferent, although, of course, his family were all still around, so perhaps he simply didn't understand, but *surely* he knew she'd *never* ask Colleen of all people for help? Yet even Conchita assumed that. The shock, Gail decided. Everything scrambled, nothing making sense. That both were simply being conventional, articulating the woman's expected role, did not immediately occur to Gail.

Forcing herself to concentrate, she began to list in her mind all the people who should be informed. "Conchita," Gail called out, louder than she intended, but her maid's movements were bothering her. "Come out of Gu Kwun's room and shut the door. Please."

All afternoon, Conchita hovered, wandering in and out of the elder Mrs. Szeto's room, straightening up, cleaning already spotless surfaces. Gail sat in the living room, holding the portable phone, but did not make a single call that Conchita could hear. It was terrible, her mistress sitting immobile. Unearthly.

Finally, just before dinnertime, she could take the silence no longer. "Ma'am," she asked. "What about Mrs. Szeto's friends?"

Gail looked up, snapped. "How do you know about them?"

Conchita started. "I don't mean anything, ma'am. I just thought since your mother was going to have dinner with them for New Year ..."

Realizing her mistake, Gail spoke quickly "I apologize," and picking up the phone to call her former schoolmate Barbara Chu, she made it clear that Conchita was no longer required.

Later, on the stairwell where Conchita met Bonny most nights for their confabs in Tagalog, she said, "Like mother like daughter, hey? Maybe the old lady didn't really have any friends either." She became thoughtful. "That's pretty sad, isn't it?"

Bonny said, "You're too soft."

"Don't be so mean. Even our enemies have hearts."

Gail stared at the table, dumbfounded. Two places were laid for breakfast. Was her maid *deliberately* trying to hurt her?

Conchita entered, carrying a tray with two bowls of *congee*, the plain rice porridge served every morning. Seeing Gail's furious glare, she gasped, "Oh my god!" and quickly removed one setting. As her maid placed just one bowl down, their eyes met briefly, and to Gail's surprise, Conchita said, "She just wanted to go home for Chinese New Year. Was this such a sin that the Lord should take her too?"

Conchita's words bothered Gail. Despite the enforced religious education at the Catholic school she attended as a girl, Gail dismissed Catholicism, and all religion, as benign superstition. She ate, hungrily, having barely touched dinner the night before. Sleep too had been fitful, her body charged and restless.

The phone rang. It was Barbara Chu, whom she hadn't managed to reach yesterday.

Even though the two women were not extremely close, talking to an old familiar voice reassured Gail. Repeating the story, that moment of discovery—*how horrible to have been so far away,* Barbara said—and it helped to know that someone who was a parent and also traveled for work would understand this.

Barbara, a senior partner at one of the "big six" global accounting firms, was horrified. "Why didn't you say something on your message?" she demanded. "I'd have called last night if I'd known, come over with our friends. You shouldn't be alone at a time like this."

"I didn't want to *ma faan* you," Gail replied.

"Come on Gail, after all these years? How can tragedy be too much trouble?"

Yet even as they chatted, Barbara recalled the last funeral and knew that it was up to her to tell the others and harness collective sympathy. Gail would be reticent about this the way she was about everything, even when her son had died from a snake bite, of all things; who would have imagined such a possibility, so tragic, and now this, this dreadful accident! But the girl hadn't changed, not really, too independent for her own good, always going it alone, *still* as ridiculously secretive, and melodramatic, as when she was a teenager—but then, that *was* Gail Szeto and after all these years, one accepted her nature and didn't ask questions. Afterwards, she rang the "old girls," their network of alumnae from their girls' school—mostly senior professionals, all Chinese, many educated abroad, plus a few society ladies, *tai tai's* married into wealth, themselves being from money—whom Gail saw five, maybe six times a year over dinners to gossip with about work, to trade family stories out of earshot of husbands, to reminisce as they pushed the boundaries of middle age, comforting themselves by recalling the girls they once had been.

Pain alleviated by the sharing of grief, Gail consoled herself with the thought that at least the old girls cared. Breakfast and the call from Barbara fortified her, and she could finally consider her mother's friends.

Those women—how to reach them? Her mother had their numbers memorized, and probably hadn't recorded them anywhere. For the next hour, Gail searched among her mother's things to no avail. Her inefficiency upset her, this inability to handle the last of Mom's life that was forced on her now. Her head ached, and two Panadol (why *hadn't* she brought home some extra-strength Tylenol from New York?) brought no relief.

At ten, Conchita left to go grocery shopping.

The realization that the flat was empty shook Gail. The truth was inescapable. She was afraid of being alone.

Gail went to her office, the excuse being to drop off some papers. The stigma of death, marked by a bit of black cloth pinned to her jacket, kept her Chinese colleagues at bay. A deep respect for superstition prevailed. Even her secretary and staff said little, unable to feign either sympathy or polite interest, something they normally did well. *Not because,* as her secretary whispered to the junior analyst, that she didn't think Ms. Szeto deserved pity, but *the death was so violent and well, you know how she is, work always comes first, and don't you think she'd rather be left alone under the circumstances?* Only her American boss openly expressed sympathy, repeating his offer that she take off as long as she wanted which, under current conditions, was generous. Yet he and Gail knew she would be back in the office on Thursday. If he felt any guilt for having just returned from his own, inauspicious vacation, it did not show.

By early afternoon, Gail gave up on work, having accomplished nothing, and went home. The office and her boss were relieved.

As she walked through the door, the phone rang. The woman Gail called Number One *A-Yi* said, "*Gay-lo,* I heard. I've been crying for two days."

"Oh, thank God you called," Gail responded. "I couldn't find your number." It had been at least three years since they'd spoken, longer since she'd seen her, but Gail instantly recognized that cough, a smoker's voice. "How did you hear?"

"My *biuhdai's* wife's brother works at the mortuary and recognized her." *A-Yi* depended on her network of distant relations, however tenuous, for information. The younger male cousin she alluded to, supposedly from her mother's side, was not actually a relative but it was the simplest explanation.

For Gail, it was oddly, jarringly, public, but then, Mom's life was like that, even at a distance. Panic set in. "I don't know who else to tell. There's so little time, the funeral's tomorrow ..." She stopped, helpless.

"No problem, *Gay-lo,* leave everything to your *A-Yi.* I'll tell people for you. If you need anything, you call. Remember, I'm still your Number One *A-Yi.*"

"Yes, okay," she replied in a girlish voice, momentarily relieved, even though this wasn't her real "*A-Yi,*" a mother's younger sister. Gail was shaken, rattled by this reminder of *that* life. Of dance halls and "chicken ladies," of voices constantly lowered to whispers, of men sneaking around in the shadows of night. Of girlhood memories, forcibly suppressed. Of a feeling worse than even the pain of regret. "Yes, okay," Gail repeated, whispered.

Just before their call ended, the elderly lady thought she heard Gail say, "No more regrets," which puzzled *A-Yi* for quite some time afterwards. But Gail was barely conscious of the words she whispered.

3

During the wake, every time Gail glanced at the enlarged death photo of her mother, she wished she had chosen a different one. One that made her nose look less flat and her hair a little less unyielding in its formidable chignon. In the cold room, air-conditioned and only slightly colder, her mother's face glowed from the open casket, as gorgeous in death as in life.

It was too soon to be back here, surrounded by these garish trappings! The last funeral had been simpler, more elegant, secular. But this one, which paid respect to Chinese tradition, was entirely for Mom.

Around her, the last of her mother's dance hall girlfriends wept. These perennial strangers of her childhood were women Gail had never completely known—Mom had made sure of that—but now, their presence, *en masse,* roused long dormant images and memories. Each woman separately forced upon Gail an envelope of money. They wanted to contribute to funeral expenses for their *daijeih,* the oldest among them who was accorded the privileged "eldest sister" status.

Number One *A-Yi* prattled besides Gail.

"We were going to have a big celebration for her eightieth birthday this year," she said, "Wouldn't that have been nice, *Gay-lo?"* All these women had trouble saying "Gail," the American name her mother insisted on, forgoing a Chinese one, desperate as she had been to win her lover's approval in the mistaken belief that this would make him leave his wife and marry her. "We were so sorry our 'crossing the new year' dinner had to be cancelled, but your mother said we'd celebrate her birthday. Did you know that?"

"No, I didn't," Gail replied.

"Yeah, we already began planning. At the Spring River's Tide restaurant, you remember, the one near your old place? We were going to order double boiled shark's fin, and bird's nest for dessert. She loved all that stuff."

Wouldn't the woman shut up? "It's very kind of you. She would have appreciated it."

"We were going to ask you to lend her to us for a day and we'd have taken care of her. We're like family. That's why she promised to look after me, you know." She stopped abruptly. She hadn't meant to bring that up, especially not here. Luckily, Gail didn't seem to have heard, and she gushed on. "It's good to see you again, my *daijeih's* girl!"

Number One *A-Yi,* who penned all the letters from her illiterate mother during the sixteen years Gail lived in the U.S., might easily have been a real aunt. All the women were elderly, except for their outfits, the too-fancy shoes and shiny clothes. Nightlife hovered around them like an unrelenting spirit, the way it had around Mom. Gail observed how the funeral director greeted these women's arrival. *So that's what she was,* his eyes sneered, for all the daughter's respectable airs. It had been so different at Gu Kwun's funeral, when his school friends arrived with their parents, classmates from International, the elite private school that taught an American curriculum for kids of wealthy locals and expatriates. And the father, Dr. Jason Chak, from one of the leading private hospitals! The funeral director had salivated over those moneyed guests, even handing out his business cards most inappropriately.

The mourning room was on the third floor of a side wing, larger rooms being located off the main corridor. Set against a stage wall, the Buddhist altar was garishly red and gold, horribly loud. Hanging in the center, framed by a border of white chrysanthemums, was the large black-and-white photograph of

Mom. Incense perfumed the air. Six mourners wailed, their robed bodies swaying as if buffeted by a persistent wind. To the left of the altar was the chilled room for the body. The temperature there was only slightly cooler than in the main room. The air conditioner rattled; in summer, it would be unbearable.

Nothing, however, could disguise the utilitarian aspect of the place. The room's tiled floor and unintentional fifties-retro design presented an unclean mosaic. Traces of the metal frame's putrid beige paint smeared the glass, an interior glass door for light, but also for staff to peer in and keep things on schedule. The store on the second floor sold Buddhist, Christian and Taoist funereal trappings, and the multi-purpose altar could be re-decorated, within minutes, into the stage of the required faith.

All morning long, her mother's friends came to pay respects. "Such a dear, sweet woman, so generous," they murmured in turn. "She didn't deserve to die." Gail hadn't anticipated this many people. How had *A-Yi* gotten the word out so fast? Much to the funeral director's consternation, Gail hadn't prepared enough money packets to give everyone and had to scramble as people left—all expected the ritual token.

Gail did not recognize most of the visitors. These dancers, policewomen and men, waiters, cooks, bartenders, gambling and massage parlor folks, a pawnbroker—all from Kowloon City, their old neighborhood—befriended her mother after Gail left for college in the U.S. Only her *A-Yi's* were familiar, the retired "sisters" from the dance hall who had taken turns watching her on their off evenings, the nights Mom worked. Number seven *A-Yi*, the youngest, was in her sixties. Number four had died young. An unlucky number, four, homonym for death.

Only the *A-Yi's* stayed the entire morning.

Number One *A-Yi* pressed a cell phone number into her hand. "You can reach me now, anytime, even when I'm out and about."

Gail murmured the socially acceptable response. "You're too good to me," and stuck the slip of paper into her purse.

Conchita stopped in briefly, saying she would offer a mass for the dead at her church. Gail's office sent a wreath. Barbara Chu was the only old girl who stopped by although the group sent an exceptionally large wreath with traditional messages of sympathy, as did the Leyland-Tangs. Gail stared at the characters on the ribbons around these flowers, barely registering their meaning. Barbara's voice, at their last get-together, filtered through her memory. *Don't talk about your job anymore. We're all sick of work.*

She was surprised when, towards the end of the wake, Janie and her father appeared. The last time she had seen Janie was at her son's funeral.

Gail did not know them well, although she had a good impression of Janie, who was generally a neat and well mannered child. Gu Kwun had often gone to Janie's to play, but the reverse was not frequently the case. It wasn't that she hadn't allowed him to invite friends over, but somehow, it seldom happened. Her acquaintance with the father was confined to small talk when he dropped her son off or she picked him up. He was always the only parent home. He was from Oregon, wrote for *The Asian Wall Street Journal,* and Gail occasionally saw his byline—E. Hammond—on the editorial pages which she glanced at but rarely read. His wife was local Chinese and ran a leading ad agency, but Gail had never met her.

"Thank you for coming," she said, but puzzled by their presence, asked, "How did you know?"

"Conchita called to let us know," he replied. "Janie wanted to come. She liked your mother very much." The girl huddled close to her father's leg, and barely glanced at Gail. He continued, "Will you remain in Hong Kong?"

Janie's father was speaking to her as a fellow American, she realized, which she supposed she was, although hardly like him and his family. No, not like them at all; her mother had once called them "a real family," which made Gail cross. She had retorted, *Isn't our own family real?*

She told Janie's father, "Why yes, I guess ... I don't know."

Rick Hammond studied her through a journalist's eyes. No lightweight professionally—he was aware of her stature—but a curious woman, difficult to befriend, who used to hurry off with barely any conversation, as if wanting to remove Gu Kwun quickly. It had been awhile since he'd seen her, although he had run into her once, about six months earlier, but she had not recognized him until he reminded her who he was. Janie once said she was afraid of Ms. Szeto, and he told his daughter she couldn't possibly know her well enough to feel that, although truthfully, he understood. "Do you have any other family?"

"No." Her eyes shifted towards the altar. "Not really."

He wondered at the brief pause. "If I can help in any way, please call."

"Thank you."

They both knew she wouldn't.

It was shortly past noon. Gail suddenly remembered last Thanksgiving, when she'd managed to take a day off because New York shut down although it was a work day in Hong Kong. When Gu Kwun had turned six and began attending International, she celebrated, ordering a traditional meal from one of the city's foreign caterers, since she had never roasted a turkey and had no desire to try. Her son had been born on Thanksgiving, and just as important, she wanted him to learn the customs of his nationality. Besides, it also made her mother happy. But last Thanksgiving, her mother had been unwell and the day passed quietly. There was no turkey. Her mother, who had had such hopes for an American life for them all, something Gail also vaguely envisioned for their future once Jason left. Now, nothing mattered. She had never even taken Mom or Gu Kwun to America for a visit. Very quietly, she began to cry.

The funeral director came into the room. It was time, he told her, to move onto the crematorium. "Only family ride in the hearse. Did you want a van for the others?"

Only family, the funeral director was saying, again, indicating the hearse and driver.

All the women had left except Number One *A-Yi,* who hovered. *Daijeih* was her family, she wanted to say, but hesitated, a little afraid of Gail. *Daijeih* had kept all the *A-Yi's* away from her daughter once Gail was in her early teens.

Gail cast around nervously, her mind scattered, unable to focus. Her eyes landed on *A-Yi's* expectant face. On an impulse, she asked, "Will you ride with me in the hearse?"

"Of course, *Gay-lo,*" she replied, pleased. "Of course I will."

Bright afternoon rays warmed the crematorium, outlining its stark newness. It had taken less than forty minutes to arrive; the hearse sped along empty highways towards Fanling. The last time Gail had been out this way was as a teenager, to buy honey from one of the apiaries. On the old road, it had taken an hour and a half by bus, more than two on holidays. Now, the new railroad transported rapidly, and highways eased congestion. Fanling was as urban as Kowloon, no longer a place of distant graveyards and rustic villages.

Gail had not been able to bear the idea of cremating her son and had buried him instead.

The hearse parked next to a side door where the caskets were removed. "Not mahogany," she earlier heard Number Three *A-Yi* whisper to Number Six as she examined *Daijeih's* casket. Gail had refused to be sold anything more than the basic box, just as she had opted for stone urns, not marble. If her mother's friends considered her cheap, let them. Mom herself said that what other people thought didn't matter.

Yet watching the workers lift her mother's coffin onto the conveyor belt that would carry it into the central oven, she regretted not honoring her mother's memory the way her old friends wanted. She could easily have rented a van and invited all the *A-Yi's* along. The unfamiliar arrangements, though, had daunted her. On top of everything, her watch had vanished into thin air, leaving her temporally unbalanced. So she had been clumsy, unable to think straight. Anyone would excuse that.

"Take one last look!" The crematorium worker intoned loudly, signaling that her mother's casket was ready to burn. *A-Yi* took her hand. Gail placed an arm around the tiny, frail figure, and took a deep breath. And then, just as the casket slid through the doors, fear surged and Gail began to sob unexpectedly, uncontrollably, lurching against her *A-Yi*, clutching her arms. "Cry, cry, it's okay," the woman whispered, stroking her bent head like a child's. "*Daijeih* had a long life."

Outside, the bright sunshine was unmarred by haze. The two women returned to the hearse. It was all so quick, over in half a day, the urn of ashes to be picked up later. The sky was deceptively clear, as if the pollutants had vanished.

Returning to Hunghom in the hearse, her mother's friend said, "You are my family too, *Gay-lo.* You can depend on me." She meant it wholeheartedly. When Gail demurred, as expected, saying she wouldn't trouble her unnecessarily, *A-Yi* smiled and nodded sagely, invoking her age. "Sometimes, death can be a way of finding out who we are. Trust me. You're young yet." Later, she declined Gail's offer of a lift, saying it would be "inconvenient." It wasn't inconvenient at all, but she suddenly needed to be alone.

Gail watched the seventy-five year old woman walk away, this unrelated *chanyan,* who was as fit and healthy as her mother had been, her mother who liked to say that she would live till a hundred and eight.

That night, on the stairwell, Conchita told Bonny. "It seems mean to abandon her now."

Bonny shook her head. "You're too soft. You should have left her last year like you were going to. The extra money isn't worth it."

"It's not just the money. She asked me to stay for her mother. I couldn't refuse. Ms. Szeto pays for everything her mother needs. A pretty good daughter, right? It's tough, you know, being alone like her, with only her mother."

"You've still got your mother too. And what about your children?"

Conchita frowned. She didn't like it when Bonny brought up family back home. Some things you didn't bother thinking about. "That's different."

"Why? Because we're not Chinese? Because Filipino women are supposed to kiss the world's ass? Because we didn't go to *Ha-Ha-Haar-vard* like her? Wake up, woman." Bonny, an out-of-work math teacher, had finally conceded to domestic work in Hong Kong because her father was ill and needed money for medical care.

"No, it's just different," she replied. "Besides, my mother looks after them."

"You're not making sense."

"I'm part of my family no matter what, you know? Her, well ..."

"Yes but you're not *her* mother, are you?" The younger woman countered, exasperated. Conchita, at thirty-five, had been in Hong Kong too long, Bonny decided. No way she'd work here *ten years*, no matter how much money she made. *No way.* Especially not if she had a chance for a real life back home, the way Conchita now had because her husband *finally* agreed to get work in the Middle East, mostly because Bonny prodded Conchita into forcing him off his butt. Filipino women, Bonny believed, were their own worst enemies. Conchita could learn a few lessons from that Szeto woman, who seemed so focused on herself that nothing, and no one, stood in the way of what she wanted.

It was past two when Gail fell asleep.

That night, Gordie took her flying. He was a man, around fifty as in life, and he didn't smile at her as the boy usually did in her dreams.

Tom Jones was singing, *Let me see what space is like on Jupiter and Mars.*

She asked, "Where's your plane?"

"Gone," her brother replied. "Like Dad's money. Like Dad."

"I don't understand," she started to say.

He interrupted. "Listen."

In other words, hold my hand. In other words, darling kiss me.

On the horizon, her mother was dancing with their father—first a tango, then a fox trot, then a cha-cha-cha—the soundtrack segued from one rhythm to the next while Tom Jones sang on, oblivious.

Her mother called out across space, *Your American brother, Gay-lo, be sweet to him. He's good looking, right, and it is only half blood, you know.* Then, she and Gail's father laughed at the lewd insinuation.

Embarrassment and disgust enveloped Gail. She tried to wrench her hand free of Gordie's, but he clutched at it so firmly that her wrist hurt and she began to cry.

Stop crying silly girl, her mother said. W*hy do you get so angry about everything? Can't you laugh for a change? I'm only joking,* *don't you know?*

"You're both dead!" Gail screamed. "Go away and leave me alone!"

Her father, whose back was to her, continued to cha-cha in the air. Gu Kwun appeared and leapt up above her father, his arms spread, and swooped towards his grandmother saying *po po, po po, aeroplane, aeroplane.* Her mother stretched out her arms to receive him, and the sleeves of her blouse floated in long waves towards Gail, like the swooping trails of satin in a Chinese ribbon dance.

Gordie yanked her hand to steer them higher. "Stop screaming Gail, you'll wear yourself out. Come on, fly with me."

Her mother was saying, "*Ngaahnggeng ngaam. Ngaahnggeng ngaam*. Gay-lo, why do you imagine you're always right? One day that metal neck of yours will break, and then where will your head be, hah?"

"You're wrong!" Gail shouted and pulled her hand out of Gordie's. "Gu Kwun," she called opening her arms, but then she began to fall. Gu Kwun, Gordie and her parents remained up in the air, diminishing in size, disappearing behind a mass of gray clouds.

Tom Jones's voice boomed. *In other words, I love you.* Gail saw a plane spin out of control as she tumbled towards Earth, thinking all the while that falling was better than flying, as she left her family in the pursuit of gravity.

Conchita knocked at Gail's bedroom door. "Ma'am, are you alright?" From within, a noisy thumping accompanied by exclamations.

Gail awoke on the floor. The persistent knocking puzzled her. Her eyes flickered to the bedside clock which read five. She replied automatically. "It's okay, Conchita, go back to bed."

"You were crying, ma'am. Shouting. Very loud."

Conchita hesitated, and then opened the door. Alarmed, she went towards her. "Did you fall?"

Her mistress glared. "Go back to bed. I'm fine."

"No, ma'am, you're not." Conchita stood over her like a sentry. "You're not well at all, Ms. Szeto. Maybe you're hurt. Please let me help you."

Gail snapped, "Leave me alone," but she remained on the ground, unable to rise.

Ignoring Gail's command, Conchita leaned forward and helped her back into bed. It was a struggle, because Gail was taller than she was by at least a head, and her body was a dead weight, uncooperative. Eventually, the maid managed to cover the mistress with the blanket, after which she tucked her in like a child.

"I'll leave you now, ma'am," she said.

Tears welled up in Gail's eyes. Turning her face into the pillow, she said, "Okay, Conchita … You may go now."

Conchita shut the door quietly. It was the first time she had ever directly disobeyed her employer, and it felt good. Later, she would tell Bonny that it was also the first time she'd ever touched Gail who, when she initially met Conchita, had not even shaken her hand.

4

Standing in the aisle of the 747, Xavier said, "We meet again." He held out his boarding pass, indicating the window seat next to hers. This upgrade to business class was more fortunate than he imagined.

Gail couldn't place him at first, but recognized the voice, flat and a little harsh, not unlike her own. She was about to rise, but he motioned for her to remain seated. Effortlessly, he slid past her legs.

He asked, "Do you always travel so frequently?"

"You obviously do," she countered, because it was less than a fortnight since they met, and a week since the funeral.

"I was bringing Kina home. My little girl, that's her name. What about you?"

"My boss was fired. I've been summoned to New York." It was indiscreet of her, but right now, discretion seemed irrelevant.

On Monday morning, Gail had walked into her office and found her boss shutting down his own, placing her in charge of the miniscule Hong Kong operation, decimated as it had been during the last months. Reluctant layoffs, because Gail's boss had opposed senior management's will—strenuously, vocally, stalling the layoffs—ultimately to his own peril.

"How awful for you." Xavier rested his palm briefly on her arm.

Her sleeve quivered. "I guess. I'm probably traveling to my own demise."

"Oh, I doubt it." He rustled the pages of *The Asian Wall Street Journal,* folding it open at "Companies in Brief." "They wouldn't bother sending for you if that were the case. Take heart. Sometimes, change is a good thing." He spoke with the authority of one who knew.

His empathy rattled her. Her eyes misted. She quickly dabbed a kleenex, and turned away, embarrassed.

That alarmed him. "Forgive me. I didn't mean to be … these moments are difficult."

She inhaled. Her instinct for privacy was disintegrating along with her life. "It's not just that. My mother was killed the week before in an accident. All my family's gone now. I'm not myself."

Xavier stared at her, shocked. Her frightening news and grief unnerved him. "I'm so sorry," he responded and went silent. He buckled his safety belt.

PA blare, aisle patrol. The raucous buzz of takeoff.

Gail normally spoke cautiously to strangers, afraid of leaking competitive intelligence. Conversations were about exchanging business cards or, if she were lucky enough to meet a challenger, sparring over facts and theories. Generally, she probed, politely but purposefully, and was constantly surprised by how much others revealed. People confessed easily given half a chance. Of her own private life, she never spoke, except to talk about her son, but now, even that conversation had been eliminated.

At cruising altitude, she reclined and shut her eyes. The flight path was smooth. Xavier read.

Gail's habit was to sleep during the first leg, in preparation for the long Tokyo to New York journey during which she normally worked. Today, she was restless. The scenario at work replayed itself, upstaging personal grief.

Downsizing had begun early last year. First, marketing went, then project finance had taken a hit. The truth was, most of their operations hadn't been profitable since before the economic downturn. She sat together with her boss late one evening, prior to the first cut, while he agonized. *I built their division, Gail, with no support from them. But I didn't complain. It was fun being the pioneer.* Now, their investment bank had a lock on securitized asset financing in Asia, *hell, we* epitomize *it*—plus a great group of people—Hong Kong staff worked harder than anyone in New York. Why couldn't New York think long term, why couldn't they see *past the tips of their goddamned noses?*

"Don't fight it," Gail had told him. "You have your family, your life, and a professional reputation to be proud of. Whatever happens, you can shape your own future."

So what about her future? Loyalty to her boss hadn't meant success. Fighting the layoffs didn't prevent them. What it meant, instead, was wasted effort with little to show for it. Now with all the regional economies plummeting, an Asia-Pacific division *was* a losing proposition. They weren't JP Morgan. Their presence was insignificant.

Don't worry Gail, they need you, her boss predicted. *But you may have to move to New York. Do it, put in your time and then get out if you want. You're good. There'll be plenty of other opportunities.* His advice, given privately to her before he walked out the door, the remaining staff stunned in his wake.

Gail opened her eyes. They had begun the descent into Japan.

Xavier was reading *The Economist*. "You sleep easily."

"When I need to," she replied, although she hadn't slept at all.

"It's important to do that on flights."

His English had only a hint of an accent. He spoke with an assured command but without the fluency of colloquialism, not unlike Gail herself.

Closing the magazine, he zipped it into a calfskin briefcase—worn, clutched often over many time zones—which he placed on his lap, and declared, "My deepest condolences for your loss."

The plane landed.

"You're very kind."

"Do you have many other relatives?"

"Only a half brother. In New York," yet she immediately regretted saying it. Why had she done so? Gordie wasn't an item for casual revelations.

"Sometimes, it's helpful not to talk. But if you wish ..." He let the offer hang.

She was about to say *Oh no, I wouldn't dream* but something about his offer, so quiet and unassuming, stilled her agitation at the unintended revelation. Xavier simply wasn't like other men she encountered in travel. "Yes," she nodded, an affirmation more to herself than to him. "I think I would like that."

They disembarked together. Both donned sunglasses against the glare along the passageway. Sunlight glowed through Narita's glass walls, lighting their path towards Transit. After the turnaround security check, Gail bypassed the elevator and Xavier followed her up the stairs towards the business lounge. The silence between them steadied her.

The lounge was full. They walked its entire length before finding a vacant corner.

Gail asked, "Is Kina your only child?"

"Yes, but please, I don't even know your name?"

"Gail," she said. After a pause, "Szeto."

Xavier extended his hand. "Pleased to meet you." This time, she gave hers and he held onto it longer than was polite. Beautiful fingers—long, manicured, unwrinkled—her pale skin was as supple as soft leather. He wanted to raise her hand to his lips.

She pulled back, almost as if she could not bear to be touched.

He said, "Excuse me."

"What for?"

"I was too familiar. We are still strangers, after all."

Somehow, that reassured her. "Xavier," she said, "my son meant everything to me."

"Then," he said, "you must tell me all about him," although he wondered at this because hadn't she said, or had he misheard, that it was her mother who had recently died? But he did not have time to wonder because Gail began to speak, and her story unwound, as she told him all about her son.

Gu Kwun, she said, had been her insulation against future grief, and she spoke of his school, his friends, his willingness to share all his toys unselfishly. Unselfish. That was what she repeated over and over. Her son was a selfless boy, not like other children today, who only cared about their own silly desires, refusing to obey parents or teachers. Her son was good. Good. About her mother, she said little beyond the fact of her recent demise. He stopped her, finally, to ask about Gu Kwun's death, unable to understand the chronology of events, unable to make sense of her scrambled narrative.

"A snake bite," she said.

He stared at her. "In Hong Kong?"

"Yes," and then she launched into an account of the local snake population. *Seven reptilian groups, fifty-four species—did you know that? A quarter venomous, even highly venomous, but as many as forty percent are at least mildly venomous. It could have happened to anyone. The one that bit … rarely seen, but hardly a rare species. The coral snake, the* calleophis macclellandi. *But it was evening, later actually, almost night and of course they shouldn't have been out there, but you cannot blame my mother who is elderly and rather useless in an emergency, and a maid, well … the cellphone wasn't charged, or the battery died I'm not sure, so they couldn't even call 999. He fainted. That happens sometimes, especially with children. Size, they say. Children are more vulnerable because they're small. By the time they got to a phone it was too late … it wasn't anyone's fault. It wasn't …* She stopped abruptly.

Xavier stared at her, fascinated but concerned. Something might seriously be wrong with this woman, and for a moment he regretted starting their conversation. Then, she seemed to come out of her trance—it was a trance, that was the only description—and appeared less off balance.

"I apologize," she said. "I didn't mean to …"

He leaned forward and lay a hand on her arm. "No, don't apologize for speaking from the heart," and he felt her begin to calm. Sitting back he asked. "How long ago?"

"November."

He started. "Only last year?"

"No. The year before last. November 24, 1996. His seventh birthday." She smiled. "Although for the longest time, a whole year I think, I felt he was still with me. My mother said she would hear me talking to him, but I didn't always remember."

Privately, he was relieved. It would have been too much to

continue this conversation if in fact the death had been more recent. As it was he wondered if he should extricate himself somehow, but her smile was beatific, oddly moving. "And now?"

She shook her head. "Now I do remember. Isn't it strange? The more he disappears, the more real my life seems to become, and the more I can love him for what he was." She paused. "He'll always be my baby."

The PA announced it was time to re-board. Grateful for the interruption, Xavier escorted her back to the plane. As they walked, he wondered at her reticence over her mother. There had been no prolonged illness after all, and the accident suggested her mother was still mobile and reasonably healthy. But when it came to women and their mothers, Xavier knew better than to ask. That relationship was often more fraught than the many bad marriages he had been privileged to discreetly alleviate.

Between Tokyo and New York, the hours rippled by. Gail found herself willing to talk now, not just about Gu Kwun but about all of her life. Xavier asked questions and was a good listener. But he did not ask about the funeral, the way everyone else had, as if the ceremony were the only thing that mattered. She appreciated that.

Over dinner, the wine relaxed her.

"You're Eurasian," he said.

For once the observation did not bother her. "Yes."

"Your father ..." He was thinking of his own parents, aging unwillingly, and gracelessly, in Paris, forcing him to remove Kina from their care because they existed in a perpetual honeymoon—*your choice, your responsibility,* his mother said, *we make no demands on you for our care, financial or otherwise.* For a second, his own existence preoccupied him. His parents were always happy to see him, as well as Kina, whom they called "their little dancer," but they were themselves *artistes* above all—his father a Greek-Chinese-American sculptor and his French-Lebanese mother the wife of art—which they never failed to remind him, just as they had repeated, all through his youth, that he had been *our greatest accident* followed by a brief laugh. Xavier still did not know, even now, how he felt about that.

Returning to their conversation, he continued. "Was he American?"

"Yes." A barely perceptible grimace.

He saw it. "You didn't know him very well, did you?"

"No. Hardly at all."

"That's too bad."

"Not really. He wasn't exactly my 'father,' except in blood."

"What do you mean?"

"Well …" She was about to tell him what she generally told everyone, the same fiction her mother perpetuated, that her father died when she was young. "My mother wasn't really his wife, even though she was."

"I don't understand."

Why reveal this? Did death somehow eradicate the lie of her mother's life? "In Chinese, you'd call her a wife."

"Qingfu?" He said it quickly, quietly. Love-wife.

His naming it, his fluency in the culture, erased the sordid. It was a relief not to have to explain. "Had my father been Chinese, she would have been his concubine, with all the legal rights that were in effect at the time."

"Yes." He did not quite believe her. "Was she a difficult woman?"

"Very."

"Did you love her?"

"As a daughter must."

He started. Had *she* been an accident too? "Well, at least you're honest."

"Isn't that the only way to be?"

But when they rested between words, somewhere over the Pacific, she did not feel honest. It was only a story of old wounds, best forgotten.

He was reclined in his seat. Asleep? The curve of his graying eyebrows arched high, and he appeared to be looking at her through closed eyes. Then, she saw the even breaths and the slight dreaming movement beneath his lids. Like watching her son sleep, beyond reach for awhile. Feeling intrusive, she looked away.

Xavier was in his early fifties, of medium height, with small hands and feet. His middle betrayed fleshy folds, although he was far from fat. The merest hint of a moustache flecked with gray. The polygenetic bloodlines—plus a little Korean, of which he wasn't entirely sure, he had confided, there being some possible illegitimacy or adoption on his paternal Chinese grandmother's side—made him look Middle Eastern. His complexion, however, was northern European, not Mediterranean, and his dark hair straight and stiff. Chinese hair. Like her ex-husband and her son.

Gail ran her fingers over her own, cropped head. As a teenager, she had let her hair grow long, mostly because her mother suggested cutting it short. But it had become too thick and wavy, and its fullness made her feel gigantic. Just before leaving for college in Hawaii, she had gone, reluctantly, to her mother's hairdresser. Afterwards, her mother said she looked sophisticated. *Going to a university in America, imagine, all grown up! Such a* leikhneuh! Pleased at being told she was a "clever girl," Gail had kept it short ever since.

Xavier turned towards the window, pulling the blanket up to his neck. He slept quietly and did not fidget. Gail leaned back and shut her eyes, wishing he were awake. In the dim light of the cabin, her face was no more or less than that of just another fatigued traveler.

The fifteen-hour flight was nearing its end. Gail had not slept. Xavier awoke, in time to have breakfast that should have been, at best, a midnight snack.

He was aware, but not fully conscious, of her presence. Fragments of a dream imprisoned him in Oslo; a trolley car ran off its rails into the fjord, liberating him. He smiled at her.

Reaching into his briefcase, he removed a business card and handed it to her. "May we exchange? I'd like to stay in touch."

"I'd like that." She handled the card delicately, with a grace cultivated by the careful reading of many business cards, letting it rest on her open palm. A nondescript company name; the title, Financial & Systems Consultant; a post office box in New York City; three sets of phone and fax numbers, in Hong Kong, New York and a third code, 47, not one she immediately recognized. *European?*

Her scrutiny amused him. Reaching beneath the card, his fingers brushed her palm as he flipped it over. Handwritten on the other side was a cell phone number. He had extracted this card from the stack reserved for women with potential—a reference only to himself of course—although lately, that stack seldom needed replenishment. "That should reach me almost anytime. Please, use it if you like."

Gail reached for her own card and wrote her home number on the back. It was only the second time she had ever done so for a stranger and a man. She handed him the card. "I really do want to stay in touch."

He noted the company, Northeast Trust, and said, "You must be good. They're tough, from what I hear."

She smiled at him. "I remember facts, and crunch numbers quickly. Plus I understand how Chinese families run and finance their businesses and lives. That's about it."

"And occasionally out-negotiate JP Morgan, right? You're being modest."

She nodded, flattered that he knew, even if it was old news from nine months ago. The HaiWai-LiangAn deal, her prize project, had been worth over two-hundred million and rated a write up in New York's financial news because of its innovative structure, winning her kudos from senior management.

He put away her card. "I hope you won't be too sad. Change is inevitable."

"But I was happy the way things were."

"Were you?"

She dodged his question. "You haven't told me about your family. Are they all in Hong Kong?"

He smiled to himself, thinking, here it was, the family questions women of a certain age and attitude *had* to ask, and replied, "Kina is. She lives with Ursula, her aunt."

"Are you widowed or divorced?"

Her question startled. It was unusually forward. "My wife's in prison," he replied matter-of-factly.

"Oh, but—" Gail stopped, horrified.

"It's been awhile. Shelley's a political prisoner, in Malaysia, her home country. A lawyer's been working on her case for sometime now." They were close, he knew, to winning her release. The next appeal looked promising. Conflicting emotions accompanied the thought of her return.

The flight attendant arrived holding white linens. "Would you both care for breakfast?"

Gail did not look at the woman. "Yes. Please."

Xavier looked up and gave her a smile, not flirtatious exactly, but neither was it entirely innocent. "No, thank you very much," he said slowly. "I don't believe I will." The attendant smiled back, apparently pleased, laid down Gail's setting and left.

"But how, why …?" She found it difficult phrasing the correct question.

He explained that his wife was Chinese from Kuala Lumpur, a former student leader exiled from Malaysia. As long as she stayed out of the country, things were fine. When her father was dying, she risked everything to visit him. Once the authorities found out, it was an immediate incarceration, without appeal. "Had I fully appreciated the meaning of her going home at the time, I would have prevented it."

"Did she understand?"

"Completely. She only told me afterwards."

"But your daughter …" Gail wanted to say—how could any mother take such a risk, since surely her child's upbringing and welfare should come before all else? She would have sacrificed anything for Gu Kwun. Yet wasn't that hypocritical now that he was dead, in part because she hadn't been around, because work had kept her late at the office and unforgivably, she had forgotten her promise for his birthday? Besides, with all the travel she did, her plane could have crashed anytime, virtually orphaning him.

"The child was an accident. Shelley didn't want one." Resignation and a trace of bitterness in his words because after all, Kina was not even his child, although it was hard for anyone to tell, given the uncanny resemblance.

"My husband, ex-husband," Gail began.

His own past receded against the waves of her presence. "He left you, didn't he? And your child?"

"How did you know?"

"You never mentioned him. Some people shouldn't be parents.

Children happen to them, and they feel guilty. But it's hard for them to feel truly responsible for something they didn't choose. In a funny way, it isn't really their fault when they run off.

"Besides," he added. "Children reject that guilt."

He didn't say much after that.

A strange relief flooded through Gail, as if the insanity of his life exorcised the pain of hers. Here was another who knew desertion. Her error was marriage, and the fact that she, not he, wanted a child. Xavier was also one of the mongrel caste, like her. Perhaps, after this awful time had also passed, he might become a friend. He seemed willing.

Dawn enveloped them. Time traveling, half a day saved. She reset her watch; awkward wearing this dainty jewel meant for formal evenings, but she hadn't had time to pick up a new one. Daylight broke apart the night. Her body felt lighter, looser, readied once more for foreign skies.

Gail raced through Immigration and Customs. At Arrivals, she headed towards the limo driver whose sign bore her name. "You got out quick," he remarked. "No baggage," she replied. She handed him the suit bag and held onto the heavier laptop case.

She spent two days in New York, and flew home on Saturday, Valentine's Day.

Her directive was brief, outlined by Josh, the managing director who was now her boss. She was to go into the office as little as possible the following week, and to stay in touch with staff by telephone instead. Josh would personally touch base with her each evening with further instructions. Dick, the VP of human resources, interjected, "Just say you're taking time off. Given your situation, no one will suspect."

The following Sunday, one of their in-house counsel would arrive in Hong Kong, someone Gail had never met. On Monday morning, accompanied by this stranger, Gail's task was to lay off all the staff and close down the entire Asia-Pacific operation. Her old job would then be over, but the company would pay her current salary plus all benefits—until April 30—to be their interim Asia-Pacific representative. She could work from home. Then, she was to do a final presentation to senior management, in person in New York, Josh said, with recommendations for a long term strategy for Northeast Trust in Asia, at, say, eight-thirty a.m., Monday, April 13? After that, she had the choice of a year's severance or a position in New York as the Senior VP of Asia-Pacific, her old boss's job. If she chose to relocate, they would like her to start, ideally by May 1, but, Dick was quick to add, we could agree to as late as June 1, given your circumstances, as if to underscore the generosity of this offer, although Dick's comment elicited a tiny frown from Josh, one which was not lost on Gail. Details of the compensation package would follow once she decided.

Gail did not voice either opposition or agreement to this course of action. The only question she asked was how long they would give her to decide about the job, and Josh said, *the sooner the better for everyone, right?* to which she instantly responded, *the end of March, then?* Afterwards, Josh told Dick that unlike her ex-boss, *she's one impressively cool gal.*

Her flight home was delayed—a connection missed—and she spent Sunday night in a Tokyo airport hotel, courtesy of Northwest Airlines.

All the next week at the Hong Kong office of Northeast Trust, rumor was rife. *Hey, the fierce nag's being replaced by someone from New York*, everyone said, because Dick *personally called* Gail's secretary and asked her to make a hotel booking at the Mandarin for a Perry Martin, because *why else would Ms. Szeto stay away like this, giving such poor excuses?* Several people gloated, *Loss of all one's face is what happens to the too-proud.* Everyone speculated about Mr. Martin, hoping he had some Hong Kong, or at least Asian, experience, and more importantly, that he not be *too* young, certainly not younger than the previous boss, who had been five years Gail's junior.

Meanwhile, Conchita boxed up the things of the deceased, separating all items for Gail to go through before discarding them. She wondered at the mistress staying home. As she said to Bonny, "She must still be in shock. Maybe she doesn't want to be responsible about anything anymore," and then, as an afterthought, added, "You know, for her, that's not such a bad thing."

For Gail, the week crawled by.

Xavier was still in line when Gail strode out of the airport. The queue at JFK for foreign nationals was much longer than for citizens. Having forgotten to bring his U.S. passport, he resigned himself to the wait. He switched on his cell phone and called Jim Fieldman, his business partner in Manhattan.

Xavier asked, "So we got the Shanghai contract, right, with Monkey International?"

"Down to us and the big boys. They liked our lower bid, although that alone isn't going to do it. But we have a shot, as long as we can move fast enough."

"I've told you, Jim, May at the earliest. You don't need to overpromise. They've told me that. Trust me on this one. They want us, not the big boys."

"Mid-April would clinch it. I mean, you'd only have to outline the project by then. They're bound to change the schedule, anyway. The real on-site work can wait till May." On Jim Fieldman's screen, the latest addition to his portfolio fell half a point. He mouse-clicked his way to "sell," and watched expectantly.

Xavier groaned. "Have you forgotten Flying Dragon? Their board expects me in Beijing mid-April."

"So hop the Shanghai shuttle, Xav. It's one, two days, max. You can handle that."

"Easy for you to say. You don't have to breathe Chinese air all summer."

"Money's too good for me to pass up. They're the biggest Shanghai company I've landed to date." He watched an eighth of a point shiver and fall. "Made any new contacts lately? And I don't mean female conquests."

Xavier tried to curb his irritation. Lately, Jim was impossible. Pushy, and worse, rather too fond of trading and "networking" which, in Xavier's mind, was simply an excuse not to do any real work. He circumvented the question. "What have you heard about Northeast Trust recently?" His partner, Xavier knew, tended to be up on information.

That got Jim's attention, and he shifted focus away from the trading screen. "Why?"

"Possibly … being acquired?"

Jim said, cautiously, "What did you hear?" Josh Rabinowitz,

his racquetball partner of many years, was an MD at Northeast and had intimated two days ago that something was in the works. Xavier couldn't possibly know that though, just as he didn't know about Jim's friendship with Josh.

"Educated guess. I talked to someone from their Asian operation. Looks like they're pulling out, going lean and mean, which usually means—well, you know how this goes." He paused. Jim's silence confirmed his suspicions. "Listen, I must get going."

Feeling victorious, Xavier crossed the yellow line towards the Immigration officer. He liked besting Jim, who was a swine about one-upmanship. The prelude to the Monkey deal still rankled. When he'd introduced Jim to the company—a well-funded designer and manufacturer of network servers, a company with real growth potential—he was embarrassed by the way his partner inflated the job beyond what was really called for. Also, he did not appreciate Jim's insinuations. What business was it of anyone whom he slept with? Jim's problem was celibacy, self-imposed since his wife dumped him two years ago, and jealousy at Xavier's willingness, and success, at indulging in the game.

While waiting at the luggage carousel, he experienced a startling insight, one rarely provoked by women who piqued his interest. Gail Szeto was not his type. Too tall, too thin, too beautifully composed. A work of art he couldn't resist. She also didn't seem like someone who would be easy to make love to. Well, maybe she'd be worth a call when he got back to Hong Kong a week hence. Then again, maybe not.

5

In a townhouse in Gramercy Park, Gordon Ashberry was eating a peach. It was Thursday, around midnight. He had only just retrieved his sister's voice message from the previous Friday earlier that afternoon. A surprise, hearing from her—it happened so rarely—even when she came to town, which he knew she frequently did. Of course, he could have checked his messages earlier, but … Gordon Ashberry was a man who lived to his own beat, which included not giving out his cell number. He did not make or answer calls when in motion or if he could otherwise avoid it.

He said, "Hi, what gives?"

The ringing phone had made Gail jump. Her staff, and even New York, always called her mobile, not her home number. "Oh, you."

"Just got back into town. Your office said you were at home. Your voice sounded upset. Something wrong?" Peach juice squirted his T-shirt. He dampened his finger and rubbed the stain.

She told him about Mom. Gordie listened, disbelieving. The peach sat, half-eaten, in his palm. "Damn," he said when she'd finished. An uncustomary anger gripped him. "Whose fault was it?"

"No one's. It was an accident."

"The bus driver though, he should've stopped. Can you sue?"

"I don't intend to do that." Gail was thoroughly disgusted. Only Gordie would think about money at a time like this!

He immediately regretted his comment. "I'm sorry, that was inappropriate." He went quiet. Then, "You're my only family now."

"Ye-es."

Gordie's voice cracked. "You are, you know, whether you like it or not."

She raised her voice. "I'm not denying it." But the idea confused her; it was surprisingly undeniable.

He said, "Sorry, this is just shitty. Don't pay attention to me. You know I shoot my mouth off all the time. Look, thanks for letting me know."

Gail heard him choke back a sob, and softened. Gordie loved her mother. Despite misgivings, she had let their relationship develop, partly because of Gu Kwun, who had adored his uncle, and there didn't seem any harm in providing this small substitute for a father. Also, her mother insisted on staying in touch. "By the way, I may be moving to New York."

"You're kidding?"

"I'm shutting down our operation on Monday." She regretted her indiscretion the minute she said it, not that Gordie would tell anyone, and he *was* family, but …

"Damn. Hey, that's great. You'll be close by." He dried his eyes. Maybe now that they were the only two left, she might warm to him a little. Besides, New York was his domain. "Whatever you need, Sis, you just let me know. Anything."

Before hanging up, he said he would possibly be in Hong Kong in a couple of weeks, and asked to see her. Reluctantly, she agreed.

Afterwards, Gail remembered that Gordie's mother had died last year, also quite unexpectedly. That knowledge was an odd comfort.

Gordon Ashberry finished his peach. The news capped an already troublesome week.

He was worried. The trip to Shanghai he had just returned from had begun optimistically enough, but proved a waste of time and money. These days, he had too much of the first and not enough of the latter. His liquid position was precarious. Trying to do business in China was despairingly slow. He missed the old days. After his brush with the Feds though—many years earlier thanks to an errant Australian partner—he'd had enough of risk. Straight business deals felt safer. All a question of how long he could hold out.

Talking to Gail put him further on edge. He suspected she did not know about the money he had "borrowed" from her mother.

The last time he had seen Gail was at her home in Hong Kong over six months ago.

"Where's Fa-Loong?" Gordie asked. He called the elderly Mrs. Szeto by her former dance hall name, "flower dragon," because his doing so made her smile, although his sister, he was aware, disliked it.

Gail said, "She's asleep."

It was only eight thirty. "This early? That's a shame." He had wanted to tell her that he wouldn't be coming to Hong Kong as often as in the past. She would ask again if it was because of money—Fa-Loong had no illusions about him, having seen him through more marginal moments than his own mother, who tied up her money in charities and from whom he didn't dare ask for loans—and he would deny it even though they both knew the truth. This time, however, he meant to ask for real help, not the small change to cover margin calls which he always paid back promptly. Seeing Gail was unexpected, because earlier, Fa-Loong told him when he called, *My angry daughter has to work late tonight so it's safe for you to visit,* and giggled like a naughty child.

Gail said. "Can I offer you something?"

"Just tea." He hadn't eaten, but dinner was over in the Szeto home and Gail had never once invited him for a meal in the six years he'd visited her apartment. This, despite his hospitality during her New York trips. Meeting Fa-Loong at her own place, without his sister around, things had been different. Gail's mother poured him "scotchoo whiskey" as she called it, "your favorite, okay?" and ordered in a feast. But now, even the upside of being able to play with Gu Kwun was gone. "So, how are you?"

"The same. You know, work."

Her voice intimated disdain. She considered him a spoilt

child of wealth who could afford to indulge his pleasures and enterprises.

He said, "I've been busy myself."

"Who isn't?"

"Gail, I ..."

"Gordie, I won't wake her up. You can't see her."

"I wasn't going to suggest that."

"Weren't you?"

Damn the bitch. Was everything with her a confrontation? He tried another tack. "Perhaps tomorrow afternoon?"

She sighed, impatient. "We've been through the schedule, haven't we? She needs to go for her walks and tomorrow is her therapy afternoon. Besides, she's so senile now she'll barely recognize you."

It simply wasn't true—Fa-Loong was lucid around him, summoning up stories of life with his father and the dance hall, for which he was always a willing listener—but he wasn't about to argue. "What about tomorrow evening?"

"That's up to you and Mom. I have to work late."

He left shortly afterwards, thinking, no wonder Fa-Loong was senile around Gail. Being normal demanded too much effort.

It was two a.m. The peach pit had dried in his hand. He flicked it out the window and watched the drop into darkness, two floors down onto the streets of Manhattan. If only he *hadn't* gone back the next day. *Guilt,* that his last encounter with Mrs. Szeto should have been because of a loan, one he should never have accepted. It wasn't as if he couldn't raise the cash himself; his assets were worth many times that amount. The trouble with coming from money was that you never had enough of the real thing.

Besides, Mrs. Szeto had such faith in him, always believing he was better than he was, encouraging him to try to succeed in something. Thinking of his own mother, he was doubly ashamed.

Then, grief roiled, swelling the quiet of the hour. He wept for his father's mistress, the beautiful Fa-Loong, the woman who loved unconditionally. He wept for his dead nephew, gone too young, too soon. He wept for his long-suffering mother, a drunk till the end. He wept for Gail, this familiar stranger, because despite the way she was and probably always would be, he wanted her as a sister, still.

Talking to Gordie compounded Gail's unease. Do something, she told herself, anything, to dispel this mood. She should go through the boxes. Entering her mother's room, she confronted the hoarding of a life.

Gail's mother was seventy-four when she was finally persuaded to move in, after much protest, because Gail's flat was large enough for all the family, and more so once Jason left. It pained her mother to part with years of memorabilia, which Gail insisted she discard. Moth-eaten and faded dresses, gold and silver stiletto heels, rhinestone studded jackets, a collection of fans and costume jewelry. The trappings of make-believe glamour. Fa-Loong! The name grated on Gail's nerves, recalling the dance hall and the lies, years of hiding her background. But some dresses survived which her mother wore at home, playacting like a child. Gu Kwun would laugh along with Grandma, clapping his hands, calling her an empress. These dresses lay in the box, limp.

My little girl, how did you become so fierce? Mom's voice, accusatory, an irritant.

Gail rummaged through the other items removed from the drawers of her mother's closet—over a dozen garters; several pairs of natural silk stockings, darned and preserved in a cloth bag; two girdles, their elastic stretched beyond use.

Separately boxed were the new clothes Gail bought her, never worn. For just a second, a familiar irritation surged. *Why could she never please* ... but then it passed, there no longer being any point to this constant emotional storm. Her mother rendered love, and congruity, impossible.

Gordie and Mom, chatting familiarly in her broken English and his broken Mandarin, her mother animated and pleased. The memory hurt. Gail had avoided intimacy with her half brother during her sixteen years in the U.S. Ten years earlier, on returning home from America to live and work, she discovered that Mom and Gordie had become friendly. He seemed endlessly fascinated by Mom's life, and had apparently been visiting for years. *They're suited to each other, both con artists,* Gail told Jason bitterly at the time. She never once introduced her husband to Gordie. How pleased Gail had been when her family could all live together at last, because that way, she could oversee Gordie's visits. Gu Kwun had just turned four, and her half-brother wasn't a good influence on them. Of course, things changed when her husband moved out, *deserted*. Gordie became family by default.

Now, a pang of—was it guilt?—that she hadn't been kinder to Mom about entertaining him, especially since she had insisted on keeping all the *A-Yi's* from visiting their home. Hurriedly, she dismissed the notion, and looked through a second box.

Four rusted biscuit tins sat inside. She prised them open. Bundles of letters to Mom from her father. She leafed through the sheets, not reading, forcing herself not to care. They appeared to be in chronological order, dating from 1950, the year after they met, till 1969, the year of his death.

Remnants of a life strewn across the bed.

Who had read these to Mom? The envelopes hadn't been saved. Had someone acted as a go-between? But Mom had been possessive, even jealous of Mark, and maintained the fiction to everyone except Number One *A-Yi*, that he was Gail's uncle, brother of a dead husband, so that her precarious status as a mistress could not be questioned. It also helped account for Mark's infrequent visits. Gail didn't recall seeing any letters arrive by mail, but she had still been in school then and her mother had usually gotten the mail. Her first instinct was to burn them all. Yet shouldn't she, an analyst and researcher, read them to seek the truth?

Conchita hovered at the doorway. "Ma'am, there was one drawer I didn't empty. It was locked."

"Wasn't the key in her room?"

"No."

"Okay, I'll take care of it." But her maid did not leave. "You can go back to your work now."

"Ma'am? Could I have the clothes? Mrs. Tang used to give me her old ones."

The remark stung. Mrs. Tang can *afford* to give away clothes, she wanted to retort, *because all she does is spend her husband's money and doesn't have any children or family for whom she's responsible.* Colleen had barely noticed that Gu Kwun died, and as much as a year later, still carried on as if he were alive, completely insensitive. Gail's temper sizzled, but then, she realized Conchita was waiting. "You're welcome to take all the things," she declared.

"Thank you very much." Conchita returned to the kitchen.

Gail pushed the door, accidentally banging it shut. Now her maid would think she was angry. Why hadn't she thought to offer? She couldn't fit into Mom's dresses, nor did she want them. Someone in Conchita's family would probably like them. Her own wardrobe was basic. Gail seldom bought anything new, believing that if she invested in each suit carefully, it would last for years. Her row of tailored suits, virtually identical, hung neatly in her closet, soldiers on parade. She hand washed work blouses, and, in the last twelve years, only had to replace two—one torn and the other stained by red wine—both during the past year. Formal wear was limited and perennial. What little casual clothes she owned were seldom worn anymore, some even dated back to college, a wardrobe for all seasons first acquired in Honolulu and later in Boston, the city to which she had transferred in her junior year and where she continued to live and work after graduation. When she and Jason were first married, they had dress-up evenings to go dancing, as well as for elaborate dinners he cooked at home. But how quickly work and life interrupted! They both started working late, their only entertainment became almost all work-related, and by the time they moved to Hong Kong, compulsory formal wear was all she needed for business and charity cocktails or balls. Only after Jason left did she buy some new casual clothes because more of her weekends were spent with Gu Kwun, driving to the New Territories, playing on the beaches, flying kites, and then even he was gone.

A lock, defiant, concealed the contents of the bottom drawer. When had Mom installed it? Inserting a nail file between the crack, she jimmied, patiently trying to trip the catch. After fifteen minutes without success, she broke the lock with a screwdriver. Wood splinters sprayed the floor.

At first, the pile of papers appeared to be more letters. But these turned out to be bank books, share certificates, and a notebook that recorded the current status of these investments in Mom's zigzag handwriting, characters formed the way a young child would—the strokes and lines made in the wrong direction, left to right drawn right to left, the vertical lines started from the bottom up and not the other way around. The last entry, January 23, 1998, was eight days before her mother's death. Although illiterate, her mother had been able to write numerals and copy characters, and she could be surprisingly accurate, able as she was to calculate easily in her head. In tiny numbers, a list of the latest share prices of some ten different blue chip Hong Kong companies. Three of the initial lots had been purchased as much as thirty years ago, and over time, more investments added.

Flipping through the three bank books, from Hang Seng, Shanghai Commercial and The Hong Kong Bank, these proved to be ordinary savings accounts in her mother's name. Regular deposits went into each—dividend checks, possibly. However, the Shanghai Commercial book was new, and showed no records previous to January 31 of the current year, except for the existing balance.

But what floored her, astounded beyond belief, was the sum total of it all. Each account contained around a million Hong Kong dollars, and the shares were worth another five, even at the current depressed prices. Over a million U.S. dollars.

Where had all this money come from?

The bank books were current, making it difficult to tell how long ago the accounts had been opened. They were dated back less than three years; each showed a balance carried forward on the first page. A business card, stuck in one of the bank books, was that of one John Haight, senior associate, with the law firm Chancellor & Chung. Unfamiliar. The card looked new.

A knock. "Lunch is ready."

She opened the door. "Conchita, did my mother ever go out alone at all during the day? I mean besides the last time?"

"Yes, ma'am. She sometimes went out when I was food shopping."

"Where did she go?"

"I don't know. She wouldn't tell me."

"But ..." She meant to say her mother was senile, incapable of finding her way anywhere. She showed Conchita the card. "Did this man ever call?"

"I don't think so, ma'am."

Her maid looked at her, expressionless. And suddenly, Gail wondered what else had been hidden from her, by staff, friends, or perhaps even Gu Kwun. Had he had secrets too?

"Did you want your lunch now, ma'am?"

"Conchita, am I a bad employer?" The question tumbled out, embarrassingly.

Her maid started. "Ms. Szeto, you've had a terrible shock. I want to help you."

"Do you?"

"Yes, even you are a good person, but tough, though you're too afraid of people."

"What do you mean, afraid?"

"You don't talk to people. Your mother …"

An uncertain silence followed. It was their most personal exchange ever. Conchita shook her head. "I don't think I should say anymore," and returned to the kitchen. Despite all her sympathy, it suddenly seemed too late to do anything for Gail. Busying herself with lunch preparations, she thought of her own son back home, happier and less troubled than the boy and old lady she had been hired to care for. Perhaps she ought to give notice after all.

Defeated, Gail sat on her mother's bed. On the dining table, lunch turned cold until Conchita eventually cleared it away, uneaten.

Late that afternoon, Gail called Chancellor & Chung and spoke to a partner, Benny Chung. He said, in Cantonese, that he was very sorry to hear of Mrs. Szeto's death, and asked when she would like to discuss the will. That her mother had one was surprising in itself, but his next question shocked—*what should he do with the trust?*

She asked. "What trust?"

"Your son's. Didn't your mother tell you? She set it up for his education in the States, and wanted it structured for the least tax liability, since you and your son are U.S. citizens."

"How much are we talking about?"

"I have to check, but it's over a hundred thousand dollars."

"U.S.?"

"Yes. Your mother was very smart. She picked good investments."

Her mother could not have done this on her own! Restraining her astonishment, Gail accepted the earliest appointment that was mutually convenient, a week hence.

Later, she felt relief that Gordie called before she learned about the money, because she might have disclosed it, unable to contain herself. Someone like him, extravagant, in trouble with the law over financial dealings—something about leasing corporate jets, she recalled—should not ever be trusted.

On Sunday night, Northwest Flight 17 from New York landed early in Hong Kong.

Xavier was in a hurry to disembark. Transpacific hauls in economy class, because his upgrade had fallen through, were exhausting. He was also anxious to get home.

Yesterday, Ursula had called, furious. "You'll have to find someone else to look after Kina. I won't do it anymore."

"Tell me what happened." He hoped this was just another of his sister-in-law's habitual tantrums, which generally dissipated after she blew off steam, unfortunately at his expense since she had no reservations about calling internationally at any hour.

"It's not just one thing. It's all the sulking, and lying, and general bad behavior. I'm sorry to say my sister's kid has a terrible character. Shelley has nothing to brag about here."

"Let me speak to Kina."

Kina's voice was barely a whisper. "I'm sorry, Papa. I didn't mean to be bad."

"But you were, right?"

She whimpered. "I didn't mean it, really I didn't."

"Alright, calm down. Papa will be back soon and then we'll talk about it. Now, can you be a good girl until I get back?"

"*Oui.*"

He tried to sound stern. "Promise you'll be nice to tante Ursula?"

She giggled. "Promise."

Ursula came back on the line and said, in English. "You shouldn't talk French. Her English will never improve this way. She is such a little actress, and yet you believe anything she tells you. We have to make some changes."

"For heaven's sakes, she's only seven. I'm sure it's quite innocent."

"Yeah, sure. Guys are all the same. You know, Shelley better take over when she gets out. This is her problem, not mine!" Ursula slammed the phone down.

Xavier grimaced. He knew this drama was about sibling rivalry, which was the real problem. What he chose to ignore, conveniently, was his own complicit behavior. Had he not had a brief affair with Ursula—two years after Shelley's incarceration, when both sisters were, in different ways, dependent on him—Ursula, the more overtly sexual younger sister, would hold less sway over him now. But three?—two?—weeks was less than brief, was hardly an affair, surely no more than a fling? Annoying how it kept such a grip on him. It was the same hold Shelley had. Any other man would have filed for divorce by now, or at least a legal separation, but Xavier couldn't bring himself to make that decision. Everything would work itself out. Things always did, eventually.

During the taxi ride home, he reflected that in his dealings with the opposite sex, the pattern was the threat of eruption, which inexplicably always simmered to a murmur instead. Like that young Vietnamese on his flight—very young, maybe even under twenty-five but absurdly irresistible—the one with the plump thighs, cleavage and cute French lisp, who practically forced her number on him yet acted indifferent when he said "I'll call you tomorrow," as they left the plane. Surely he was meant to … *elle baise donc je nique?* Meanwhile, Shelley, teetering on the brink of release—an on again, off again, nerve-wracking process—assumed everything would go back to "normal." At least, that was the message her lawyer conveyed by telephone from Malaysia the day before yesterday, not for the first time.

Over six years as an absent wife—had she ever truly been a "wife"—during which he had only been allowed to see her four times. What kind of marriage was that?

And then, Gail Szeto. Why even consider her, especially when instinct told him she invited trouble, complications?

There were too many difficult women in his life! A daughter was more than enough for one man to handle.

Meanwhile, Perry Martin, in-house lawyer at Northeast Trust, a business class passenger on the same flight, checked into the Mandarin which assumed, as it had for years, its privileged prestige, located as it was in Central near the waterfront. The porter led the traveler to a harbor view room, and drew open the curtains onto an irresistible night view of the water and the hills of Kowloon. Despite fatigue, the guest gazed, amazed at this first sight of the teeming Asian port, and the porter left with a sizeable tip, as he knew he would.

6

On Monday morning, Perry Martin surprised Gail's staff because "he" turned out to be a woman. At ten thirty, when the mass layoff was over, surprise gave way to shock. By noon, the office echoed like a cavern. Gail and Perry were the only two people left.

At Perry's suggestion, they had split the task of finishing paperwork to "move this thing along faster," which they did at the conference room table, although there was, in fact, very little to do that required Perry's assistance.

Perry said. "Wow. Glad that's over." She was in her late thirties. Mostly, her job was to keep management out of trouble. This was only her second hatchet assignment. She continued, "They, the staff I mean, didn't seem to take it too badly."

Gail didn't look up. "You deal much with Hong Kong professionals?"

"No. It's the first time I've been here."

"Figures."

That annoyed Perry. She had tried, all morning, to be understanding, but now, Gail was pushing it. "Hey, only doing my job, okay?"

"Sorry." Gail regarded her from across the table. "It's just that … never mind. It isn't your problem." She stacked the finished paperwork into a neat pile.

"Stupid, isn't it, my having to come all this way just for one announcement, but you know how it is, they like to have counsel present."

"So who fired my boss?"

"Josh did that one. He flew out and told him in person on the Sunday."

"When do you go back?"

"Tomorrow." Perry rose and stretched. "I'm beat. Jet lag's catching up. Besides, I know this must seem real unfair to you."

Her words mollified. Being deliberately cool was the only way Gail knew how to survive the morning. She could almost hear the staff—*selling us out, going over to their side.* The hardest moment was when the office administrator disappeared to the Ladies. The woman's husband, an accountant at Federal Express, had cancer and was on long term, unpaid leave. They had two teenage children and his parents to support. Worst of all, she was already in her fifties, so a new job, especially during this recession, would be difficult to find. The woman had been an employee for over ten years, since the division's inception. She cried when Gail's boss had been fired.

Of course, Perry couldn't be expected to know all this. Still, it had been awkward when she wondered, aloud, why the woman was taking so long in the bathroom, holding up their meeting.

Perry pushed back her dark blonde hair. Pretty in a healthy sort of way, she was of medium height and looked as if she regularly exercised. In this humidity, her sleek, blow-dried cut degenerated into a mass of disobedient curls. An indentation on her ring finger marked a recent removal. "Is there some place I could get souvenirs? I promised my daughter."

Visiting executives treated their Hong Kong trips as part pleasure, earned. Gail wouldn't have dreamed of doing likewise when she traveled anywhere on business. To make up for her cutting remark earlier, however, she offered. "Sure. I'll take you. We'll grab lunch on the way. How old is she?'

Perry whipped out a photo of a four- or five-year-old, caught in forward motion on her rocking horse. A shock of dark curls and whirl of skirt. Flying, laughing. Perry held the print out proudly, her eyes devouring her daughter.

The glimpse at childhood joy was almost too much for Gail to bear, and she was grateful her colleague continued to look at the photo and not at her. "What's her name?"

"Persey, short for Persephone." Her eyes stayed on the picture. "The father's part Greek. We're separated."

"Sorry to hear that."

"Don't be. He deserved abandonment."

"I'm divorced."

"Infectious, isn't it? But enough of that. Do you have any kids?"

"Had one. He died."

Perry stared at Gail in disbelief, dumbfounded.

Calmer now, Gail reassured her, "I'm sorry. I didn't mean to shock you." Then, after a brief pause, she added, "I still don't quite believe it, even though it was quite awhile ago. I apologize."

"Don't be silly!" She touched Gail's arm lightly.

The two women, strangers till this moment, smiled wanly at each other.

Perry stared at Gail, unconvinced by her apparent calm. "Come on, let's blow off the afternoon. It'll do you good," Perry urged. The crisis of emotion Gail provoked was best dealt with by action. Besides, she was eager not to waste her precious few hours in Hong Kong. "So where to?"

"What kind of toys does Persey like?"

"Doesn't have to be toys. She likes whatever no one else has."

"Okay. I know a place."

Northeast Trust was on the 47th floor of the ineptly named Central Plaza, which was actually in Wanchai along the waterfront, a few miles east of Central. This invariably confused staff from New York, who insisted on staying at the Mandarin because it was in Central, despite the more convenient proximity of the Grand Hyatt. As the two women rode the elevator down, Gail could not help reflecting on their Hong Kong-New York divide, one that sometimes struck her as similar to the separation between the Island and Kowloon. On the water's surface below, the noonday light leapt in sparkles like so many Tinker Bells. At Gail's suggestion, they rode the Star Ferry from the Wanchai pier across to Kowloon, which delighted Perry. A short walk by the harbor in Tsimshatsui brought them to the Art Museum store where Perry pounced excitedly on a set of pencils with a retro

Shanghai design, as well as other similar gifts. "These are terrific," she kept saying.

Perry Martin proved talkative. From useful gossip about their senior management, she moved on to intimacies, the way women do, unfolding life history. "Guys at work don't talk, you know, *really* talk. I love my job, but it gets dreary discussing work all the time. Maybe I'm not ambitious enough. But I jumped out of a pretty safe career in law early on in favor of investment banking. The money was an incentive then, but it wasn't just that. I wanted the risk and the challenge.

"Having Persey changed things, which was why I joined the in-house counsel group. Quasi-admin. If my marriage hadn't fallen apart, Persey would have a baby sister or brother by now. I've got two older siblings, a brother and sister, and one younger sister, only she died when she was eight. Boating accident at camp. Believe me, I really feel for you.

"But I love law, and that keeps me going. I'd always wanted to become a lawyer, ever since I was a kid. Kind of a namesake thing. Mom was an Earl Stanley Gardner fan, know who I mean? She read all the Perry Mason books and turned me onto them too. Now I read all of Grisham's."

Perry paused to take a breath. They were moving, prowling the aisles of merchandise. "Persey's my whole world. I'd die if anything happened to her." She caught herself and stopped short, stricken.

Gail had been listening, fascinated at the way ideas and revelations rolled off Perry's tongue, as if words and more words could somehow untangle the knots in life, or at least, clarify her chosen path. Among Barbara and the other "old girls"—her only girlfriends, really, all Chinese—there was a deliberateness about their Cantonese conversations, despite the jokes and laughter of a common school life. Did the English language somehow allow her more freedom? The very directness of American conversations demanded at least the semblance of a true human connection. She reassured Perry, "Really, it's fine." Yet the flicker of an idea, *a daughter*, reminded her of what she had once wanted so badly. Willing away grief, always precariously near the surface, she asked, "So what happened with your ex?"

Perry went silent a moment, then said, "Fortune 100, investment VP reporting to the CFO, managing their pension fund. Seems he 'borrowed' funds to cover a personal margin call and got caught. He was allowed to resign in exchange for his keeping it quiet. Don't you love the way things get done?" Glancing at Gail, "I didn't tell anyone at work except to say we split up. His friends think he's just going through some kind of 'finding himself' or mid-life thing. Hell, I don't even know why I'm telling you all this."

Gail said. "It's okay, you can trust me. I won't say anything," but she was shaken by Perry's situation, which made Jason's betrayal almost pale by comparison.

"Peter, my husband, isn't even contrite, says it wasn't that big a deal. Gail, after five years, it was like being married to a complete stranger."

"I'm sorry."

They continued walking.

At the cash register, Perry said, "Persey asks why he's a thief. How do you tell your child that her own father can't be trusted?"

"I know what you mean."

Perry stood, poised, holding her credit card that the clerk had returned. "It was the worst breach of trust. You know, I could have forgiven him an affair."

Gail said. "That's why mine left me."

"Oh Gail, I didn't mean …"

The two women stared at each other, strangers again for the moment.

A child's voice, crying, caught Gail's attention. She turned and saw, surely, wasn't that, that *was* Kina? But it couldn't be. The girl was accompanied by a young-ish couple, thirty-somethings, a Chinese woman and Caucasian man, evidently her parents. The woman raised her palm as if to smack her bottom, but the man stayed her hand. They left the store, the girl sniveling, but Gail thought, again, that the resemblance to Kina was quite uncanny. The trouble was, although she didn't like to admit it, that Xavier Dopoulos, and Kina, occupied rather a lot of mental space, something she didn't understand, something that made no sense in the midst of this seemingly unending sorrow.

Perry was asking, "So, you seeing anyone?" What she *wanted* to ask was how Gail's boy had died, had he been alone or had she been with him. However, the invisible wall around Gail appeared impenetrable.

Gail demurred. She had waited four years after Jason left, two since the actual divorce, to remove her own wedding ring. Dating was a subject about which she remained reserved, even with women.

Perry Martin was voluble. "I wish I were seeing someone, but where do you meet reliable men? In the personals? Certainly not at work. Let's face it, you do miss it, the sex I mean, and casual encounters, well, they're better if you're twenty-something and then, they're not much good in the end, are they, either for dignity or life; besides it wouldn't work bringing anyone home what with Persey, so, then what, on the road? And then most guys who are interested are married anyway, so forget them." She paused for breath. "It's been simply *ages* since I've had decent sex."

When Gail brought Perry back to her hotel that afternoon, Perry told her. "Listen, life's been pretty awful for you, hasn't it? You may not believe this, but I will be thinking of you. I like you. Thanks for today. It was really generous."

Her openness disarmed Gail. It felt honest, like an invitation to intimacy that did not make her wary. Gail thought it would be nice to have a friend in Perry. "I'm glad you're the one they sent," she said.

"I hope we'll work together in New York. You're relocating, aren't you?"

"I don't know." And then, "My mother was killed in an accident twenty-three days ago."

"Oh my God! Gail, I'm so sorry."

"It's okay. She was old. She had a good life."

Perry was still reeling, furious that Dick hadn't bothered to brief her, since surely he must have known. Things made more sense to her now. Gail was experiencing a surfeit of deaths. "Hey, forget the relocation. You've got too much to deal with right now."

"You're probably right," but even as Gail said this, the idea seemed real for the first time. "Although maybe change wouldn't be the worst thing."

She air kissed Gail's cheeks. "Look, call me when you get in next month. I'll show you more of New York than the guys will, plus tell you all the gossip that's fit to know," and scribbled her home number on a card.

Perry watched Gail stride off. What was it that Dick said about her? *Super smart, a fighter, but coldly serious to the point of being rude. Like Medusa with a head of nails.* Funny how the guys just didn't get it, but when it came to a woman *and* colleague, guys seldom did.

Back in the office, the empty cubicles accused her. Gail walked through the space, switching off computers, copiers, paper shredders and lights.

Lucky Perry. She could fly back to a real life. Why *had* New York bothered? She didn't seem the type to propose junkets. Local labor laws didn't demand much of foreign companies. All the staff really cared about were their reference letters and severance. It was a question of trust. Management preferred to believe in one of their own, an employee from New York, rather than a foreign "local" staff.

Despite the welcome break that afternoon, Gail couldn't help thinking how easily Americans disrespected their jobs. No one's identity seemed tied into respect for the corporate or business entity, except in a superficial way. Yet willingness to accept personal responsibility—or blame for mistakes—was commonplace. *Initiative,* as her former boss used to say, *locals lack initiative.*

In Hong Kong, respect cut deep for "face" and a well-paid, respectable position provided that identity. Locals—how divided her work world was—took everything to heart, especially when it came to admitting mistakes. No one voluntarily "shouldered the *wok*"; a personal sense of responsibility was the province of foreign managers, or just for people like her, neither a real local, despite her being a senior local hire, nor an expatriate.

Which side could really claim the high ground of moral superiority?

From her private office, Gail gazed out at the empty area. The landlord hadn't been able to find a renter for the unused portion after last year's layoffs. Even less likely now. All this space in a city where the sea regurgitated land from its depths.

Josh's parting words, in New York, accompanied by a light squeeze of her shoulder, *It'll be hard, but we're counting on you. Remember, Gail, it's not personal,* had left her with a nagging sense of ambivalence.

Her first day at the job—six years ago, a "step-up" position—had been such a proud and certain moment. Even the sky that day had been startlingly clear. Once, when Gu Kwun was six, he had asked Gail to describe what she did at her job. A few days later, she overheard her son telling Janie, *my mother finds money for companies who need cash. She gets banks to give it to them.*

"That's ridiculous," Janie had replied. "Banks don't just *give* away money."

Gu Kwun explained. "Suppose I were a company. I'd have 'assets' like the stuff in my toy box, right? My mother could figure out how much they were worth and get me that amount from the bank. The toys would be like a promise to pay, a security. As long as I didn't wreck them or give them away, the money's safe. Get it?"

Janie frowned. "But that's like a loan. You'd have to pay your Mom the money back eventually. How would you do that?"

He gave her an exasperated look. "Well, I could sell my toys, I guess. But like you know how Caspar and Kazuo sometimes give me a cookie or candy bar when I let them play with my Game Boy? Or when I win at marbles how I end up with more marbles? I could give my mother all those things since they're worth money. That way, she wouldn't have to spend anything to put a cookie in my lunch box or buy me more marbles.

He paused dramatically, and then declared. "Remember what we learned in history, about barter? Goods instead of money."

Janie did not argue back.

Gail had listened, amused by her clever boy, although a brief anxiety, *wasn't this just a little* too *precocious,* but pride quickly prevailed. Her son, as she later told her boss, had redefined the process of securitized assets financing.

Now it all felt like ancient history.

Tomorrow, she would negotiate the end of the lease and arrange for movers to pack and ship the files.

Her private line rang. The echo bounced across the empty cubicle spaces and against all the inner walls. An inchoate hiccup of a wail, ringing, persisting. She let it ring. It could only be Conchita or Gordie, and she did not feel like talking to either one. The call rolled into voicemail.

Gail leaned against the window. From the 47th floor of Central Plaza, Hong Kong's tallest building for the moment, only the sky was real. Roars and odors did not penetrate the sensory-resistant glass. But its shadowy tint could not discolor the gray-blue canvas wrapping the earth. The dirty sky looked chilly.

It was a quarter to five. Five-thirty was official closing time. There was no reason for Gail to stay, because the main phone line's message announced Northeast Trust's "relocation" to New York and a management contact number, that being her cell phone which was also on voicemail. No more responsibilities insinuating themselves into her every moment. Unwilling to break routine, however, she remained.

Winter's afternoon light haunted.

Change is inevitable. Xavier's utterance, timed for truth. An ache of despair surfaced, at the absence of anything that felt real in her life. Leaning her cheek against the cold pane, she cried until twilight ended. The glassy chill spread through her as night encroached, the only invader to privacy.

7

The lobby of the Mandarin Hotel was quiet but not deserted. It was just past eleven at night.

Gail crossed the wide expanse, leather clicking on marble. Nearing the front entrance, she glanced right at the raised dais, where she had left Perry yesterday afternoon. To her left by the doorway of the Captain's Bar, Xavier Dopoulos was switching off his cell phone.

He smiled. "Hello. This is a nice surprise."

That voice again. Its level flatness, at a pitch below expected, evoked a suggestion of intimacy.

She asked. "What are you doing here?"

"Waiting for you, naturally." His moustache creased above his smile. Funny, these compensations of fate. He had waited an hour to call the young Vietnamese woman who had stood him up, and her unapologetic innocence did not sit well. "It's quite late. Are you usually out at this hour?"

He stood slightly above eye-level though she wasn't in heels. "I've just had dinner in the coffee shop," she replied.

Xavier motioned towards the bar. "I was just leaving, but if you'll have a drink?"

She hesitated. Bars were too much like the dance hall, and she did not frequent them except to meet Gordie or other foreign guests related to work.

Taking her elbow, he guided her in. "Come. Three accidental meetings deserve further exploration, don't you think?"

Perhaps it was the loneliness, or the effect of a long work day now finally at an end, but Gail followed him and, as soon as she was seated at the bar with a glass of wine before her, felt suddenly exhausted.

Xavier noted the slump in her posture. "So are you in demise?"

"I beg your pardon?"

"What you said, that you were 'traveling to your own demise'. Did it happen?"

"Oh that, yes, although I've been spared." Seeing his questioning look, added, "They offered me a job in New York."

Interesting, he thought. What he said, however, was, "I was going to call you."

"Really, why?"

"To ask you out, of course."

She straightened up. "Do you mean for a … date?" The word felt foreign.

Her tone of voice amused him. "Yes. Is that so strange?"

"Ye-es."

He leaned in. "You *are* attractive, you know."

Drawing back, she knocked over her wine.

"If a little clumsy." Taking a napkin, he wiped up the spill and signaled the bartender for another glass. "Was I being too familiar again?"

"No, yes … sorry, I'm very tired. I shouldn't have come in here."

"Poor Gail." He paused. "It's hard, isn't it, being the hatchet woman?"

"Don't call me that!"

Her exclamation, slightly too loud for the surroundings, startled him. "Pardon me, I didn't mean to be rude. It's just that, well … nothing personal, you know. Isn't that what they always say?" He was afraid she would withdraw. He reached for her arm, rubbing it lightly. "But it is hard, especially given your situation. I'm sorry."

Gail leaned both elbows on the bar and placed her head in her hands. "Very, very hard. That and everything. It sometimes feels like more than I can handle." Draining her glass, she raised it to the bartender who poured her another. She smiled at him, wryly, slightly cross-eyed. "The wine's good, though."

He said, "Perhaps I should take you home." Then he added quickly, "I didn't mean that the way it sounded."

"Xavier," she said, "no one's asked me out in six years."

He felt a sudden desire to embrace—*no, not embrace*—but to console her. Embarrassed by her revelation, she looked away.

Later, he offered, again, to accompany her home, but she refused, saying that taxis were safe enough in Hong Kong. Xavier could not deny the elation he felt because she agreed to meet him on Saturday, for dinner.

There are those moments in some men's lives, rare though they may be, when opportunity, if correctly seized, transforms existence. The coincidence of running into Gail that evening was such a moment. For the rest of the week, the question that teased Xavier was who could be buying Northeast Trust, and more importantly, why?

After their last joint consulting job was completed in mid December, Jim Fieldman had said, "You miss the real opportunities, Xav. It's that bad habit of yours, getting distracted by women. That and lousy timing."

They were at the McDonald's in Causeway Bay, near Jim's hotel on Hong Kong Island, having a late breakfast. Jim's choice. Xavier was trying to curb irritation at what passed as food. Xavier never ate fast food of any nationality if he could help it. "What kind of opportunities?"

"To get your life on track, make money."

"What's the problem? This job paid."

"But you took twice as long as we planned to get your end done. Besides, that's not what I'm talking about."

"So what are you talking about?"

"This business with Shelley. You should deal with it. You can't just go back to being a husband again when she gets out, and you know it."

"And you're doing so well? That's why your wife left you? At least mine's in an unavoidable separation."

"Leave my personal life out of this."

"Ditto, Mr. Psychoanalyst."

Xavier understood the root of his partner's self righteousness. Jim made contacts, got work easily, acted on the right stock tips, owned a huge apartment in Manhattan he had bought for a song *and* a summer place up at the Cape, while Xavier was satisfied with a modest retirement portfolio from his last corporate job and that he could cover rent—well, almost—in two expensive cities. In the seven years they'd known each other, his life careened from one crisis to the next as Jim navigated, with seeming ease, the humiliation of being the cuckold—and how *public* since friends and even clients knew, his wife having made a point of broadcasting it—after a fifteen-year, childless marriage, while leveraging a former academic career and practice as a psychiatrist into executive training and consulting for multinationals. Despite Xavier calling himself a partner, the business was actually Jim's.

Gail Szeto could help change things. There was money to be made on Northeast's stock if he timed it right. An insider—not that he expected her to disclose anything—but there were ways to ask. Besides, Gail would be much more than merely a stock tip if things went well. She was in a position to make introductions if she chose.

Wednesday morning.

His daughter was coloring pictures opposite him at the dining table, which also served as his desk. Ursula was out buying groceries.

Xavier said. "Kina, don't you like your aunt?"

She continued coloring and did not look up. "I love Auntie Ursula very much Papa."

"Can you look at me when you say that?"

There was a long silence. Xavier sighed, knowing only too well what would follow. "You're not very nice to her, are you?"

His daughter began to whimper. "I don't like it when you go away."

"Enough. You know there's nothing I can do about that," he said sternly, but already his heart gave way, and all he wanted was to promise her the impossible.

Kina looked up. "You could take me with you," and then quickly bent her head and began coloring again.

He watched her work. Kina was a remarkably controlled child, although she could throw tantrums suddenly, without warning. Xavier's father had once commented that she acted like a rapist, which Xavier dismissed as absurd. But then, his father was like that, thoughtless, careless with words, although affectionate when things were going well. As for Xavier's mother, unless something was a *cause célèbre,* her attention was difficult to maintain—her daughter-in-law's situation, which initially fascinated, quickly bored her once she realized how marginal it was, and though she wouldn't say so, Xavier knew she favored his divorcing Shelley. Her two greatest contributions to his upbringing had been giving birth to him in Chicago, his father's hometown, hence bestowing upon Xavier dual citizenship, and secondly, sharing her passion for things *Chinois,* including the language. His father, ironically, the part Chinese, spoke virtually no Mandarin. Thus did his parents ease Xavier's path into an international career.

The door opened and Ursula entered loaded with bags. "Can't you help me with these, Xav?"

He sprang to his feet, but she had already taken everything to the kitchen herself where she began unpacking.

"Listen," Ursula called out, "I'm going out Saturday night."

Xavier said, "Sorry, I've already got plans."

"Well, change them. Marcel has tickets to a play."

"You don't like plays. And who's Marcel? *Paramour du jour*?"

"Just change your plans," she retorted. She went to her room and shut the door loudly.

Without looking up, Kina said, "Marcel's the nice one, Papa. He won't last."

Irritated, Xavier did not fully register what his daughter said. Meanwhile there was the problem of Kina's schooling in Hong Kong, which he had yet to arrange, and the question of where he should stay in Shanghai, since it looked likely that the Monkey International contract would come through. A good thing too, because this was a big strategy job and not training. Strategy was Xavier's strength, not Jim's.

Wednesday afternoon, Gail paced around the empty office.

She was going mad! This was about Xavier. Her long, perfectly manicured nails, were almost all gone. Years, decades since she'd bitten her nails, not since … Harvard? She rolled the tips of her fingers into her palms, unable to witness their ravaged state.

The doorbell sounded. Nervous about her isolated state—ridiculous really, but the office was ghostly in its vacancy—she had locked herself in to wait for the movers.

A foreman stood on the threshold, consulting his paperwork. He was almost a head shorter than she was. All her life, Hong Kong surrounded her with short men. This man was muscular, stocky and tanned, and wore his company's T-shirt and tight jeans. He held out the form on a clipboard for her to sign. Gail imagined his hands clutching her wrists. Absurd! Her thoughts were roaming towards places where they had no right to go. She tried to refocus her thoughts on business.

After a quick survey, he declared, "This won't take more than a couple of hours. By the way, what should we do with the cabinets once we pack up the files? You didn't want those sent, right?"

She shrugged. "I don't care. Throw them out, or take them if you want."

"Whatever you say, *missy.*" On the back of his shirt the company's motto read, in Chinese, *Customer Is Boss No Problem!*

With everything organized, Gail wandered around the fringes of their activity, feeling useless, but grateful for the racket the movers were making. She stared again at her bitten nails. It wasn't just Xavier. The absence of noise—in all her familiar spheres—was daunting.

She took refuge in her office. The phone rang.

"Gail." Xavier said. "Did you sleep well?"

His voice! A perilous caress. His voice blew kisses between her thighs, which she tried, unsuccessfully, to ignore. She bit her upper lip. "Oh, hello."

"About Saturday," he began. His email inbox surged on screen. Fifteen new messages.

She interrupted. "You know, maybe that isn't such a good idea."

"No, wait …" Fieldman's message distracted him. *Monday April 15, Monkey International, Shanghai confirmed. Be there.* Xavier consulted a calendar, noted the public holiday dates for Easter in Hong Kong, and replied: *tell them April 19. promised Kina the long holiday weekend,* and, after adding a brief note about Northeast Trust, opened the second email.

Gail heard the computer keys but did not mind his divided attention. It contained life and connection. The lack of human contact was suffocating her. "I'm lonely," she said before he could speak. "Like you."

His next message did not distract him. "We can just be friends," he proposed.

From below the pit of her stomach, a tiny ache nudged its way to the surface. Goosebumps skittered across her legs and arms. She stared out at her slice of view, distant patches of green between buildings and sky. "Sometimes, lonely people want … foolish things, things they'll regret."

"Desire is human, Gail." Dahlia Jiang had replied to his earlier request to crash at her place in Shanghai, *no problem,* to which he responded, *bon! Kina will be happy to see you again. zaijian. soon.*

She could feel herself giving in, but held firm. "I don't know if I should see you."

That made him pay attention. He did not like being thwarted. "Gail, meet me Saturday. Please?"

She closed her eyes. A headache commenced. "You're married."

"Even husbands must eat." He would have to enlighten her, apparently, but there would be time enough later. Xavier turned back to his screen. The third message, from May, his flatmate in New York was an unexpected *do you mind but* … She was the unpredictable type. Now she'd gone and invited some painter to their loft where she promised to *model for him isn't that exciting?* "Gail, we all need friends," he said, not noticing that she hadn't spoken. "Can't you keep that option open for me?"

She had thought, hadn't she, that he could be a friend. There was more to intimacy than sex, after all, and she wasn't her mother. "Alright. Dinner at seven." That way, they'd be done early and could go their separate ways to avoid creating the wrong impression.

"Beautiful! Till then. *Zaijian.*" He typed *no*, but before opening the next mail, he found himself wishing May were less of a tease, because he did not want to jeopardize their amiable, and platonic, roommate situation.

"*Zaijian.*" She responded instinctively, but how absurd, Gail thought, that they should use Mandarin, since it was hardly his language and certainly not, despite a reasonable fluency, her dialect of choice.

He couldn't possibly have suggested changing their date, Xavier reflected when he hung up, not given her reluctance. A sharp, brief throb shot through his back left molar, where a root canal required attention.

"Who was that on the phone, Papa?" Kina asked from behind.

He spun round. "Darling, you gave me a fright. Don't sneak up on me like that."

She giggled.

He said, "Do you remember the lady at the airport?"

"The tall one who gave me the ribbon?"

"Yes. That was her."

She thought a moment. "She's a nice one," and then ran off to play in her room, taking full advantage of these school-free days which, she suspected, would not last.

What Xavier had told Gail, that Kina lived with her aunt, was not strictly true. The flat the three of them lived in, on Observatory Road in Kowloon, was one he had rented only from the beginning of the year. Prior to that, Kina lived with him in New York, May being a nutritionally irresponsible, albeit affectionate nanny in exchange for free accommodation; she had gotten Kina off to school and brought her home each day. His frequent trips to China made Hong Kong a suitable base, especially since it was where Ursula was breaking up with her last lover—Italian this one, another of her Eurotrash finds, Xavier gloated—and needed a place to live.

But mid-academic year transfers were difficult, and Ursula, a former primary school math teacher turned real estate salesperson, was both a lousy nanny *and* tutor, albeit a nutritionally balanced one. Ursula, who should have been able to help facilitate his daughter's entry into schools, instead gave Kina sums to do, with percentages and fractions to calculate her sales commissions, which were much too difficult.

"It's not a problem," Shelley had written in response to his concerns about their daughter's schooling. "Besides, the life experience is good for her," and then had gone on at length about the latest activity of the Oslo group who were working on her case and would Xavier please contact them again as soon as possible, even though he had already told her that he'd been in touch with them, weekly, since their efforts began.

He could not help thinking that a woman like Gail would have been much more worried about Kina, even at the expense of her own well-being.

A more immediate concern, however, was the pain in his tooth, which he hoped would not require further attention.

"*Missy.*" The foreman stood in Gail's office doorway.

Gail started. She despised that "Canto-lish" form of address.

"We're done," he announced proudly.

"That was quick."

"My guys work fast. We're not allowed to stop long outside the building, you know, because of the taxi stand." Customers, his boss said, should understand your constraints, otherwise they'll make all kinds of unreasonable demands.

He walked her through the office, pointing out emptied drawers which his crew left partially open. The boxes packed with reports, files and disks had all been removed for shipping to New York, except for the three boxes that would go to Gail's home.

"You didn't really have much here," he commented. "It wasn't a big company."

"No."

"So, does *missy* still have a job?"

Nosy, Gail thought, yet she felt that he was, like so many others, only articulating the fear that accompanied this unexpected economic slide. "I go back to America." She didn't mean to imply a return, but in Cantonese, it felt natural.

"Oh, so you're ABC. Your Cantonese is very fluent," he complimented. "Most American-born Chinese can't speak well."

"Ngoh haih Heung Gong yan."

"Really?" His puzzlement furrowed a path into his brow. "You don't look local."

"Well, thanks for everything." Opening her wallet, she handed him several, red, hundred dollar bills. "Here, treat your guys to 'tea.'" It was overly generous "tea money" for the little work they'd done, but her company could afford this tip.

Not so that it was obvious, but his thumb flicked through four bills. Not bad for less than a couple of hours work, he thought, although his crew would later disabuse him, their new foreman, of that notion. He nodded an abrupt thanks and left.

Gail began locking up. The phone rang, and she was about to let it roll over to voicemail, but then decided, one last call. It was Janie's father.

He said. "Hi. Just thought I'd call to see how you were doing."

"Oh fine, thanks," but her first thought was *journalist, he's fishing*. The media could read their official releases. She wasn't prepared to discuss Northeast Trust's situation. "Listen you caught me at a bad time."

"Well, I won't hold you up. Give a call sometime. Let's have coffee."

"Sure. Say hi to Janie," although she wondered why he really called.

Gail finished locking up. Tomorrow, the furniture would go and the phone and fax lines transferred to her home.

The elevator shot downwards to the lobby of Central Plaza. She headed for the taxi rank. Easier to be ferried by an unquestioning chauffeur. Lately, she hadn't felt much like driving and her new Volvo sat unused in the garage at home.

The taxi raced towards the south side. Gail leaned back and closed her eyes.

Why shouldn't she "go back" to America? Coming home had changed everything in her marriage, something she still found inexplicable, even after all this time. And now … now there wasn't anything left, nothing.

The taxi was at a standstill. Her building cast a short afternoon shadow, offering minimal shade.

"Hey you, we've arrived," the driver said. "Get out."

His rude interruption dispelled memory. Taking her time, she counted out exact change and didn't close the door. He cursed as she walked away.

In New York, Jim Fieldman was pissed at Xavier's reply. *Damned slacker.* Always some personal drama. Maybe it was time to find someone else, like that Tony Dong from Beijing, with an MBA from Stanford; he was young, bright and eager. Well, a bit too eager.

The alarm clock in his office-cum-bedroom had stopped five hours ago at midnight and there wasn't another C battery *in the whole goddamned apartment!*

Jim had other reasons to be upset. Tokyo's close was discouraging and the Hang Seng equally unfavorable. London—but nothing much was happening there either. Josh's admonition, late last year, *futures, my friend, forget this other crap.* The trouble was, Jim didn't fully understand futures. The Chicago Board of Trade, home of the largest futures exchange, conjured up herds of cud chewing cows and rows of cornfields against an endless horizon, the very vision he'd left the Midwest to escape. Also, too many variables, too complicated to calculate and, if he were completely honest with himself, way too fast for him. Jim Fieldman was a man who needed to understand and most of all, to be in control.

He yawned. Coffee didn't keep him going long enough anymore. It was hell being fifty. He turned off his computer, lay down on the sofa bed and shut his eyes.

The perplexing thing was Xavier's continual interest in Northeast Trust. *Btw,* his email had also said, *NTE movements worth watching.* And what possessed him to use the ticker symbol? It was unlike the man, who barely kept track of his own stocks. Might be worth prodding Josh Rabinowitz on the subject next week at the club.

8

"Ma'am?" Conchita did not move away from the table after serving Gail's breakfast. "Can I talk to you?"

"It's not convenient right now," Gail replied. Ten minutes earlier, she remembered her appointment at ten with the solicitor, Chung, and was preoccupied with how to rearrange her morning. Inconvenient, not having a secretary.

Her maid stood her ground. "It's important, and it won't take long."

Impatiently. "Okay, what is it?"

"I'm very sorry, ma'am, but I want to give notice. I mean, now that your mother ..." she stopped abruptly.

Gail's first reaction, like a speeding car suddenly forced to brake, was violent. *How dare you,* she wanted to shout, *can't you see this is the worst possible time?* But Conchita's expression—hard, almost angry, markedly different from her usual placid demeanor—arrested her.

Conchita added, "Well, it's not like you really need me anymore."

Calming down, Gail flicked her wrist to check the time but could barely read the tiny watch face. *Going blind, too soon for reading glasses, surely?* Looking up. "Can we talk about this in the afternoon? I ... I have a few problems this morning."

Conchita's face softened. "Okay, ma'am. Thank you," and

hurried back to the kitchen. Removing the saucepan from the stove—odd making such a tiny portion of congee in the small pan instead of the larger one she'd used for years—she washed it by hand. There wasn't much need for the dishwasher these days.

The look in Ms. Szeto's eyes—pleading, almost frightened—was unexpected. She had braced herself for a tongue lashing or a similarly unreasonable response. Bonny's advice, last night, that she must remain firm under any circumstance, seemed irrelevant now. Besides, after all this time, she could wait a few more hours.

Entering the offices of Chancellor & Chung, Gail pictured her mother walking through these doors, sitting at this same conference table across from these two men in their early to late thirties. John Haight, an American, was the younger of the two, and Benny Chung was a local who had spent time in the States. They specialized in Hong Kong probate, international tax and U.S. trust and estate law for wealthy people with complicated global lives.

They had met her mother three years ago when she showed up, asking them to help take care of her American business.

"She came alone, and kept apologizing for her bad English, and requested that my partner translate. I thought she spoke quite well," Haight said.

Gail shrugged. "She manages," but privately, she was incredulous. Three years ago, her mother was virtually senile, forgetful and muddled over the simplest things. That she found her way to this exceedingly foreign place and conducted business with these two professionals … and what on earth did they mean by 'her American business'?

He riffled through the folder of papers, pulling out documents to review. "The will left everything to you, except for …" He paused. "She said you'd understand what she meant about taking care of your *A-Yi*. She fixed an amount in a separate letter but wouldn't give us your aunt's name."

"She's not my aunt, but I'll take care of that." Gail knew her mother often covered *A-Yi's* gambling debts. *Like family.*

He continued. "She had us structure a trust fund for your son's education. Also, since your mother is a green card holder ..."

"My son's dead," she said, and then registering what he'd said, added, "Green card? What are you talking about?"

The two men exchanged glances.

And that was when she understood why an American law firm was necessary, because a permanent resident would be subject to certain U.S. tax laws which a foreign national wasn't. Haight was saying, the inheritance was complicated, there were U.S. and Hong Kong taxes to satisfy, and since the portfolio was now worth ...

She stopped Haight, mid-sentence. "What portfolio?"

Chung interjected. "Her investments in the U.S. stock market."

"You mean the trust?

"Oh no, her brokerage account. She had mutual funds, some individual stocks and a few treasury bonds. She appointed us custodians. Said she was getting too old to take care of these things anymore."

"How much are we talking about?"

"I don't know exactly, but it's roughly three million, possibly a little more. U.S. dollars, of course."

Dollars from heaven! Money was pouring over her, raining down in more than one currency. Her IRA, her one-time carefully invested college fund for Gu Kwun, paled by comparison. Years of scrimping, to pay off the loan for her MBA, the painstaking financial planning she took such pride in, her careful budget to avoid incurring even the smallest credit card debt—everything was a vast comedy of wasted effort. Even the remaining mortgage on her flat, the one unavoidable debt, could be paid off entirely with less than a fifth of Mom's money.

A surplus of wealth, making her giddy.

Haight took a deep breath. The funny, clever, unconventional woman who had been their client bore little resemblance to her daughter, this severe, composed professional who was courteous but did not smile, whose expression was difficult to read. This woman hardly seemed like a daughter in mourning, despite her somber tones and Chinese widow weeds. "You really didn't know?"

Gail shook her head, willing herself to remain calm.

Benny Chung asserted himself. "Ms. Szeto, perhaps we ought to start over."

At the end of the hour, Gail's mind was racing. She asked, "By the way, how did my mother find you?"

The two men frowned at each other. "We're not entirely sure," Haight said. "She called and requested an appointment. My older brother Harold—he's with Merryweather Lind here—handled her U.S. dollar brokerage account. He didn't refer her though, never met her. They conducted business entirely by phone. Harold speaks minimal Chinese of any dialect, but his assistant translates brilliantly."

"You didn't think it odd when she produced all this money?"

Chung interjected. "In Hong Kong? Hardly."

He was right, of course.

"But I was a little surprised she wanted to make a will," Chung continued. "Old folks here don't, as a rule. They think it's bad luck to test the gods." He broke into a smile. "I remember asking what if *she* survived you, and she laughed and said, *Then who cares where the money goes!* Your mother was one wild old lady."

Gail took this in, her thoughts flicking through possibilities. Her father, or another of his relatives? Or some other benefactor, her mother's running joke a reality, *got to find a rich man?* But what baffled her most was why her mother had continued to live the way she had before moving in with Gail, in that rundown old flat, if all this money was hers.

"Oh, there is one other thing." Haight handed her a Redweld. "It's a letter from a Mark Ashberry. Your mother didn't want you to have it till after her death."

Gail untied the ribbon and flipped open the cardboard folder. In it was a sealed envelope addressed to "My daughter Gail Szeto Ashberry." Christmas, 1956 was written in the bottom right corner. She held up the yellowed envelope a second, then dropped it, unopened, into her purse, thinking, *Did Mom actually get some of the Ashberry fortune?* "What did my mother say about this?"

The two men exchanged glances. Haight said, "She wouldn't explain much, just that it was among your father's things that were sent to her when he died. I guess they lived separately?" When Gail didn't answer, he continued. "Is he your father?"

"Was. He died when I was seventeen." She did not hesitate in telling them the truth. Her mother's lie was pointless in the face of all this reality.

"Well, that's all we have on file," Haight concluded.

Chung said, "Would you like us to handle the probate? We have a partnership with a U.S. accounting firm as well who can deal with American taxes. Only if you'd like them to, of course. John's brother still handles the brokerage account, more or less."

It was just business to them, these two lawyers who looked at her as merely another potential client. Overwhelmed, despite an exterior calm, she said, nonchalantly. "Why not? Someone has to."

Afterwards, Haight said to his boss. "What planet's she from?"

One Exchange Square, where Chancellor & Chung were housed, ended at the ground level as a vast atrium in which Gail stood, unsure of what to do next. On the outdoor concourse facing the front door, a Henry Moore offered comforting curves, familiar in its public largesse. The building rose from a concrete platform above the Central bus depot and train station for the new airport, embracing the reclamation that extended into a shrinking harbor. On an impulse, she called Barbara Chu, whose office was in Two Exchange Square. "I'm in your neighborhood," she said. "Any chance you could take an early lunch break?"

Barbara, besieged by work, was not sure she heard Gail correctly. "Today?"

"Right now. I've been more or less laid off, by the way."

The news, startling, over and above the surprise of hearing from Gail who almost never called, *and* given her old school chum's tragic circumstances, stopped Barbara long enough to reconsider her schedule. "It's an awful morning, I'm afraid, meetings one after another, big new client project we weren't expecting, my youngest girl's out with the flu and hubby's in China so somehow, I've got to get out long enough to take her to the doctor, *and* the nanny's on vacation, worst timing, well, you know how it is … but if you want to talk for a few minutes, why don't you come on up?"

"Okay."

Minutes later, Gail was seated in the large corner office with its commanding view of the harbor and Kowloon. Piles of papers and files were spread all over Barbara's desk, as well as along the top of a cabinet beside the desk and on a table behind her. It surprised Gail that her friend could be disorderly and yet hold such a powerful job *plus* manage three children, two of whom were teenagers, a dog, *and* a gaggle of in-laws as well as her own family of, was it, *six* sisters and elderly parents?

Gail said. "Sorry to burst in on you like this."

"Don't be silly, what are friends for? How are you coping?" Barbara was thinking, *such a dreadful thing, one death after another, so unlucky,* and was glad Gail was reaching out, finally.

"My maid's giving notice. Such a pain."

It was the last thing Barbara expected to hear. "You can get a part-time one to clean. I mean, it's not exactly like you need one full-time anymore, right?"

"Well ..." Gail stopped, not knowing how to continue. What was it she expected? A bitch session, perhaps, to relieve all the tension and uncertainty, although *had* that been the reason for her call? Now, taking in her friend's reality, she suddenly realized, Barbara didn't know her any more than she knew this woman seated opposite her, despite their long acquaintance. Barbara had no idea about her mother's life or her own secret shame. Glancing down at the array of photo cubes on the desk, she spotted one of Barbara and her husband, surrounded by their children. She said quickly, "I suppose you're right," she added, "Nice photo," and pointed at it.

Barbara turned the cube towards her. "Oh, I'd forgotten that was still in there. It's old."

"Yes, I suppose so," Gail repeated vaguely. "Your kids are still young, not much older than ..." She stopped again, Gu Kwun's name on her lips, afraid of bursting into tears.

"Are you *sure* you're okay?" Barbara's maternal instincts rose to the fore. Gail seemed like another sick child. "Why don't you come to my home for dinner tonight? We can relax and talk then."

Gail got up to go. "No, really, it's okay. You're busy. I've taken up too much of your time already."

Barbara began to rise from her seat. "Wait, hold on, let me see about lunch …" The intercom buzzed at that moment and her secretary's voice *boss man's calling, sounds mad.* She gave Gail an apologetic look but Gail was already at the doorway, leaving.

There seemed nowhere in the city to go, now that she no longer had an office. Furniture removal was happening this very moment at Northeast Trust, overseen by the building management. As the elevator carried Gail down to the concourse, she considered calling Kwok Po, whose office was nearby, but then thought otherwise. Better to make an appointment and not upset old habits. By the time the doors opened at ground level, she had already recovered her composure.

The chilly outdoor air sent her in search of a warm place. Remembering the coffee shop, mezzanine, where she'd once met Gordie, she headed there. The morning rush was over and it was almost empty. She ordered a *cappucino* and sat down.

Her purse was still open and, as she was about to close it, she saw the slip of paper with Number One *A-Yi's* cell phone number. The money, she had to tell her about the money.

A-Yi exclaimed, joyful, "I knew *Daijeih* would take care of me. A million dollars! Surely that's too much. What about yourself, *Guy-lo?*"

It wasn't much, Gail knew, not even a hundred and fifty thousand in U.S. currency and less than four percent of the inheritance. "I can take care of myself," she replied.

"Let me treat you to dinner at least. We'll have double boiled shark's fin, okay? You like that, just like your mother. *A-Yi* remembers."

The raspy voice, despite cell phone's static, pulled Gail back in time. *Yes, yes,* she wanted to say, let me stay with you *A-Yi,* the way, as a child, she had begged her aunt when she couldn't stand being around Mom, and *A-Yi* would let her, for a few hours, until Gail was ready to return home.

"Come on," *A-Yi* said. "I know you're busy, all you girls today, such important jobs, not like us old birds. But you can make a little time for your *A-Yi*."

Yet now, Gail was afraid to impose, afraid perhaps that *like family* merely meant obligation. "No *A-Yi,* that won't be necessary."

Afterwards, she wondered, did *A-Yi* know the source of the money, and if she did, would she consider her portion less than generous? Yet her ignorance—of Mom's life, of what *A-Yi* knew or didn't know, of "family," Gordie, her *dai gor,* the "big brother" Gail reluctantly agreed to know after her marriage ended, wise guy, scammer, *untrustworthy*—now, her ignorance was finally beginning to trouble her, worrying its way into issues she thought long resolved, forcing out feelings that set her on edge and made her uncomfortable, causing her to lose control.

At four that afternoon, Gail and Conchita sat down at the dining table.

Gail said. "So when is it you want to leave?"

If this were victory, to Conchita, it felt Pyrrhic. "As soon as possible, if you don't mind. At the latest, I'd like to be home with my family for Easter. It's important for us Catholics, you know."

"Yes, I do know." Gail looked around the flat vaguely, not certain what she wanted to see. "I went to a Catholic school."

"Did you, ma'am?" Conchita's interest was piqued. "And all this time I thought you were Buddhist, like your mother. I graduated from one too and studied secretarial."

It was Gail's turn to be surprised. "Really? Did you work as a secretary?"

"In Manila, for six years before I came to Hong Kong."

"You know ..." Gail began slowly, "How would you like to stay till Easter as my secretary? I'd pay you more, of course, off the books, and your domestic work would be much less anyway." And then, she explained her company's situation, adding, "I probably will be leaving Hong Kong myself, perhaps even as early as May."

They talked for almost an hour, a real conversation, Conchita felt, as if her mistress were actually seeing her for the first time. Conchita asked to think about Gail's offer overnight, although in truth, she had already made up her mind.

That night, Gail removed the sealed letter from her bag and deposited it in one of the tins with her mother's letters, unopened. Should dead voices speak? She didn't know. She was afraid to find out.

Talking to Conchita that afternoon—how animated, responsive she'd been—had made Gail feel good, even made her laugh when she said. *Let me think it over. The resurrection can wait for me one more night, don't you think?*

This day of so many unknowns, where only instinct, not logic, prevailed. A day where you couldn't know wrong from right, where any certainty of being right, *ngaam,* had all but vanished. She wanted to call out, explain to someone, anyone, even Jason, that this hollowing out of all she was, was painful. She had only one self, the one sure thing that kept her going. This hollow hurt even more than the feeling of regret, a feeling that overwhelmed Gail when she was younger, certain as she was that if she had only done such and such differently, she would have suffered less or succeeded more, despite what her mother said. *Melodramatic, girl, that's what you are, scaling Everest when the only obstacle is an anthill. What on earth do you have to regret?* Gail had refused to listen, knowing her mother was simply wrong and that she, Gail, was *ngaam,* right. That night, sitting at her desk at home, Gail stared out at the sliver of view, the affordable sliver of her overpriced flat in her property-mad city, the home she insisted upon buying against Jason's and her mother's wishes, wondering, had she ever been even a little bit right about anything?

Now, everything gone, everything except her mother's refrain, an unforgiving echo. *Ngaahnggeng ngaam.* And the nagging echo-question—*no more regrets*—now no longer the conviction it once had been.

"She's offering *how* much?" Bonny's voice bounced around the walls of the stairwell that night. "Are you sure?"

Conchita nodded. "Of course I'm sure. Do *I* make mistakes about money?" She was pleased to be able to lord it over the younger woman who was at times too sure of herself, even though she meant well. "Besides, didn't I tell you Ms. Szeto can be flexible, and basically is fair even though she's difficult? This thing with her company, so terrible. But I can learn a few things from her, and it's only for what, not even two months?"

"Maybe I was wrong about the bitch."

"Hey, don't use that kind of language. It's not nice. And another thing, you shouldn't make so many judgments when you don't really know someone, *di ba?*"

"Okay, okay. But listen, what if it's just a trick to make you stay longer and then she reports you for working illegally. I hear stories from other girls. The Chinese can be like that. You know, right, on our visas we're only supposed to be domestics, not do other work?"

Conchita gave her friend a withering glare, thinking, such petty jealousy was beneath her. "For such a clever girl," she said, "you say some pretty dumb things sometimes."

9

On Friday morning, Gordie called. “I’m in Singapore, transiting at the airport from Jakarta. I’ll be in Hong Kong in a few hours. Want to meet for dinner tonight?”

He had said a couple of weeks, but Gordie was like that, unpredictable. She said, “Just a drink, if you don’t mind.”

“*Such* enthusiasm.”

But she heard the laughter in his tone, that irritating optimism he flaunted. Wanting to deflate it, to throw him off guard for a change, she said, “Gordie, I found a letter from Mark for me.”

“Oh yeah? Where was it?”

“Among my mother’s things,” she lied. No, not the money. She wasn’t going to tell him about that.

“When was it written?”

“The year I met him.”

He recalled, with a lingering sting, the letter Dad had left for him, written the year before he died. His father never wrote or spoke much to him, not after Gordie burnt his draft card. The letter had been the closest thing to forgiveness, although even that exacted a price. “So what did it say?” But then thought, *why would she bother, being the way she is,* and added. “Or didn’t you read it?”

Gail started. How did he guess? Annoying the way he could strike these almost familial claims. “I didn’t read it.”

"Lucky you," he muttered.

"What was that?"

"Oh, nothing," he said, adding quickly, "Family history, nothing you'd be interested in." He reverted to logistics. "So, say six o'clock? Would you mind doing Felix? I want to see it."

Inconvenient, having to cross over, and such an "in" place held little appeal for Gail, but she knew Gordie always stayed in Kowloon. "Fine. Six."

"It's a date."

Gail was puzzled. Why hadn't Gordie been surprised by the letter? As reluctantly as she had agreed to see him, she was now grateful for a chance to probe.

Her brother. A problematic relationship from the first moment they met.

It had been an evening in October of 1969, three months after Mark's death. Gail was seventeen. The young man in a suit who turned up at their doorstep after his phone call had just turned twenty one. He was tall, a little over six feet, and had pale, smooth skin that burned.

Mrs. Szeto wore her best *cheongsam* to greet him. Gail had continued studying after his call, annoyed that her mother so readily changed plans for this person they'd never met and refused to put on "something pretty" despite her mother's wishes. She did, however, oblige by translating their conversation, although she avoided speaking directly to him.

"There was a will," he said, after accepting tea in a glass tumbler which Gail served. "I felt it was my duty to tell you personally." He leaned forward as he spoke. His hands were large, but he handled the hot glass gracefully, holding the rim to avoid burning himself. In their living room, he seemed at home.

Mrs. Szeto smiled before Gail finished translating, having understood most of what Gordie said. "Then your father kept his promise."

"I don't know about any promise but …" In short, there was a trust fund for Gail and an acknowledgement of her birthright. "You're eligible for U.S. citizenship, Gail, since you're not yet twenty one. I'll stay and help you apply if you'd like. Our family has friends at the Consulate." Gordon Ashberry studied his half-sister curiously. She was exotic and intensely striking, and had her mother's intelligent eyes.

Gail did not reciprocate his gaze.

Mrs. Szeto spoke through her daughter's confusion. "Now do you believe me, *Gay-lo?* Like I always told you, just a question of time." Turning to Gordie, she said. "Tell Mark's son that he too is an honorable man and that I take him as my son."

Gail's temper flared but she kept her voice level in front of this stranger. "He's not your son. I won't do it. We're Chinese, not *gwai.*"

"Silly girl, where do you get such crazy ideas from? From these Hong Kong bumpkins, so backwards, not like in Shanghai. *Gwai* are people too. Obey me, *Gay-lo,* or I'll find someone else to tell him. Don't make me go outside the family."

Gordie said. "Cantonese sounds so different from Mandarin. I've studied Chinese, you know. At Yale. But I'm not very good."

"See, he's a smart boy. Went to Yale, knows Chinese. You better do as I ask," Mrs. Szeto said. "Otherwise, he might figure out what we're saying." Her lover's language filtered through, and, despite not having seen him for a couple of years, and hence not practicing English, some vestige retained.

Tethering her fury, Gail translated, wishing her mother would speak for herself. Why didn't Gordie stop staring? His eyes, green as Lion Rock Hill behind their home, seemed to see right through her. He was making her blush, the way American sailors did when they ogled and whistled.

Gordie stood up, spread open his arms and gave Gail's mother a hug. She laughed and hugged him back. "Not as fat as your father," she said in English, patting his waistline. "His *toe laam*—how did he call that?—his 'spare tire' too big. Too much beer!" Then she pulled away, frowned, and asked. "What about your mother? Is she angry?" There was genuine concern in her voice.

He nodded. "She's very upset at me for coming here." His betrayal weighed heavily. Mrs. Mark Ashberry, the only one completely in the dark, would never see the light and a painful tremor stopped him. Surely his mother had deserved more than merely the position of first wife? Surely there had been some love once?

Mrs. Szeto squeezed his arm, bringing him back to the moment. "You're a brave boy," she said. "Just like your father."

Gail folded her arms, desperately forcing back tears. After all this time, she had stopped believing that one day, the shame of her illegitimacy would disappear. *Mark knows I don't want anything for myself, but I made him promise to do the right thing for our Gay-lo.* And here it was, finally, with even an offer of the Ashberry name. All those years, her explanation to friends about her name had been what her mother taught, that a person ought to keep a Chinese name because after all, even Mom kept hers. Gail Szeto, younger sister to Gordon, Gordie. Daughter of Mark and Fa-Loong, the "flower dragon," the only name her father used, having never known her real one.

That seedy dance hall, where women's bodies were their priciest asset. The shameful life that was a lie, all lies, to teachers, friends, acquaintances, everyone who wasn't a part of her mother's underworld. A mother she learned not to trust.

Tears erupted, against her will.

Gordie reached out his arm. "Hey … Sis." The word felt strange on his tongue.

"You crying again, *Gay-lo?*" Her mother asked in Cantonese. "*Ai-ya!* Such a sentimental girl, even sniffles over movies. Come be nice to your big brother. Their family has money, didn't I tell you?"

It all came down to money with Mom! "He's not my brother!" and she ran to her room, slamming the door.

Gordie said, "Wow, what happened?" He shook his hair—sun-streaked pale blonde—out of his eyes.

Gail's mother laughed and replied in English, "Girls, so much trouble. Not like boys. Pay no attention. I take care of her later. Come, you practice your Mandarin with me."

Later, Gail could not remember if she'd shouted in Chinese or English.

Conchita was saying, "It's for you, a Mr. Dopoulos," and handed Gail the phone.

Gail took it distractedly. Why did talking to Gordie always affect her out of all proportions?

Xavier said, "Ah, at last. Didn't you get my message?"

The accentuated "ss" sprinted off his tongue, French style, making her shiver. "Oh, yes." His voicemail, *please call back as soon as possible,* retrieved late last night. She had meant to call first thing this morning and forgotten. "I'm afraid I've been busy. Also, it was too late to call yesterday by the time I got it."

"It's never too late for you to call me."

His provocative tone discomfited and teased her. She asked, "What can I do for you?"

All business again, he thought, and said, "About Saturday, I don't suppose there's any possibility you could make it tonight instead?" He hesitated. "Only if it's convenient. Otherwise I'll keep tomorrow's appointment."

It disturbed her, his calling it an "appointment." Was that, after all, really how he saw it? "I have to meet my brother tonight."

"Your half brother? From New York?"

"Right."

"Well, perhaps afterwards? We could have a drink."

"I … we might be late," she lied.

"How friendly."

A bite in his voice, or was she imagining? "Well, see you tomorrow then."

"Surely, please don't let me hold you up."

The phone clicked, cutting off Gail's goodbye.

What, Gail wondered, had that been about? She regretted, almost immediately, having lied. Unaccountable, her behavior. Why did everything seem so fraught? Her son's voice, *I know we're lucky you have a job, thank you Mummy,* stabilized her, brought her back to a known center of certainty. When in doubt, work.

Xavier frowned, conflicted. Now what to do? Earlier, having cajoled Ursula into postponing her date with Marcel—a most accommodating man who actually managed to exchange tickets for the play to Sunday—the problem was over when, out of the blue, the young Vietnamese had lisped, in French, back into his orbit. *Saturday,* she said seductively when she called, *you can buy me a drink. I must go with these people to Visage and wouldn't mind being rescued.* He had offered dinner Friday but she demurred, and he knew, right then, if he wanted to sleep with her, it would have to be on her schedule, not his and not, as he would have preferred, because *he* took her out.

The trouble was, when it came to women—trouble, regardless—she reminded him of May, and to a lesser extent, Ursula.

Two years ago when May, daughter of a friend of a friend's, showed up in New York and looked him up as a contact, Xavier had been deprived for an extended period. The brief fling with Ursula had ended eighteen months earlier, and he wanted to break his habit of going to hookers since Shelley's incarceration. Had work allowed him to live in Western Europe—Amsterdam, for instance, where he at least felt safer about diseases—where the trade was less appallingly pitiful than in Asia—such *young,* sad innocents—and less expensive than New York, this habit would have been less of an issue for him.

"It's an arrangement," he told Jim at the time. "May needs a place to stay, Kina needs someone to look after her. Nothing else."

"Oh sure. You're going to have some twenty-year-old Malaysian bimbo sleeping one door away from you."

"She's twenty-six, and Malaysian Chinese. All I said was that she was 'cute.' Jesus, she's a kid and a nice girl. Besides, Kina really takes to her."

"And you're a midlife walking hormone."

"At least you're being polite, for a change." But he knew Jim's real problem. The man was horny as hell.

"You, pal, will end up with blue balls." Jim chortled at his own joke.

Xavier winced. "My mistake."

He wouldn't concede, no matter how much his partner needled, that Jim was partially right. Pushy women, willing to go after what they wanted with naked aggression, unafraid of their sexuality, *were* his type. The more Rubenesque, the better, youth being the icing. That defined Ursula and May in varying degrees. What Jim didn't appreciate—what Jim, not being a parent, would never appreciate—was that you automatically kept some things out of the home, *especially* when raising a daughter.

Besides, May truly was a nice girl, with zero interest in him. The young Vietnamese, on the other hand, whose name he couldn't recall—she hadn't scribbled it along with her phone number and identified herself over the phone only as *"c'est moi"*—was not at all nice, and probably available.

Meanwhile, Gail. Guaranteed good conversation, perhaps even appreciative of wine and cuisine, and, if nothing else, a business contact. The trouble with ladies was that courtship took time. Had it not been for a new, *unexpected*, hunger for order—the habitual chaos perpetually surrounding him had gotten old, *perhaps*—Xavier Dopoulos might simply not have bothered with the likes of Gail Szeto.

At Felix, situated on the top floor of the tony Peninsula Hotel, Gordie cruised towards Gail who, having arrived seconds earlier, was seated at the bar. He was unseasonably casual. Khaki slacks, black short sleeved T-shirt and a pale beige lightweight jacket, loafers, no socks. On anyone else, the combination would have been hopelessly wrong, but on Gordon Ashberry, somehow it wasn't.

Gail, business-suited in charcoal gabardine, glared at his naked ankles.

"I love this place," he said, "especially those goofy urinals and crazy wide windows. I'd heard it would feel like you were peeing into the Hong Kong harbor. It does."

All the familiar irritations that were her brother—crude language, incessant jocularity—upset Gail, but this time, there was a strange comfort in the routine of their encounter. Scotch, his only drink. The way he could rattle ice in the glass, hard, but without spilling a drop. His ordering her a Chablis without having to be told.

He offered his place in New York—a townhouse in Gramercy Park belonging to the family which she didn't know existed—while she looked for her own. "As long as necessary, Gail. It's yours too, in a way."

"Thanks," she said. "But I'll manage if I decide to move."

"Hey, let me help you."

"I don't need help."

"Yes you do. Death is rough enough. You don't have to go through everything alone."

Gail said, "These life passages are normal. Everyone goes through them."

"You're in shock, doll. Stop being such a …" he tried to stop himself but said it anyway, "such a fuckin' rationalist."

Such language! And those unwelcome endearments. She winced. "I'm not," she replied, coldly.

Abruptly, "Look, I know you only tolerated me because of your mother and maybe even Gu Kwun. If you never want to hear from me again, say so. I'll disappear. You don't owe me anything."

She hadn't expected a confrontation. "I'm sorry if …"

"Skip the apologies. You want me out of your life, right? Now's the time. All you have to do is tell me." He hated talking that way but Gail was confrontational, like Dad. "So," he concluded, "is that what you want?"

"I'm not sure what I want." Then, "You *are* my only family," she said, awkwardly.

"Look at me." He lifted her chin. "We both have our father's mouth."

She looked down, embarrassed. The past, a childhood of not belonging, welled up.

"Hey," he said softly, "we can do this slowly." He stood and opened his arms. "Can I give you a hug?"

Gail stiffened.

"Come on," he said.

Uncertainly, without rising, she leaned into his embrace.

Gordie pulled back first, surprised by the intensity of his feelings. He signaled the bartender for a second round. "Wow, glad that's over. So how *are* you doing?"

She sipped her wine. "There are times I don't know what to do next."

"When in doubt, do nothing."

That's not the way I am, she wanted to say but instead, "By the way, why do you suppose Mark would leave me a letter like that?"

"You're kidding, right?"

"What makes you say that?"

"He probably just forgot to post it. I mean, he wrote you all the time."

"Whatever gave you *that* idea?"

"But your mother, she said, well what I *understood* was, that Dad sent you letters telling you all about America, and that he spent time with you in Hong Kong. When I was a kid, he brought me here several times, but I had no idea, until much later, where he'd disappear to when he left me with Uncle Jimmy. You know him, right?"

Gail shook her head. "Never met him, but you mean Jimmy Kho, don't you? Mom used to mention him." Gordie nodded. She continued, "Mark visited Mom, but he didn't come to see me. They usually went out. I think he only actually talked to me three times."

They studied each other in silence as their respective histories rewrote themselves.

Gordie finished off his drink. "Are you sure you won't have dinner?"

"I think," Gail began uneasily, "maybe I will. You and I, we ought to talk," and drank up her Chablis.

He watched approvingly. "You're a good Ashberry, Sis. You hold your liquor well."

They talked till past one in the morning.

Alone in his hotel room afterwards, Gordie regretted this foray into the past. It aggravated ghosts. After years of going it alone, in the space that was "family," blood had thinned. Perhaps it was a mistake, asking to see his sister again tomorrow.

In his entire adult life, Gordon Ashberry had never held a job. He traveled constantly, piloted gliders and small planes, sang baritone in *a capella* and with jazz bands, and collected expensive vintage, and new cars. To maintain liquidity, he played the international stock, futures and currency markets. To appease his mother, he squired debutantes or other ladies requiring an escort to social functions for charities that Mrs. Ashberry supported as a board member and active fundraiser. Occasionally, he fell in love with exotic women, meaning red-blooded, not blue. These relationships fell apart when he wouldn't bring them home to Mother.

Around his father, Gordie knew he never measured up.

After the war, Mark Ashberry had flown for Pacific American as a commercial pilot, though money was hardly a reason. Flying was his passion, and an airline as good as it got in peace time, since Mrs. Ashberry eschewed the idea of a career military man as a husband.

In the eighties, Gordie had started a business, ostensibly to lease aircraft to corporations. His Australian partner traded arms on the side and Gordie liked the excitement of the black market, which cut through bureaucracy and was amenable to bribery. When the Feds caught up, his partner vanished to Portugal, via Bermuda, under a new identity, and Gordie only managed to evade prosecution because his best friend Harold Haight, a Wall Street tax lawyer, had taken care of things for him by cutting the right deal. A sizeable portion of his inheritance went towards the IRS in fines, although his main assets remain untouched.

The loan from Gail's mother had been to stake a business venture—timber contracts between Indonesia and China—and was his second attempt to do something resembling work.

Only at home did he work. For reasons neither of his parents ever understood, Gordie insisted on doing all his own domestic chores—food shopping, cooking, laundry and ironing—refusing to hire even a part-time cleaner. In hotel rooms, he straightened up after himself, and frequently made the bed. If asked why, he would only say, *no reason*.

For the women who *didn't* care about meeting his family, this was what they said drove them away.

Family, Gordie had long ago decided, especially the richly insane tree from which he had sprung, was like a willow, its branches flailing in the winds. Ironic that Dad died before acknowledging Gail. She and Dad were similarly parsimonious, and Gail much more like the child he had wanted, the son Gordie had never been.

10

At home by daylight, the night before with her brother felt surreal.

It was almost eleven. Conchita brought Gail the phone. "It's Mr. Tang," and then laughed, "he was surprised to hear me as your secretary."

"Thanks," Gail replied with a smile. In only a matter of days, the temporary arrangement with Conchita was proving satisfactory.

Kwok Po said, "So it's home office, is it? How are you faring?"

Busy, she almost said automatically, but stopped. "I don't have that much to do, other than busy work. Truthfully, everything's temporary until I make up my mind about whether or not to relocate to New York."

"I've been worried about you and would have called sooner, but things are tough right now. You know I don't work on Saturdays if I can help it. But you called yesterday?"

"I did. About money."

"Money?"

"You're rich, so you're the best person to ask advice from about money," and she told him about her mother's legacy. "What I really don't understand is how she could have had a green card all this time without my knowing."

He was sanguine. "You know old folks. Your mother probably got it years ago and never mentioned anything. She didn't really want to go to America, but it was insurance." Gail's family background was complicated—exactly how Kwok Po wasn't quite sure, or perhaps couldn't remember—but given her private nature, it was no surprise if her mother had been the same. However, when it came to the older Chinese generation, some things were universal.

"I suppose that's possible. I'm not sure I want to go back myself, especially to New York." What she really wanted to discuss was work.

"Gail, you needn't move to New York if you don't want to. There are plenty of options here. What about Shanghai? My partner and I have tons of contacts." For as long as they'd known each other, he had been intrigued by Gail. Talented, unusually independent and not weighted down by family—especially now—she had all the choices in the world. "Besides, you needn't decide right away if you're not ready. Tell them you want an unpaid leave of absence. They'll do it if they want you badly enough. It's not like you need to make a living anymore."

She said, "You're probably right."

Kwok Po was solicitous but matter-of-fact like about the money. She was only just beginning to comprehend its magnitude and how it could affect her life. But unlike Kwok Po, who came from wealth and understood how to be rich, she was, for the first time in her life, confronting that prospect.

"You should travel, take time off, Gail. Everything's been such a nasty shock. You need to re-group. Take a cruise or something."

When had he begun sprinkling English words like "re-group" into his Cantonese? It wasn't like him. "Maybe. There's no place I really want to go to though."

The trouble with Gail, Kwok Po thought, was that she had never learned to have fun. Although a workaholic, Kwok Po knew how to enjoy himself. "Then what about a spa or resort? That way, it doesn't matter what country it's in, as long as the place is pleasant."

Reasonable suggestions, perhaps, but they seemed wasteful, self-indulgent. "I'll figure something out. Thanks anyway."

"No problem. Anytime. We're friends for life, right? Let's have lunch next week. Whatever you do, don't let some second-rate investment bank push you around. They're lucky they have you. I mean that, Gail."

How she appreciated his recognition of her abilities! Just like the old days at Harvard, when they had argued about cases, challenged each other, debated the future of China's development against the disadvantage of America's global dominance.

"Thank you," she said, feelingly, but he had already hung up.

Kwok Po caught that slight emotion in her voice—he knew her well, after all—and regretted cutting her off, which he hadn't meant to do. Never mind, Gail would understand. Afterwards, he was surprised at how uncomfortable she had made him feel. This was *Gail*, whom he'd known forever, who had suffered unbearably. Imagine losing a son *and* a mother one right after another. Well, almost so. Yet a jarring thought, one he had never considered before, surfaced. The Gail he knew was the discreet, reliable Professional and a long time Friend. She wasn't someone's Mother or Daughter, and certainly not anyone's Wife. He suddenly remembered, the mother's funeral, he should have said something, apologized for not stopping by. Had she been insulted, upset, hurt? Why didn't he know? But then the illogic of these competing thoughts confounded him, and eventually, they sank from view, and Gail resurfaced as the woman he'd always known.

Later, Gail wondered whether or not Kwok Po, in the over twenty years they'd known each other, ever spared a moment to recall that she had once told him she loved him (long, long before Jason or Colleen showed up in their respective lives)—and she had, secretly, for two years, or thought she had, desperately loved this perfect Chinese man—and he had told her, *Gail, we're not that kind of friends,* repulsed by her advance, cutting off all hope for love and marriage as she craved it. Later, he dismissed her apology with *Ngoh dei ying goi mohng gei—we ought to already have forgotten*—adding, *between friends, some things need never be said.*

It wasn't till Tang Kwok Po married Colleen Leyland did Gail finally begin to accept that it *hadn't* been, as she believed, that his rejection was because she, of mixed blood, wasn't Chinese enough. Wealthy men, she decided, simply preferred their wives young and dependent, because Colleen was thirteen years his junior and had never held a job or earned an income in all her life.

Gordie said. "So why won't you read Dad's letter?"

It was late Saturday afternoon. They were standing in front of Gail's childhood home, a two-story, traditional shop house on Nam Kok Road in Kowloon City, the residence above what was now a hardware store. Overhead, airplanes droned, as they took off and landed at Kai Tak Airport down the road, northeast of *nam kok,* the "southern corner."

She countered, "Why did you want to come back here?"

So be like that, he thought, and said. "It reminds me of Fa… your mother, and Uncle Jimmy." He pointed at the store. "Used to be a beauty parlor, right, faded Marilyn in the window, and every time we passed, Uncle Jimmy and I—of course I didn't know it was your place then—he got a real charge because I'd say I didn't see any Chinese blondes."

"You can, nowadays," she responded, laughing, although she was thinking, *except for number four A-Yi,* the one who had plied the U.S. naval R & R trade and wanted to look Eurasian to get more customers. She had dyed her hair an ugly, platinum blond. The one who died young. "Who was Jimmy exactly?"

"He flew together with Dad under Chenault."

"From the … Flying Tigers days?" Reference bytes scrambled through her brain, memory chips in the wrong slots, random access hard at work. Talking to Gordie helped straighten out the facts of her father's life, without the haze of Mom's storytelling.

"That's it. Jimmy introduced Dad to your mother, you know, at the racetrack, although he didn't tell me that till much later."

"He's still alive?"

Gordie flinched visibly. "Been in a coma since the early eighties. Family won't pull the plug. Good thing too," he added hastily.

"Is it? I mean, what comfort is there in that?"

"One of his daughters, Rose, visits him weekly." He became wistful, nostalgic for an impossible romance. "She's a doll, that one."

Gail experienced a faint curiosity. A whole other tale. She never recalled any mention of girlfriends; and her brother had remained, as far as she knew, a bachelor. This man dipped into her blood and navigated her past, touching some sacred fount of knowledge. Yet how much could she honestly care? He was still a stranger.

Gordie barely missed a beat. “But hey, she’s married, so forget that.”

“How ethical of you,” she remarked, but the situation with Xavier nudged, nagged.

Gordie went silent and stared at the dwelling which stirred such remembrance. Watching him, Gail felt almost guilty that she was not as deeply moved.

Approaching dusk did not soften the building’s dirty exterior. The window frames were rusty, but new drainpipes hung down one side. Jammed between two taller buildings, it looked puny. The verandah was a half-story platform below the roof, an outdoor refuge on sultry nights. The hole on one side of the barrier remained, where the carved stone façade had crumbled. Like a paper cutting, the barrier comprised a symmetrical pattern, circles like sentries across a sheet of stone. Though old, there was a solidity about the building. The distinctly Chinese curvature of the cornice was quaintly out of date.

Gail suspected it survived demolition only because a stubborn owner wouldn’t sell. Or perhaps not. What, after all, did she know about their landlord, this building, or how Mom ended up there? It had been home, with its high ceiling and bank of windows that faced the rising sun. She had slept on a wooden bed with no mattress and studied by a naked bulb at a folding *mahjeuk* table while her mother costumed herself each night for work. She had hand washed laundry and hung it out on bamboo poles, the water dripping onto the street below. The rack was still there, although no poles were in sight.

Gordie interrupted their meditation. “It’s getting to the cocktail hour.”

She was still hanging laundry, the dampness in winter wrinkling her skin. Rousing herself, she glanced at her watch and exclaimed, “Oh my God,” realizing she had barely enough time to run home and change, which upset her.

He asked, "So any plans this evening?" Gordie's weekend was open, which was how he generally kept his schedules. Revisiting the past had its moments, but in his books, the present and future were what counted.

"I have a … date," and she blushed.

That delighted him. "Then you shouldn't be wasting time with your brother, should you?" He hailed her a taxi.

She offered. "Can't I give you a lift?"

For the first time, he looked at his half-sister as prey. Gail possessed a quirky kind of glamour—body almost like a model, but cursed with a brain—although she was too leggy for his tastes. A wicked grin lit his eyes, and just as quickly, extinguished itself.

"Never mind. Some other lifetime." He pecked the edge of her lips. "Stay in touch, okay? And call me when you get to New York."

At the Captain's Bar, Xavier was beginning to get annoyed. It was seven-fifteen, and Gail, he imagined, was not the type to be late. The tonic water was too sweet and irritated his tooth, which was proving a nuisance. Swishing the sweet liquid towards the right side of his mouth he turned on his cell phone and speed-dialed Kina who, when he'd left the flat, was throwing a temper tantrum.

The bartender pointed to the door, and he complied, stepping out to the lobby across which Gail was rushing.

"Xavier," she was limping. "I'm so sorry, but the traffic … no taxis, so I drove, then the parking! And then my heel." She pointed at her shoe. The heel was wobbling precariously.

Gail was wearing a short, thin wool, pale green dress, which exposed shapely—and surprisingly long, Xavier noted—legs, and a calf-length, off-white coat. Her scarf was colorful, with a hint of spring. Out of the business suit uniform, she was slimmer than he expected, almost thin. But her broad shoulders made her seem larger boned than she really was. It was physique for netball and basketball, both of which Gail had played competitively as a girl.

Xavier switched off his phone, took her by the hand and assisted her down the steps of the entrance towards the bar. "I thought you weren't coming."

"Oh of course not!" She hadn't meant to exclaim, but what she was thinking was that normally, she would have called, *naturally*, but realized, too late, she'd forgotten her phone. On top of everything, an unexpected period. Perimenopause scrambling her regular cycle, *such* a nuisance. Things had a habit of going haywire whenever Gordie entered her orbit.

Xavier said, "You look pretty."

"Do I?" She thought, *how stupid, as if fishing for more compliments,* and bent down to fiddle the heel, securing it firmly back in place.

"A Chardonnay for the lady," he told the bartender.

She interjected. "Chablis." Glancing at Xavier. "If you don't mind."

"No, why should I mind?" But it piqued him, her assertion, and thought that perhaps the young Vietnamese must remain, after all, an option for later.

She said. "So where …?"

He said. "Nice to …" and stopped, "Ladies first."

"Where should we eat?"

"There's no hurry, is there? His tooth throbbed, and he pressed two fingers to his left cheek. The last thing he wanted was food

"I'm starved," she said. "We could go to the Banker's Club. It's near here."

"Gail, that's not exactly what I had in mind."

"Oh, but the food's excellent. I'm a member. I'll be happy to sign for us."

He took both her hands firmly in his and said, softly. "You know, I'm not dangerous, and … Oh my god, Gail! What happened to your nails?"

She pulled her hands away, embarrassed. "I didn't think men noticed things like that."

Xavier shook his head and began to laugh. It was infectious, and Gail began laughing as well. He said. "Are you really very hungry?"

"No," she admitted.

"Come on." He picked up her coat and draped it over her shoulders. "Let's walk by the harbor. The air will do us good."

Along Queen's Pier, languid waves lapped the concrete walls, a rhythmic, laundering swish of sea. The evening was warm for February.

She spoke first. "Tell me about your daughter."

He was prepared. Women needed to know these things, although, with Gail, he had already decided to take a chance with the truth. Much later, he would question this unusual frankness, wondering if it hadn't been misguided. "She's not my child."

"What?"

"Shelley, my wife, was raped in Paris. I was away for three months on business. Kina's the rapist's child. He was French. The police didn't find him."

"That's ..."

"What, Gail? Horrible, awful, terrible, frightening? Indescribable? *Incroyable,* as my countrymen say?" His voice was edgy but without bitterness.

Chronology. Events. She tried to focus on facts. "So after she had Kina, when did she go to prison?" He had said, awhile. The girl looked about five or six.

"She left for Malaysia two months after Kina was born and never came back. That was over six and a half years ago."

"Then she ..." She was about to say that Shelley did not really know her child, this offspring of violence, all of which mitigated, somehow, the abandonment.

He interrupted. "Yes, Kina has become my child. Shelley's Catholic. She wouldn't hear of an abortion." His wife had won that battle, one he lacked the will to fight, the way it was with all Shelley's wars. What choice did he have?

Gail said. "It isn't easy raising a child alone, and in this case ..." Her voice trailed off in sympathy.

"I appreciate your understanding."

They stopped by the guardrail and faced the water. Gail was moved. Her own shame seemed hardly shameful at all.

Looking straight ahead at the water, she began to speak. "My mother was a prostitute. She was sold as a girl to people in the Shanghai sex trade who later sent her to a Hong Kong brothel, but she managed to run away. By the time I was born, she was a dance hall hostess. You know, a taxi girl? Many don't sleep with customers, at least she claimed she didn't." Her lips stretched taut as she spoke.

"And did she?"

"Yes." It was something she had never admitted to anyone, not even Jason, that her mother sold herself regularly to rich or otherwise useful Chinese men. She turned and leaned her back against the rail.

He stroked her arm gently with the back of his fingers. "Difficult lives."

She told him then about her father, the Flying Tigers pilot who later flew for Pacific American, although, she emphasized, he didn't need to, being from a wealthy family.

"And did he acknowledge you?"

It was as if he had touched the darkest points and scattered light everywhere. Was *this* it, the reason she was drawn to him, this understanding that came from a parallel life of secrets and shame?

By nine-thirty, Gail realized she had been talking nonstop about herself. She was hungry. "You know," she said, "we really ought to eat."

Xavier had been only half listening, thinking it fortunate, her asking about Kina, because it gave him an opening. He liked revelations, the best kind of foreplay, and, in Gail's case, possibly the only kind. She remained propped against the guardrail. He was leaning beside her, his hand playing with the sleeve of her coat.

His phone rang, jarring him out of his laziness. "Sorry about this, my daughter, you know."

The reminder of life as it had been for her was reassuring. She said. "Don't ever apologize for responsibilities," and turned to the sea, allowing him privacy.

His shout made her turn around.

"… stop, you're being ridiculous. She's only a child!" At which point the line went dead, because Ursula had hung up.

Xavier glared at the phone in his palm. "Gail, I …"

"You have to go, don't you?"

"I'm really very sorry …"

She stretched out an arm—long, proportional to her legs—and, reaching for his free hand, maneuvered him towards her and kissed him like a lover, the way she once had—*shamelessly*—kissed Kwok Po, except that instead of backing away, Xavier closed in towards her, held on, while around them, the Saturday night revelers thronged.

11

The dream would replay itself in her waking moments—Mark, her mother, Gordie, Gu Kwun up in the sky as she fell—and Gail wondered, was real life a thing of the subconscious, existing in a place where fiction reigned, and the only element making her conscious self tick the marching routine of work?

On Monday morning at seven-thirty, Josh Rabinowitz rang. Gail had been at her computer for the past hour and a half.

Josh said, "Not too early, I hope?"

"Not at all," she responded brightly, but he put her on edge, this man she had seldom dealt with directly, this boss for whom not even Sunday evening was sacrosanct for leisure.

"Wasn't sure you'd be in yet."

Testing? "I'm at home."

"Call forwarding?"

"No. I've already broken the office lease and moved everything out."

"That was quick."

"A kill fee's cheaper than a live rental. No point paying more than we need to, is there?"

"Good girl. Well that makes what I have to say even easier."

He needed her report earlier, third week of March if possible. They settled on the end of the month. When she asked why, he did not disclose the real reason—a close-to-final merger—except to say that the board wanted it, which was, essentially, true.

"So," he said after she'd given him a rundown on the outstanding deals, "have you decided?"

"No."

He cajoled her, amused. "Gail, what's the matter? Don't you like me?"

Her ex-boss' advice, *If you ever have to talk to Rabinowitz, get to the point right away. The man has the attention span of a flea.* She inhaled deeply. "You haven't made me a real offer yet, have you?"

That impressed him. He scrolled through his electronic diary. "Lady, get yourself to my office next Monday, two-thirty, no, make that three, and you'll *have* your offer."

Afterwards, Josh made a mental note to speak to Dick in the morning about drafting the package terms and then added Perry Martin to his list of people to get Dick to consult, thinking, *it takes a woman.*

Conchita said. "Breakfast is ready, ma'am."

Gail was still recovering from her own audacity. Her first thought, *Call Perry,* but decided to wait till after she ate. Meals were sacrosanct. Gail did not eat and work simultaneously unless it was absolutely unavoidable.

Also, there was another thing. "Conchita, you don't need to call me ma'am anymore."

"Okay, Ms. Szeto."

"What about just Gail?" She had tried, when she first returned to Hong Kong, to get secretaries to use her first name, accustomed as she had been to Boston's more casual office environment. By now, she had long since given in to local formalities. Conchita, however, wasn't local.

"Sure."

Uncertainly, Gail added. "You wouldn't be willing to eat with me, would you?"

Conchita hesitated. Even with the Leyland-Tangs, who had been far more relaxed—in their home as a domestic, the "ma'am" business had been dispensed with from the start—she never ate with them.

Gail said, "I'd like the company."

"It's kind of you," Conchita said, "but no, I'd rather not, if you don't mind."

She was disappointed, but not about trying. "Well, it's up to you," and began to eat her congee.

After breakfast, Gail called Perry.

"So I hope I'm not breaching company policy by asking your opinion," Gail said after telling Perry that Josh was pushing her to decide.

"Don't be silly. I'll be the first to tell you if we ever shouldn't talk."

Gail said. "I just don't know New York."

"What's to know? It's the greatest city in the world." Perry, a native New Yorker, saw little reason to live anywhere else.

Shyly, Gail added. "There is a man who lives in New York … well I'm not sure but … oh, why am I even telling you this?"

"Tell, tell."

Gail told. Perry listened to the jumbled narrative, interrupting to ask an occasional question. At the end of it, she still wasn't certain how long Gail had been seeing Xavier.

Perry said, "Dopoulos? A consultant?" and mentally ran through her husband's Greek acquaintances. "Can't place him."

"He's more French, I think. The only problem is he's sort of married." Gail hesitated. It made her uneasy, confessing to the possibility of such an affair. "What I mean is, he's separated."

"Aren't we all? So what's the problem? Is he good in bed?"

"Well …" Gail did not complete the sentence.

Perry said, quickly, "Forget it. I'm just being nosy." For an intelligent woman, she thought, Gail seemed almost naïve about men, a bit like a teenager with a crush. Or perhaps, Chinese women were unusually conservative? Somehow, she didn't believe that. She added. "But then there's incentive to move here, right?"

"Maybe. It's still a big move."

"That it is," Perry conceded. "Listen, come for dinner when you're here. We can talk some more. Persey would love to meet you."

"Thanks, I will."

Afterwards, Gail thought that it was more than the city. The country itself daunted her. Most of the years she had spent in the U.S. was as a foreign student, or among other foreigners like Kwok Po, a pattern that repeated itself with Jason during her professional years in Boston. Hong Kong was home; or at least an idea of order. She knew how to be Chinese. Being American still felt artificial, despite the passport she had been pleased to acquire, the *only* Ashberry legacy she cared about. Citizenship meant being able to support herself by working through college without visa problems. Gail had rejected both her father's money and his name.

Her thoughts about Xavier, on the other hand, were more than merely foreign. They were—as hard as she tried to suppress them—obscene.

The night she met her father was the first time Gail understood why she wasn't all Chinese.

She was four. Her mother knocked on the door of her room. By then, her mother had already instilled in Gail the habit of locking her door, to prevent problems with the johns she occasionally brought to their home, a practice she ended as Gail got older.

"Gay-lo, someone wants to meet you."

"*Yahplaih.*"

As the door opened, her mother instructed. "Speak English." A tall man stood beside her. "Gay-lo, this is your father."

She had stared at him, uncomprehending. *"Ngoh mo bahba."*

"Silly girl," her mother admonished. "Of course you have a father."

"Hi there," the man said. He knelt beside her and scrutinized her face. Looking up at her mother, he said. "She has my mouth."

"I told you."

The tangy whiff of Old Spice. He asked. "Will you give me a kiss?"

Gail shook her head.

They stayed a few minutes longer. When they left, he gave her money in a red packet, saying, "Don't spend it all at one time."

That night, her parents went out. "If you need anything, go downstairs and knock on Number One *A-Yi's* door, okay?"

Mom said in Cantonese. *A-Yi* rented a room in the back of the hairdresser's. Gail nodded obediently. She waited all night, expecting her mother's return. At three, the flat was still empty. Gail sat in the living room, afraid to fall asleep, afraid to go back to her room. Eventually, she drifted off.

She dreamt that her father was a giant, towering over the park near their home. He kept growing taller and taller until eventually, his head hit the clouds and disappeared into the sky. His voice boomed like the roar of thunder, asking for a kiss. She put her hands over her ears to shut it out. *Ngoh mo bahba, ngoh mo bahba.* She repeated this louder and louder until she drowned out the sound of his voice. By morning, *A-Yi* was shaking her awake saying, W*hat are you doing in the chair?* She looked around her home, but Mom was nowhere in sight. *Why are you crying, Gay-lo, what's the matter?* But she shook her head violently, and refused to reply.

What dogged Gail as the week progressed was Xavier, or more accurately, the possibility of a lover. After a celibate 24-7 life, her current workload left too much free time, and she often found it difficult to concentrate. Dangerous.

What she had implied to him, that there had been no man in six years, was not entirely true. A couple of years earlier there had been Vince, a divorced American photographer, to whom she was attracted. No sex, though. He hadn't been interested in her romantically, and she managed to avert disaster by withdrawing gracefully. They remained casual friends. Then there was Gu Kwun, Mom, and a much more demanding schedule to distract.

By Wednesday morning, Xavier had not called. Repressing the impulse to phone—she had already given away more face than she probably should have—she rang Kwok Po for lunch instead, after which Benny Chung rang to follow up with her on the probate and other matters.

Chung said. "On that Shanghai Commercial bank account, we've requested the transaction history. We'll start with five years. The printout should come through from the bank in about a week or two. But the probate's another story. That will take awhile."

"How long is 'awhile'?"

"Maybe six months, a year. Perhaps not that long. In the meantime, all the Hong Kong bank accounts are frozen, unfortunately."

That did not seem terrible. She hadn't needed, or used, her mother's money, not in a long time.

"Pity you didn't have access to her accounts," Chung added.

"Why?"

"Oh, you know how it is. The banks can't stop you withdrawing cash, as long as you do it quickly, before they're officially notified about the deceased, that is. People do it all the time."

His *laissez-faire* attitude annoyed her. "You mean breaking the law."

"It's perfectly legal."

Ignoring his huffy defense, she asked about U.S. estate taxes. Those, he said, would be more burdensome, although her mother not being resident in the U.S. might mitigate the problem.

This asset deep freeze relieved her. She really had no idea what to do with all that money, other than the bequest for *A-Yi*. The longer the probate took, the more time she had to make decisions. All these decisions! She wished life could be as easy as working for Northeast Trust. The future for their Asian operation pointed in one obvious direction only. North, to China, and all that implied.

At lunch, Gail was appalled by Kwok Po's diet. Red meat was *much* too heavy, and at his age too, what *was* he thinking? It had been awhile since they'd seen each other. Was it her imagination, or had his complexion become even pastier than she remembered? But she said nothing. After all, she wasn't his wife.

Kwok Po said, "What does it feel like, being rich?"

"Why ask me? You should know."

"But I've always had money. What I want to know is how it feels to become rich overnight."

Their salads arrived. Gail found the dressing excessive, and wished she had requested it on the side. Kwok Po appeared unfazed by the drenched greens.

"To be honest," she said, after swallowing her first mouthful, "money now seems rather pointless."

He grinned. "Coming from you, that's refreshing. Seriously, I'd love to see you spend wildly, frivolously. It would do you good."

"It's not so easy. I tried to buy myself a new watch yesterday. Walked around for hours, looking at shops. Amazing how many different kinds of watches there are now, I had no idea. In the end, I simply couldn't buy one. Consuming doesn't come naturally."

"Try. You might like it," he urged, and asked. "So, when are you coming to work for me in Shanghai?" The best way, he knew, to get Gail to talk about what was *really* on her mind was if presented with a red herring.

She laughed, knowing full well they would never jeopardize their friendship by working together. "Don't you think I should go to New York?"

"Only if that's what you want. Frankly, there's more happening in Shanghai and you know it. Forget the money. Think how much more fun work could be. You'd never have to crunch your own numbers again, that's for sure. Or work for *gwailoes* who have less qualifications and experience than you, but presume to tell you how to do your job."

It startled her to hear him say *gwailo,* since his own wife … but Gail knew what he meant. At foreign companies, things were different. Even though she was American, she would never be treated the same as a white person. She'd been headhunted on several occasions for top management positions with Chinese companies in Hong Kong and China, the kind of power no non-Chinese, no matter how qualified, would ever be given. Previously, however, she couldn't consider the option since her mother didn't want to go back. "Maybe," she ventured.

"Have I ever steered you wrong?"

"No, you haven't." He was right about that much. In November of 1987, when a pink slip appeared on her desk after Black Monday, Kwok Po had persuaded her to give Hong Kong a shot; he had returned earlier that year to work for his family. It had been the best career move she had ever made.

"And Gail, you do realize, don't you, that you don't ever have to work again as long as you live? Lady of leisure isn't so bad, is it?"

"Now that," she said, "is a novel thought."

It wasn't till the wee hours, when she awoke drenched from a heat flash—another hiccup of being a woman—that she wondered, and what about a lover, since a husband was pointless. Where was the man willing to take a chance on her? Or was she—as the *A-Yi's* and her mother used to laugh about number four *A-Yi,* the Chinese blond, behind her back—cursed with "so big an itch" that only the *gwailoes* "devil men" dared approach, the ones with "tools long enough to scratch"?

Gail's mother had liked Jason. He shrugged off her dance hall past with a democratic smile. *A doctor!* She told Number One *A-Yi,* when Gail called from Boston to say she had gotten married. *Gay-lo found a doctor! And he's Chinese. I knew she could do it.* His being six years Gail's junior and only at the start of his career did not immediately trouble her, despite always having advised her daughter to marry an older, established man, one who could look after her. Jason's family wondered about this daughter-in-law who got married abroad—no *chanyan,* even, bereft of blood—who didn't believe in banquets, and was *jaap jung* to boot, whose only saving graces were her foreign passport and Harvard degree. But Jason, a youngest child and only son did not suffer, never suffered, censure or shame.

The affair was another matter.

After he finished blaming himself for it, Jason had turned the tables on Gail. She was abnormal, he said, and ought to see a psychiatrist. They had met, prior to the court date, to discuss joint custody for Gu Kwun.

"You need too much sex," he told her.

She said, "Are you insane?"

"It's no use, Gail. You can't say things like that anymore. I won't listen."

What things, she demanded, just what things did he mean? She was always reasonable, only insistent when she knew she was right.

"You're always right. Don't you ever think you might be wrong?"

Well of course she knew. No one was always right. Such a child sometimes, irritating her, needing constant guidance. Even now, he was running away from home, pretending to be in love with that silly woman. A receptionist, not even a university grad. How could he stand such a partner? Could she afford a maid, raise a child correctly, satisfy him in bed? No. Gail Szeto was the only wife for him. "You're a fool, you know. Gu Kwun will never love you now." She spat the words at him. He had walked away, saying, That's up to you, Gail and never looked back. And then she was alone and Gu Kwun no longer had a father. Life went on, a little sadder perhaps, while Gail clung to her sense of righteousness with a vigor that was almost pathological.

By late afternoon the next day, Xavier still had not called. She had just finalized her travel plans for New York. The frenzy of the day was over and she was thinking about going to her health club for a swim when Rick Hammond called.

"Hey," he said. "How're you doing."

"Fine." She waited, wondering what this was about.

"I was thinking maybe you and I could have a coffee sometime?"

She remained on alert, a protective radar against journalistic inquiry, since what other reason would he have for contacting her? But if he thought that because Gu Kwun had been his daughter's friend, that meant he had an "in" with her, she needed to put him straight. "Rick, what is it you want to know?"

There was a loud silence. Then, "Gail, you misunderstand. I'm not calling you as a journalist. This isn't about work."

That was when something exploded in her. *Another married man!* What was this, a surfeit of unhappy marriages circling around the divorcée? She wanted to shout at him, *What do you take me for,* but restrained herself with difficulty. Her mother's laughter rang out, mocking her. She shut her eyes briefly. "Mr. Hammond," she said. "I don't have coffee with married men."

"Oh hell, Gail I'm sorry, of course you didn't know, did you? I'm divorced now, have been for eight months."

Her face flushed. She felt like crying. What was wrong with her life? Nothing was working anymore, everything was splintering, glass shards gashing her insides until she bled. What more would she have to deal with?

"Gail?"

"I'm sorry. I didn't mean to be rude but you're right, I didn't know. Look, it's not a good time right now."

"Okay, perhaps another time."

"Perhaps."

That night, Gail's body raged with uncontrollable desire which, try as she would, she could not satisfy. She was *not* her mother! She would never be like that woman! But no matter what she did to shut out the images—first Xavier, then Kwok Po, even Vince and now Rick—the *lust*, there was no other word for it, raged. *You need too much sex!* That horrible accusation, as if she were some kind of freak, a she-devil, abnormal in her desire. And all because she was the daughter of a whore, a bastard, a birth that should never have been. Was this why her life was falling apart? Through her sleeplessness, her mother's laughter mocked her. *Ngaahnggeng ngaam, ngaahnggeng ngaam, ngaahnggeng ngaam.* A never-ending echo. Iron-necked, and hardly *ngaam.* No, nothing about her life was remotely right at all.

When Barbara Chu rang Thursday at noon to confirm their old girls' get-together for Friday night, Gail grabbed at the phone before Conchita could answer it.

For the last five days, Conchita had observed Gail's nervous behavior, the way she started every time the phone rang. She wondered if her mother's death had finally unbalanced her, melting away all that pain and terror she kept frozen inside, and thought also that perhaps, it really hadn't been such a good idea for her to stay on after all, despite the money. Gail was less rigid as an employer of a professional than as the mistress of a domestic. Yet as she told Bonny, only two nights ago, *Hong Kong and Manila, two different worlds. Even secretaries here are treated like slaves, just like domestic helpers. Doesn't matter* what *she says my job is or how much she pays me.* But she was committed now, until Easter, and there was nothing she could do.

Late Thursday afternoon, Xavier still had not called.

Part Two

New York to Hong Kong Hong Kong New York (or JFK–HKG RT)

12

Meanwhile, Xavier's week had begun with a call from Jim and then slid progressively downhill.

"It won't be for another couple of weeks, probably," Jim said when he woke Xavier too early on a Monday morning, "but I'll hang out for three, maybe four weeks. It'll be easier for getting to and from Shanghai. I've borrowed this great house in Shek-O, belongs to an old college buddy. He and his family will be on vacation."

The idea of Jim being in Hong Kong infuriated Xavier. It was like forcing an open wound into a bowl of salt. On top of everything, Jim would be living in luxury, near one of the best beaches on the south side of the Island, in contrast to Xavier's straitened urban circumstances in Tsimshatsui. The only consolation was that his trips to New York could be eliminated.

On Tuesday, Ursula packed her bags to move in with Marcel. She stood by the door, a triumphant look on her face. "I've had it with you and that brat. Find someone else to do your dirty work."

"Please," he said. "For the family."

"Family, my foot!" She glanced at Kina, who stood silently by the door of her bedroom. "That girl should never have …"

"Don't," Xavier cautioned. He raised his hand, readied to slap her face. "I won't think twice if you dare say another word."

Ursula picked up her bags and rushed down the stairs. In the streets below, her current savior awaited in a Toyota Corolla.

Xavier looked at his daughter and sighed. "Now, *chérie*, what are we going to do?"

Kina came next to her father and ran a finger over his knuckles, one at a time, repeating the movement in a steady rhythm as she spoke. "And the man and his little girl went over the first hill, then the next, and the next." She smiled as she whispered the bedtime story Xavier told, the one he made up for her when she was two. "And at each hill, there is a different monkey. The first is bad, the second is *plus mal*, but all of them are what monkeys are, naughty just like me."

Laughing, Xavier picked her up off the ground in a sweeping embrace. "Ah, *mon petit chou,* just *what* am I to do with you?"

Kina nuzzled her face into his shoulder, happy to be rid of her bossy aunt because she could speak with Papa in their own language, hoping this meant moving back to their place in New York, and May, with whom she gladly spoke English because May let her do what she wanted and didn't tell Papa.

He set her down. "Now, will you go to your room and be a good girl? Papa has to think."

She pecked him on the cheek. "*Oui,*" and disappeared, content to be obedient and to amuse herself for several hours.

Xavier leafed through his notebook. Surely there was someone whose domestic could be spared part-time? He pondered several names and settled on one, a former lover, Italian, married, who would be more than anxious to help, partly because she hadn't quite given up on their affair even though he had, but also because she didn't want her husband, who had been a client of Xavier's, to know. He was aware such help would pose him no complication and her no hardship, affluent as she was. She came through, as expected, solving the cooking and cleaning part of the equation. After that, he rang a Filipino woman acquaintance who was manager of a babysitting service for several of the hotels in Tsimshatsui as well as for expatriates on short-term assignments, and pleaded for help. *Just a few weeks until I sort something out*, and offered to pay the girls off the books. She agreed, reluctantly, a little afraid of getting caught, but unable to resist the power it gave her over the girls in her employ. Xavier Dopoulos was a man who knew how to appeal to women when he had to.

At four-thirty the next morning, a call from Oslo roused Xavier from a turbulent dream of Paris and his parents.

The female voice on the phone exclaimed in accented English. "It could happen as soon as this week, maybe even today!" In the background, a male voice admonished her in Norwegian; she said, flustered, "Oh dear, it's too early to call, but I was so excited that I had to tell you right away."

Xavier said. "It's alright, thank you."

"Your daughter will be happy to have her mother back, won't she?" The voice continued.

"Yes, yes; of course she will," he replied, trying to remain civil, and grateful, to this group of well-meaning activists who were *so* inspired by Shelley's case, and by the persona that was Shelley, even though they failed in the common sense department. With Shelley, it was all about persona, the heroic, long-suffering political prisoner, the martyred mother who cried over being wrenched away from her child, at least before what small public was interested. It was not in that public's interest to know Kina's origins, or Shelley's lack of true maternal concerns.

Afterwards, he could not go back to sleep, not properly, and at five-thirty, Kina woke him, as was her habit. If he must raise this child of an unknown father, he mentally groaned, why did she have to come with the genes of an early morning riser? But then she hugged him and said, "Papa, *je t'aime,*" obviously pleased that Ursula no longer interrupted their mornings, and any annoyance he felt vanished.

At noon, the lawyer from Kuala Lumpur rang. The judge had denied the appeal.

She said, "Will you tell your friends in Oslo to go save the albatross or something else instead? They've just undone weeks of my hard work with their stupid publicity threats. We were so close this time."

"Talk to Shelley. They're not *my* friends."

"She's terribly distraught. The doctor gave her a sedative. She said you'd know what to tell them. Besides, you're the one who has the freedom to arrange things, you know."

Her patronizing tone grated. "No, I *don't* know. Half the time I have absolutely no idea what they're up to. Shelley's the one who insists on letting them interfere."

"Damn, Xavier, surely you can appreciate how she must feel! Don't you want your wife freed?"

"I'm paying you, aren't I?"

"Some nerve. You're an asshole, you know. If I were Shelley I'd have dumped you ages ago. You don't deserve her, that's for damn sure." She hung up with a loud click.

He shouted at the dead line. "Just do your job!"

Late Thursday afternoon, it dawned on Xavier that he hadn't called Gail. He had meant to, but in the scheme of things, his priorities lay elsewhere. Recalling the taste of her kiss—fruity, redolent of summer's absent-minded ease—he wondered why *she* hadn't called.

She said, "Saturday evening? Could we make that brunch instead? I fly out early Sunday."

He heard the slight edge in her voice. His apology had not been well received. "Tonight? I know it's short notice, but you know how weekends get, childcare, I mean." He played for sympathy by skirting the truth.

Concerned at appearing over eager, she hesitated. "Sorry, dinner with old classmates." She added, "I am free Friday night."

"Business dinner."

"Oh, then later, perhaps?"

"Impossible I'm afraid, but very well, brunch then," he said hurriedly, afraid she might cancel completely.

His certainty threw her. "Okay, I have to go," and hung up quickly before she could embarrass herself further.

Gail was upset. Why hadn't she simply agreed to this evening, and cancelled on the old girls instead? They wouldn't mind; they all did likewise. She had bailed on lunches and dinners at the last minute in the past, for work, Gu Kwun, Jason,

Mom, even for that photographer Vince. Why did Xavier throw her so far off balance?

Afterwards, she rationalized that brunch was the better choice. Late night drinks, replete with possibilities, led to unnecessary humiliations, like the time in Shanghai, over a late night drink when Vince had said, "There's a friend of mine in New York you should meet," signaling his own lack of interest. It wouldn't hurt to get to know Xavier first. The problem with Vince, after all, had been her not knowing him well enough, and hence not realizing how completely unsuitable he had been for her.

Xavier wasn't entirely sure why he was keeping his options open. Why waste Friday evening on the *possibility*, only, of *Ma'mselle C'est Moi* instead of seeing Gail, especially after their kiss?

Gail's forward behavior surprised him, but her sensuality did not.

When it came to women and their bodies, Xavier Dopoulos was rarely wrong. He reckoned Gail to be one who would be good in bed because she was discriminating. In his experience, there were only two kinds of women worth the effort of lovemaking, the discriminators or the "frequent flyers," which was why most prostitutes were good. *Ma'mselle C'est Moi* was merely indiscriminate.

Shelley fell somewhere in between that spectrum.

His wife. The mother of his child. How could he prepare Kina, never mind himself, if and when she was released?

The first time he had told the truth about Kina and Shelley was to a prostitute in Amsterdam. It was six months after the incarceration. He was just beginning to accept the idea that Shelley might be away for a long time.

He handed the woman the money. "It's been years since I've done this." It was true. The last time had been fifteen years earlier, in New York.

"Alors, qu'est-ce que vous voulez?" She asked, hoping he would not insist on "talking."

Perhaps it was the intimacy, albeit make-believe, in his native French—Shelley was not fluent and had a *terrible* accent—or the lonely aftermath of catastrophe, but during the paid hour, he did not fuck the woman. Instead, Xavier treated her as if he *were* in love, making love slowly, with enormous tenderness, pouring all the exhaustion, frustration and pain of being alive into a catharsis of the body, until the woman exhaled, without faking. She was astonished, this no longer young professional who had given up on surprise.

They spent the night together, and he told her that he married Shelley *only* because she was pregnant from the rape. At the time, they had been together a couple of years but he had been planning to end their relationship. When it happened, he simply didn't have the heart. The situation was not, as he had led Gail to believe, that Shelley was already his wife.

In the morning, the woman said, "You can come back anytime. No charge."

"Thank you," he replied. "I don't come to Amsterdam often, I'm afraid."

There was joy and even satisfaction, however fleeting, in sex without complications. After the week he'd had, *Ma'mselle C'est Moi* would be exactly the ticket. Besides, there was that other doubt, one he didn't fully understand which was this: he did not quite trust Gail Szeto.

On the phone with Jim the next morning, Xavier was frantic. "You don't understand, I simply cannot leave Hong Kong right now, *and* on such short notice." What he really wanted to say, to shout in fact, was *How dare you commit me for a meeting on a Sunday!*

Jim was unmoved. "They're impatient," he said.

"It's Ursula …" he began.

"What did you do? Screw her again?"

"Fuck you, Jim," and he slammed the phone down, startling Kina. It was a lousy way to begin the weekend.

In New York, Jim was shaken. Xavier had never hung up on him or sworn with such intensity. Within seconds, the phone rang.

Xavier said, "Listen, apologies but …"

"No," Jim said, "I'm the one who should apologize. It was rude … tasteless of me." Despite his constant barbs, these were mostly in jest. At heart, Jim was civil, and one reason he worked with Xavier was because of his partner's Old World European civility. He said, "What's the problem, Xav?" And he listened as Xavier explained the situation.

"... so you see, I don't have someone to be with her full-time, and she's too young to leave alone, except for short periods, like at most an hour or so."

His partner considered a moment. The contract was too big to jeopardize. "You can stay at Dahlia's in Shanghai, right? So why not bring your daughter?"

"But ..." There were complications with Dahlia, not untenable, but he did not want to go into those with Jim.

"I'll even be a sport and spring for her ticket. What do you say?"

He wanted to say no—indebtedness to Jim did not sit well—but he knew how much Kina loved to fly. It would be a treat for her, one he couldn't afford to pass up. Besides, he needed the money from this new job, especially given another appeal for Shelley, which was already in the works. There was a strategic reason as well. He wanted time for more personal contact with Monkey International. "Done. What time and where?"

Afterwards, Jim mused that age was making him go soft in the head. His partner had probably—well, more than likely—screwed, or otherwise compromised himself with that sister-in-law of his. It was typical.

Xavier thanked whatever goddess who ruled his destiny for this Friday as he delighted in Kina's excitement over the trip.

She asked, "Will Aunties Dahlia and Lilith take me out to eat?"

"If you're polite to them."

"Oh, I definitely will be, I promise," she said in Mandarin. "Papa, they took me to a beautiful garden last time with Aunties Xiao Ling, Cherry, Lisle and the one with the funny name, Aunty Piña Colada."

Xavier laughed and replied, in English, "Yes, you had a good time didn't you?" He wished he had his daughter's memory when it came to names. Dahlia, the unofficial leader of the lesbian crowd in Shanghai, couldn't do enough for Kina, just like all the other "Aunties." Although he had some reservations at the way Dahlia and her girls fussed over his daughter—*bordering on lust?*—but he quickly dismissed this since Kina was just a child after all, and he had known Dahlia too long and too well to be truly worried.

Kina remained happy and obedient all day.

When *Ma'mselle C'est Moi* rang around five, as promised, it was to tell him that she now had a sudden appointment for dinner but *peut-être après*, for drinks?

He replied, nonchalant, "Perhaps."

"So see you after my dinner then?"

"You're a cocktease," he told her, which caused an outraged exclamation that made him laugh. He did not promise her anything one way or another.

A woman who crossed the line from temptation to merely available no longer intrigued. This one was too young anyway. Fuckable, yes; necessary, no. Then, he realized he had to cancel out on Gail, since he was flying out Saturday, or perhaps, might she be available tonight? He picked up the phone, knowing it did not really matter what her answer would be. Ensuring his daughter's happiness and well-being surpassed whatever joys any woman could offer.

13

At seven that evening, Gail skittered around her room nervously, trying on different outfits. Why was she meeting Xavier on such short notice? This was foolish. Surely the man didn't warrant such attention or anxiety?

At eight-ten, wearing a pale gold dress in which she was not entirely comfortable, she arrived at the Szechuan restaurant in Happy Valley where she had agreed to meet him at eight. Her thin lips, slightly parted, were moist. As she hurried forward, her nylon ran down the back of her left leg.

Xavier was at a table and rose to greet her, a bottle of wine in his hand. He waved away her apology for being late. Holding out her chair he said, "How very lovely to see you," and kissed her cheek, stopping just below the ear.

She sat down quickly, under the watchful gaze of the all-Chinese restaurant staff.

Still standing behind her, he ran a hand lightly down her side. She started. "You Americans," he said, "are so dreadfully puritanical, aren't you?" Popping the cork on a bottle of Chardonnay, he poised it over her glass. "Wine, *madame?*"

"I'm not really American, anymore than you are, and why are you pouring wine like a maître d'?"

"My dear Gail." He slipped the corkscrew into his pocket and sat down. "Must you turn every encounter into a confrontation?

But, so, in answer … you gave me the impression you were American, and I brought two bottles of my own, which are better than anything they serve." He displayed the Nelson, New Zealand label.

She didn't know the wine, but knew New Zealand ones weren't particularly expensive. It also wasn't what she drank. "That doesn't explain your pouring it."

He saw her disdainful glance. Women knew nothing about wine, *especially* Hong Kong women. "In my younger days, I wanted to be a sommelier. I used to be a wine waiter. It was a profession, perhaps, it would have been better for me to pursue." Handing her the menu. "Here, you order."

It was not the respectful request from foreigners to her, the resident expert, but a command, much the way her mother used to say, exasperated, about any number of things, *you do it then,* missy, *since you think you know everything.*

Xavier was already regretting the evening.

Gail hid behind the pages of the menu, feeling like a fool. The ladder in her nylon spread, split and tore completely.

She stood up. "Excuse me, I have to visit the ladies."

He rose also, wondering if she would pull a disappearing act by feigning illness.

In the toilet stall, Gail rummaged in her purse for a spare and found none. Curbing a mounting temper, she pulled off the pair she was wearing and discarded them. Her mother's silk stockings, neatly darned, preserved in a cloth bag, suddenly seemed infinitely preferable.

At their table, Xavier was ordering dinner, speaking Cantonese with a fluency that would have surprised Gail.

At the end of the meal, he poured her fourth glass of wine, emptying the bottle. Gail sat back, satiated. Her bare legs no longer felt naked. The four-season beans had emerged piquant and crisp from the wok; the double-boiled pork that followed was tender and not too fatty; the tofu coated in shrimp roe was pan fried to exactly the right consistency. The balance of the meal he ordered, and his choice of restaurant, impressed her.

"About earlier," she said, "I'm sorry you found me confrontational." Upon her return from the bathroom, he behaved as if nothing were amiss, saying only, "You know, that dress is very becoming. The color suits you." During dinner, she told him about her career and the sacrifices she'd made to get where she was and the trepidation she felt about possibly moving to New York. She mentioned the inheritance in passing, saying only that it was "unexpected" without any indication of its scale.

Xavier listened. Only once did he interject a question about Northeast Trust, trying to probe, but she either didn't know or wasn't saying, he couldn't quite tell. Her willingness to talk about her personal life—curious how much she said given a chance, the wine, he supposed—placed few demands on him. He signaled the captain to clear the table and bring the second bottle.

She protested. "No, please. I'm driving."

"There's always a taxi," he said. Taking the bottle from the captain, he uncorked it and poured. Her dubious expression amused him. "What's the matter? Can't the game plan change?"

Provoked, she retorted. "What do husbands do when they've eaten?"

"Kiss beautiful women."

"I didn't mean …"

"What *did* you mean, then?"

She tipped her glass and drank up. He watched, frowning.

She said, "I was too … forward. It was wrong. You're married."

"You keep saying that."

"But Xavier, you *can't* expect me to ignore that fact."

"Why not? I do." He poured her another glass. His own glass, his third of the evening, was full. "I don't mean to be flippant, but come on, Gail. We're both adults!" He glanced at her mouth.

Looking down, she played with the stem of her glass. The heat between her thighs, or perhaps a hot flash, or both, made her flush and she shifted uncomfortably. She bit her upper lip. "Perhaps this wasn't such a good idea."

"You keep saying that also."

She emptied her glass and tried to stand. "I think …" She sat down, hard.

He reached out to steady her.

In the taxi, she fell asleep against him. He stretched her out as comfortably as possible, admiring the smooth, fair, unblemished skin of her face and neck.

It was dark when Gail woke. All she knew was that she wasn't in her own room. She was still dressed, but her dress was hiked up to her hips. She sat up, tugged at the skirt, her head dizzily woolen. Struggling to stand, she realized she was in her mother's bedroom.

The door was ajar. In the living room, Xavier was watching a Chinese period drama on television. "Are you feeling better?" He clicked the mute switch on the remote.

"What time is it?"

"Late."

Only the floor lamp was on, dimmed to low. The living room looked different—warmer, less bland—without the glare of the overhead light she normally used. Conchita's room door was shut. "What happened?"

He laughed gently. "You fell asleep in the taxi. It was quite a job bringing you home. I believe we shocked your maid."

Her dress hung loosely. Reaching round the back, she zipped it up and fastened the hook.

"You're attractive like this." He leaned back against the sofa.

She slid into the armchair opposite. Her mouth was parched.

"Would you like me to run a bath? It'll make you feel better."

She nodded. He sprang up and set to work. It was as if they had been friends, or lovers, for a long time. Yet … she saw her bare feet. Also, she wasn't wearing any underwear.

He returned to the sofa. "It'll be a few minutes, *madame.*"

"Why …?" She stopped.

"It's not what you think."

"Why was I in my mother's room?"

"You insisted on going there."

"And then?"

"You started undressing when I put you on the bed." Having glimpsed, and being aroused by, her drunken dishevelment, he felt uncomfortable. "Believe me."

The sound of running water pounded its way to the forefront.

"The bath!" They exclaimed together.

He arrived first and turned off the tap. The water was just beginning to splash over the rim.

He watched television while she soaked. Her headache eased. Why had he made her drink so much? The hot water seeped in between her legs. No, she hadn't succumbed to drunken sex. Xavier was a gentleman, fortunately.

Steam curled upwards into her nostrils, clearing her sinuses.

What time was it?

The light bulb popped and died. Moonlight illuminated the square of glass. Gail slid under and wet her head. Beyond the locked door, television voices burbled. It soothed her to bathe in the dark, in the almost silence.

Her extra long tub was her single greatest luxury. Custom designed, it allowed her to stretch her legs out straight. As a child, she hadn't had a tub. Bathing meant filling a basin and pouring water over herself with a plastic ladle. A floor drain handled the runoff. In winter, she had to put a full kettle on if she wanted hot water, which was never enough. The bathroom floor retained a perpetually damp chill.

A tentative knock. "Everything alright?"

"Fine, thanks. I'll be out in a minute."

"Take your time. I didn't see the light under the crack and just wanted to be sure you were okay." He remained by the door.

How long had it been? The water was tepid and stars still lit the dark. She ought to get a new watch. The dainty jewel watch wouldn't survive day-to-day abuse, unlike her old Seiko. Pity. The one major purchase saved for out of the first money she'd earned. Sixty U.S. dollars. A huge sum in 1974. Hadn't she been proud, showing it off to the Chinese waiters at the Dragon Palace Restaurant in Boston, where she was a waitress while in college. All of them crowded round to see it. *Wa Gay-lo! It even tells the day and date.*

Outside, stars faded as the water cooled.

Xavier met her when she emerged, clad in a robe, and led her by the hand to the living room. Barefoot, she stood level with him. He had rolled up his shirtsleeves. His black and gold cufflinks were on the coffee table next to his wedding band.

He said, "I have to go. Kina, you know."

"What time …?"

He stroked her cheek. His leather watch strap rubbed against her skin. "Gail, you have to learn to relax." Taking her by the waist, "Come on. Let's dance."

"Without music?"

"Without music. You're romantic enough."

They danced. She felt his breath on her face. "Xavier, we shouldn't …"

He interrupted her. "Will you do me a favor?" His lips found her earlobe.

"What?"

His fingers eased deeper into her back. "Please. Don't speak."

Very gently, he kissed the vein in her neck.

14

That night, Gail's dream did not recur, either in its original or in the revised versions. Years earlier when she and Jason were engaged to be married, she had told him about her flying dreams. She said she flew alone and did not mention Gordie. He was just beginning his Masters in Psychology and said, "You can be my first patient." She had responded, sharply, "I'm not crazy," to which he replied, "Sweetheart, I've never thought you were."

At three-fifteen on Monday, Gail sat facing Josh Rabinowitz in his office. On the walls hung baseball paraphernalia, evidence of a rabid Yankees fan. Gail, who understood baseball only in theory, had never been to a game in her life.

Josh saw her alone. He had kept her waiting ten minutes. For the last five, he had been outlining their offer. It was a forty percent increase over her current salary, included the benefits package with stock options and 401K previously denied her as a non-U.S. staff, plus a generous relocation allowance and bonus. "That's it, Gail. Happy?"

It was far more than she expected. Money, she realized, would never be her problem, regardless of the inheritance. "Thank you. I'll give you an answer as soon as possible."

"You don't sound impressed," he said. Before she could answer, he continued, “Look, since you are our top Asian management now, you need to know something.” He walked round and closed his office door. “We’re on the block.”

Gail asked, “We, or you?”

He returned to his seat. “You don’t pull punches, do you?”

“No point.” She stared hard at him. “Is there?”

“Lady, I don’t *back* loser deals. You should know that. It’s more like a merger, actually. Part of their operation with part of ours, so we protect our European and domestic fronts. Over time, we lose a few folks in New York and they bring in theirs.”

“So who gets to stay?”

“You would. You *are* on board, right?”

She hesitated. “I thought I had till the end of the month to decide?”

He spun his chair round to face the window. “Gail, I’m leveling with you here.” He paused. “The board needs to meet you next week.” He turned slowly back round. “Catch my drift?”

Her former boss’ words echoed. *They need you.* She said, “The deal’s done?”

He leaned his head back and looked away. “More or less. We ne… we’d like you as part of the team.”

“So which board am I meeting?”

He looked her in the eye. “Theirs, of course.”

“And who …?”

“Shanghai Industrial Bank.”

This pressure to have her say yes made sense at last. Shanghai Industrial already had their own offices in Hong Kong which explained the shutdown. More importantly, Northeast Trust had no one in management who could deal with the Chinese on their own terms.

“And how do you know I won’t jump ship in the meantime?”

“We checked. If you’d wanted to bail, you would have six months ago. You had the opportunity.” His voice was terse. “So Gail, we can move on this?”

She looked down briefly, then raised her head and smiled. To someone who didn’t know her well, especially a man, it would have seemed like a sweet surrender. “The board meeting, Josh. When and where?”

Afterwards, Josh told Dick that he hadn't been sure, up till the last minute, that she would play ball. Dick, accustomed as he was to the vagaries of Human Resources, was not entirely convinced that she had from Josh's description of the conversation, but he did not voice these doubts to his boss. In these uncertain times, who was he to analyze the motives of the highly paid? As long as they did their job, the why of their existence in the organization was not really his concern.

Gail returned to her hotel room feeling almost happy. *Leikhneuih,* her mother used to say, *your brain's going to be your meal ticket.* Ironic, really, because this had little to do with intelligence and much more to do with luck and timing. The offer was flattering, but more than that, it was the power inherent in being who she was that was exhilarating.

She called Gordie to say she couldn't see him this trip since she was leaving the next morning, but would be back in a little over a week, although she was careful not to elaborate. "I'll be able to stay over the weekend," she added. "They're being nice to me. My boss told me to check out the sales in New York."

Gordie laughed. *Doll,* he started to say and corrected himself. It didn't seem quite the right term of endearment for her. "Gail, somehow, I don't think of you as a shopper."

"My boss's wife is, or so he tells me."

"I'll take you to the Block."

"The Block?"

"I'll explain when you get here. Call me, okay? There are other things we need to talk about as well." He was thinking of the money he owed Gail's mother, something he wanted to set right. It would be difficult right at this moment though. He had just lost a huge amount in currency contracts going long on the Euro.

"Okay."

Later, as she made her way to Perry's, a lightness prevailed.

Perry Martin lived on the first two stories of a three-story brownstone in Brooklyn Heights. Her tenant had the top floor.

Gail was struck by her colleague's presence in this space. She was like an exactly right flower arrangement, one that enhanced a room, neither overpowering the space nor dwarfed by it. Gail could not remember the last time she had had dinner at someone's home. Probably with Jason—*had* it been that long?

Persey stared curiously at her mother's friend. "Are you really from Hong Kong?"

Gail smiled. "Yes."

She held out one of the pencils from the Art Museum store and a sketch pad. "Will you write my name for me in Chinese? My mother says you can."

Perry said, "Persey, don't be pushy. Let Gail have a drink first."

"It's okay," Gail said. Kneeling next to Persey, she rapidly wrote four characters—*bai li* "white beauty" and *bai xin* "white angel"—remarking, "there, now both you and your mother have Chinese names."

"That's so lovely," Perry said, when Persey showed her the pad. She set a salad on the table. "They look like drawings."

Their delight pleased Gail. In school, she had been proud of her Chinese brushwork, painstakingly forming her large characters correctly within the frame of nine squares. Mom had always nodded approvingly. Even after she realized her mother couldn't read, Gail still felt exceptionally pleased with the A's on her homework. But there hadn't been any need to write in Chinese for a long time, not since she'd moved home and no longer had to write letters to Mom.

Persey tore the sheet off the pad and began jumping around, showing off dance steps. "And this," she informed Gail, "is a pirouette." She spun around and fell on her bottom.

The girl was making Gail dizzy. Kina had been like that. She heard Xavier's child saying, "Papa *look* at me," insistent and petulant as he tried to settle her down at the airport lounge and his voice, protesting weakly, "Kina, *please* keep still," to which she replied, "but Papa, can't you see I'm *dancing?*"

"Persey," her mother cautioned. "That's enough. Gail and Mommy are going to talk now. Can you please go to your room and read a book, or hey, didn't you want to watch *The Little Mermaid*?"

The child frowned, looking as if she were about to refuse, at which Perry stuck both hands on her waist and stared down her daughter. Persey slunk away, unrepentant, but behind the closed door, Disney magic captured her attention, much to her mother's relief.

Perry held up a bottle of Pinot Grigio with a questioning look and Gail nodded. "Kids," she said, rolling her eyes and then stopped, embarrassed, thinking her colleague must be hurting something awful at the sight of this domestic scene. She wished now she had thought to meet Gail anywhere else except home; but then, sitters were difficult to come by and unreliable … "So what gives?"

Gail was thinking about Gu Kwun and how much more obedient he was than Kina or even Persey; but then thought, *had* it been a good thing, his obedience? She sipped her wine and said, "I think I'm in," she was about to say *"love"* but corrected it to *"lust,"* thinking that would go over better. Americans preferred to joke about serious things.

"No kidding? But what about the job?"

"Oh that." She was nonchalant. "The money's good."

Perry waved Gail towards the dining table. "Tell me over dinner," and disappeared into the kitchen to get the lasagna.

An antique mahogany dining table—"My ex had taste, if not ethics"—was laid for two. Persey had already been fed, although she came noisily out of her room as soon as the adults were seated. "But Mommy, I just want to *look* at the table," and then turned around and went back in, shutting the door loudly. Perry shook her head. "Sometimes," she said, and stopped.

"It's okay. You can talk about …" Gail waved one hand in the air "… motherhood. Really, it's okay." She nodded hard, trying to convince both of them it was.

Perry said, "No. It isn't what you need to listen to right now. So tell me about," what she really wanted to know was whether or not Gail meant to take the job, but instead said, "your man."

Gail smiled. "He'll be my first non-Chinese lover."

The future construction did not elude Perry. She said, "Oh, so you only … knew Chinese guys before?"

"Guy. One. My ex."

Perry said, slowly, "How long did you say you'd been going out with this man?"

"I, that is, we had our second date last week. He was in Hong Kong, on his way to Shanghai." Besides saying he had a child, she had not revealed much else of Xavier's personal situation.

Perry controlled her shock. Gail's innocence made her feel almost … *slutty* by comparison, which she *hardly* was, only five, no wait, six, before her husband, and that summer but *those* didn't count … It was difficult to connect this woman at her table with the one she'd first met. "He'll like it then if you move to New York, right?"

"About the job, well I'm sort of doing it, but you see," and she told Perry about her inheritance. "The problem is, it's not about the money. If it were, the decision would be easy."

Perry was envious. "Heck, I'd quit in a flash and go work part time for a non-profit. I even know which one. The point is, you wouldn't catch me working in your situation."

"You're fortunate. You know what you want."

"But Gail, surely you knew what you wanted once, right?"

"Love," Gail replied without hesitation. "And family."

Perry flushed. "Look, I can't hide this. Josh asked me, through Dick, to check you out. I told them we were having dinner." Her eyes avoided Gail's. "I'm sorry if you think me deceitful."

The admission relieved Gail. She suspected—it was a logical assumption—but something about Perry pulled. *Friendship?* "Forget it. You're doing your job." And she knew, on her part, she couldn't say anything about the merger. It was likely Perry didn't know, given her non-managerial status.

Perry said, "It's a good thing, being in love, that is, or even in lust." She hesitated. And then. "Does the job matter more than …?" She stopped. Perry was younger, another generation, one that was already liberated.

Gail, a pioneer, wore the name, *feminist,* comfortably, and with pride. "Just a job, in the end, is that what you mean?" she asked, adding, "I liked being married."

"Gail, so did I."

The two women reflected quietly. Was opportunity a privilege or a curse? Were they still writing their golden notebooks?

Perry asked, abruptly, "Do you also hate your ex still?"

"Yes, I suppose I must, although I dislike thinking of myself that way."

"Me too. Funny, that. It wasn't him I couldn't forgive, but marriage. Marriage let me down, with all its promise of stability, of being properly grown up and socially acceptable, and what he did made our whole marriage suddenly 'wrong.' But he made a mistake, that's all."

"Such an unforgivable one though, right?"

"Truthfully, Gail? It was just as much me. When it came out, I told Peter he was a fool. I was right, of course, and everyone agreed, but what good is being right?" She drank a large draught of wine, holding back tears. "I miss him. I'd do anything to make it all go away." She began to cry quietly. The revelation, unsaid till now, deserved tears.

The younger woman wiped her face with the back of her hand. Gail stretched across the table and rested a hand on Perry's shoulder. "It gets easier," she promised. "I wish I'd understood sooner what you already do. Perry, it's been over six years, and I still can't let go. At least you left him."

Perry gazed at Gail but her eyes were focused elsewhere. "Persey misses him." She emptied her glass in a single gulp. "Gail, I miss him so much."

"It really does get easier," Gail repeated.

"He wants to come back."

The two women stared at each other.

Perry refilled their empty wine glasses. "Come on," she lifted hers. "Let's drink to, what is it we are, Gail?"

"The reluctant feminine mystique?"

Perry laughed. "Yes, I could drink to that."

When the dishes had been washed, dried and put away—a joint operation—they tucked Persey in. Gail watched mother and daughter as Perry read and sang to her child. Except for her pale blue eyes, Persey could have been Perry's clone, as if the father's image had been eradicated completely. Xavier's girl, her greedy, undisciplined expression, all energies drawn towards herself to ensure happiness; that petulant girl in the shop, Gail suddenly knew, *was* Kina. Compared to Persey, or even Gu Kwun's friend

Janie, Kina lacked the certainty of these other two girls, a certainty that said—*I am loved, unconditionally*. Gail felt sure she was right about this. Some things you just knew.

Afterwards, "Thanks for the home cooking."

Perry smiled. "We like company. It gets lonely."

"I know."

The unasked hung between them.

"So, what do you want me to tell them?" Then, "I'm tired of being a lawyer all of a sudden."

"Tell them whatever you want. It's okay, really. I won't let on."

"But Gail, what do *you* really want? Shouldn't you figure that out first?"

"I wish I knew, but I will figure it out." She grinned. "They tell me I'm good at problem solving."

"Take heart." Perry air-kissed Gail's cheeks. "At least you're getting some."

Gail shrugged. "It doesn't help me think, though."

Perry stepped back. She wore a mock-thoughtful look. "Gail, think of it like booze. Desirable, necessary, but only in measured quantities."

On the flight back, Gail could not sleep. Her brain buzzed with everything that was changing, so rapidly, around her. Grief seemed to have submerged, underneath the rush of her present actions. Yet all the while, an insistent imperative: her personal history *demanded* scrutiny whether or not she wanted to do so.

Did she hate Jason?

Like booze. Was that what love was as well, best in measured quantities?

The first time she and Jason Chak made love, they were both virgins. He was twenty six and she, thirty two. When he rolled off her, way too soon, Gail had said, *we need a lot more practice*. From that moment on, she needed to possess him completely and, until he left her, she made sure she did.

And now, Xavier Doupoulos—with whom intimacy was still foreign—*was* she, could she really be falling in love with Xavier?

15

It was an enormous bouquet, too large for Gail's coffee table. An assortment of blooms—orange snapdragons, indigo lilacs, salmon and lemon roses, golden-red tulips, tiger lily orchids—nestled in verdant splendor with the message, "Gray is not an option. X."

Conchita said, "You have an admirer."

"I suppose I do," but she stared at the flowers, thinking, *how extravagant.*

"It's that European gentleman, isn't it, from last weekend?"

Gail nodded, feeling slightly overwhelmed, and fatigued, having slept little after arriving home last night. She said, abruptly, "I've never been sent flowers before."

"Not even from Mr. Chak?"

"We couldn't afford flowers." Then, uncomfortable at the slightly too personal turn in the conversation, she added, "So what do we have?" signaling the start of their work day.

Conchita handed her the morning's pile, wondering, *"we"?* Surely this wasn't a joint decision? Surely a doctor could afford to send his wife flowers, *would* be a little romantic from time to time? But with Gail, what was expected was not necessarily what you got.

"You surprise me," Xavier said, when Gail called to thank him and invite both him and Kina to her home for dinner Friday. "Unless you mean that we won't ..."

Gail smiled into the mouthpiece. "You Europeans are so puritanical. Besides, all children sleep eventually."

"You Americans," he countered, "know nothing of romance."

"And what about the Chinese?"

Xavier said, "We Chinese make love, don't we?"

She *was* in lust, Gail decided. It was almost a relief to admit that to herself, because it gave her permission to get what she wanted. Perhaps she wasn't very romantic, inviting a lover to dinner this way. Too pragmatic? But she dismissed the thought. A relationship, she decided, survived on something other than romance. Her own parents proved the rule.

The night her father died, Gail had discovered what love meant to her mother.

It was May, but unseasonably warm. Gail returned late that night from the movies with her girlfriends to find her mother in tears. "Mark *bu huilai. Ta yi hou bu huilai.*"

"What are you going on about?" At seventeen, Gail was accustomed to her mother's theatrics, performed always in Mandarin. When her mother was happy or wanted to flirt, she sprinkled her conversation with pidgin English; when she wanted to make a point, it was Cantonese. But when heaven and earth shuddered, she affected Mandarin, doing her best not to slip into her native Shanghainese.

"Uncle Mark's dead."

Gail stared at her, feigning indifference. "How did you find out?"

"Jimmy Kho called." She dabbed her eyes. *"Wo sheng ming wan le, wan le!"*

Irritated, Gail demanded. "What about me? Don't I count? Your life's not over. You still have me."

Mascara ran down her mother's cheeks. In Cantonese she said, "You're a heartless girl! How can you close your heart to your father like this, to your own flesh and blood?"

"He never opened his to me." She went into her room, slamming the door.

Less than ten minutes later, she heard the rustling of dresses.

Gail hovered in the doorway of her mother's room. "If you're so upset, why are you going out?" Her mother was at the dressing table mirror, fixing her eye makeup, drawing the long cat tail Gail despised. "That looks cheap, Mom. Do you have to do that with your eyeliner?"

Her mother did not turn towards her. "Leave me alone, *Gay-lo.* Don't you have something to study?"

"School's out, in case you hadn't noticed." The news she had been harboring all week felt stale. "I got ten Distinctions and one Credit in my School Cert, although of course, *you* wouldn't know since you've been gone the last two nights. The results were posted Tuesday. *And* I got the Imelda Scholarship for Form Six, since I was top of my class, although what good is that?" What she didn't add, since her mother wouldn't have cared, was that she had taken more subjects than anyone in the entire colony and had had to get special approval for that.

Her mother was dabbing rouge. *"Lekneuih.* So much cleverer than your mother. But keep your voice down, please, the neighbors will complain. I keep telling you, it's not ladylike to shout." She painted her lips vermilion.

Gail folded her arms, holding back her temper. "Where are you going?"

Her mother got up, smoothed the skirt of her *cheongsam,* and picked up her purse. In her three-inch heels, with her teased hair, she almost reached Gail's chin. She squeezed her daughter's arm. "Now, I know you're upset about your father, but life goes on. I have to go to work. We still must eat."

Gail's anger flared. "You're not even his concubine."

Her mother started. "What did my daughter say?"

"You're not upset over 'Uncle' Mark—why must you call him that? My wonderful father hasn't been to see you for *how* long now?" Her voice rose. "Do you think I'm totally stupid? That I don't know anything?" She unfolded her arms and stuck her knuckles on her waist.

"Shut up, girl," her mother said, and left.

It was still dark when Gail awoke to the sound of her mother's return. Her wooden pillow had been pushed aside, and her nightgown sat folded on the chair by her bed. The covers were around her feet, kicked away during the sultry, humid hours. Her nakedness soothed.

A man was speaking Shanghainese. She recognized his voice, that moderately high-pitched, slightly nasally tone. The painter, the "friend" since "Uncle" Mark stopped visiting. The only other man who came to her mother's bed for free. Cultivated, Mom called him. *Not what you think Gay-lo, he treats me delicately, with refinement.* Gail had refused to meet him, she did not even know what he looked like. But she could not block out the sounds of his presence.

That night, the bedroom noises were unsettling.

Gail turned away from the thin wooden wall separating their rooms. Her father's figure—his back—always leaving, stepping out their front door with Mom. In the blackness, an imaginary Gordie knelt beside her bed, staring at her naked body, a prelude to her night flights with him since puberty. But then she saw her father instead—a memory of his hand fondling Mom's rear—and the image vanished into the night.

Her mother was speaking softly. "Thank you. I needed a friend tonight."

Gail wiped her forehead. Her body was damp with sweat. A mosquito buzzed in her ear and she shivered. She sat up. Next door, a rustle of clothing. Tonight, she could not ignore them, could not simply turn around and shut them out. She knelt on her bed and pressed the front of her body against the wall, imprinting her dampness onto the wood.

The wall was made up of six vertical panels, joined by thicker strips of wood, creating the effect of a screen rather than a wall. Along the top was an opening which once had comprised several transom-like windows, evidenced by the hinges left in the frame. A row of bamboo slats, running vertically across, covered half the opening. Frosted glass windows were set in the other half. It was an odd divide, the logic of which Gail never understood. Her mother said it provided cross ventilation for light and air, since her room was in the back and had windows, while Gail's had none.

More than a year ago, when Mom's friend first started staying over, Gail had carved a slit into the midpoint of the second and third panels, on either side of the joining strip. If she peered through it, she would have a perfect view of her mother's bed. The hole was unnoticeable from the other side, positioned as it was at the top of the dresser. But she was afraid to look, despite a gnawing curiosity. Life beyond the wall frightened and confused her, even though she felt herself drawn to it.

Tonight, she dared.

The man's back faced her as he pulled down his trousers. He had a fleshy rump and pale, hairless legs. Her mother, still wearing a nylon slip, pulled aside the mosquito curtain and climbed onto the platform that was her bed, on which was spread a bamboo mat. It was framed by four tall wooden poles. The bed was across the room next to the windows. Gail's heartbeat sped up. As he turned in profile, she gasped, then quickly ducked back down onto her bed—two wood planks covered with a sheet—and turned her back to the wall. She shut her eyes. Her mother said, *what was that,* but then nothing happened and after a few minutes, the familiar rhythms began.

Gail lay on her side, her heartbeat returning to normal. She opened her eyes, afraid that the stolen sight would replay itself. As the man had turned, his hand moved aside, revealing his erection. He was of average height and build. But that long, thick, *awful* thing. How could it fit into Mom?

Next door, the knocking rhythm increased in intensity.

Her hand slipped between her legs. That wetness was there. She touched her breasts; the large nipples, shaped like Mom's, were stiff and sensitive. Moving in time to the sounds from the other room, the rhythm found its groove. Those times before, when her fingers searched, rubbing herself sore, trying to find something, *what?* But this time, her thighs trembled, and the climb, beyond her control, aching, until the explosion—relief—before the chill that followed her first orgasm.

That night Gail dreamt she flew alone. Gordie flew beside her, but he did not take her hand as he usually did.

On Friday morning, when Gail called to reconfirm dinner, Xavier said, "I have to go to New York next week."

She said, "How nice. I'll be there too. You can show me New York."

"I'll be very occupied, with my business partner, I'm afraid, but I'm sure we can fit something in." The thought of working around the clock, which was Jim's style, wearied him, as did the prospect of the unanticipated trip. "He's one of those work hard, play hard types," he added, not wanting to seem like a workaholic himself.

"So am I," she said. "By the way, what did your card mean? About the gray?"

"Your wardrobe," he said. "I like it when you wear colors."

She protested, but scanning her closet before that evening, she saw the dominance of gray and wondered why it took *him* to show her.

16

Kina curtsied as soon as Gail opened the door. *"Bonsoir, Madame Szeto,"* she said.

Xavier instructed. "Speak English, Kina. Auntie Gail doesn't speak French." He ushered his daughter in.

"I do a little, actually," Gail said.

Kina said, in English, "You have a very beautiful flat, Auntie Gail." She smiled prettily and walked a circle around the living room, pointing her toes in ballet steps. "It's *much* bigger than ours."

"What's your flat like?" Gail asked.

"Kina," Xavier cautioned, "Be good."

"Oui, Papa," she replied, her eyes twinkling mischievously.

At dinner, Gail was extremely impressed by Kina's manners. She was quiet, never interrupted the adult conversation and ate everything she was served. Only once did Xavier admonish her, when her swinging foot kicked Gail's leg. She kept still right away and looked so contrite and upset that Gail said, "Don't be angry, Xavier, it was an accident," at which Kina gave her such a warm smile that Gail felt her heart melt.

Conchita, who had reverted to her role as a domestic helper who cook and serve dinner, observed these guests. That evening on the stairwell, she said to Bonny, "I wouldn't trust that man, or even his little girl, one bit." She paused and became thoughtful, adding, "Especially the daughter."

Bonny, still peeved at Conchita's extra income, responded, "You're just jealous."

"Me? Come on, you know me better than that. He's real nice looking, but I think he's the sly type. He was so extra, *extra* nice to me, telling me what a good cook I am. You know the kind, eyes always smiling at you like a singer from on stage so that you think *you're* the only woman he's looking at? Can't trust that. Not like Janie's father. Now he's genuine. I wish he would ask her out. But I suppose you can't blame Ms. Szeto. I mean, how long can a woman hold out?" She laughed.

"I'm astonished," Xavier said, as they settled together on the couch after Kina had been put to bed in Gail's mother's room. "I've never seen her so well behaved around a new person. She must like you."

"You're a good father," Gail said. She removed her shoes and tucked her legs up under her. "It must be hard dealing with her on your own, although I suppose her aunt ..." She was curious about Ursula, but didn't want to ask.

"Ah, her." He leaned back. The week, like all his weeks recently, had been exhausting. "She's moved out."

"Good heavens! But what do you plan to do?"

"Something will work out. It always does."

"Xavier, surely you must have *some* kind of plan. What will you do next week, for instance, when you're back home in New York?"

He closed his eyes, thinking, *this wasn't a good idea,* and all his earlier trepidation at the awkward nature of their "date" resurfaced.

Gail was still speaking. "You know, Conchita's here. She's a marvelous nanny. If you like, Kina can stay with me until you sort something out."

Her offer seemed unnecessarily generous. He said, "I wouldn't dream of causing such a bother, really," hoping his words would close the subject.

She continued. "It's really no bother. You know ..."

He leaned over and kissed her then for a long while. It was the only path to silence. When they moved to the bedroom, he said, *"Alors, tu parles français?"*

"Oh no, not really, I mean I studied …"

"In that case," he said, reverting to English as he began undressing her, "I will make love to you with a foreign tongue."

Afterwards, when Gail's heartbeat had returned to normal, she said, "So tell me, what is it you do, exactly?"

Lying on his back, Xavier stretched. He felt better than he had in a long time. A smile lifted his face—invigorated, less wearied than earlier—crinkling his eyes. "Exactly? I'm not sure I can be so precise."

She sat up. "You know what I mean."

He suppressed a smile at her business-like voice and continued. "I'm an independent. I was with Anderson's consulting division, but broke out on my own a few years back. Can't handle structure and the compromise of benefits." He glanced up; she did not appear amused. "Usually, I work with associates and partners. The one in New York has a background in organizational psych, and runs training courses for executives, while I do systems consulting and strategize IPO's or other financing. For a few dot-com's, but multinationals mostly, especially their China operations, although recently the business from Chinese companies is growing."

Gail was pleased. He wasn't a lightweight. She said, "China's lucrative these days."

"She certainly is." He propped himself up on one elbow and traced a finger over her breasts. They were small for her stature. "But you. You're quite the dragon lady, aren't you?" because his expectations had been surpassed. Gail proved responsive and surprisingly easy to please.

She shifted, creating a space between them. "So do you work out of your home in New York, or is there an office?"

"Home."

"Really? Do you own your apartment in New York?"

"What is this, Gail, the grand inquisition?"

She started. "I'm sorry, I didn't mean …"

He tugged her closer to him. "I'm a consultant. I make a living. I raise a daughter. What else do you need to know?" He made love to her again, more forcefully this time, refusing to release her until he could make her come several times, hoping that this, if nothing else, would slow that relentless mind.

When Gail woke, the sun was bright, and she was alone in her bedroom. Xavier and Kina were gone.

Conchita said, "Mr. Dopoulos apologized but he had to bring his little girl home. He said he'd call you later." She handed Gail a cup of tea.

"Thanks." Gail looked around distractedly and stared at the clock. "What time is it?"

"Eleven."

"Thanks."

"Don't mention it," but Conchita wasn't sure whether to smile or worry.

Gail stepped out to the little-used verandah and sipped her tea. She was tired the way she used to be after a strenuous netball match at school. Unused muscles ached. Her legs and arms felt bruised. In her head, Mom laughed—*Find a man who adores fucking and food, Gay-lo. They make the best lovers, remember that*—words she wanted to forget.

What had they talked about? She vaguely recalled teaching Kina the cha cha and waltz. Gail liked to dance. The *A-Yi's* and Mom had brought the dance hall home, practicing steps, teaching Gail all the latest ones of the moment. Also, she and Jason had once been the king and queen of dance among their Boston circle of mostly Chinese or foreign graduate students and professionals. Once they returned to Hong Kong, however, work and family had eliminated dancing from their lives except on rare occasions.

The evening was a bit of a blur. She hadn't drunk much, just a couple of glasses of the wine he brought. Even after the most prolonged sex with Jason—and they had been wonderfully compatible—her body never felt as it did now.

She wasn't sure she liked this overwhelming physical imbalance. This strange sensation of having been, not just made love to, but utterly … utterly and truly fucked.

Her first non-Chinese lover. Despite Xavier's mixed blood, she thought of him as European.

When Gail was seventeen, a Portuguese boy had kissed her. It was during a party in Kowloon Tong, a moneyed district, at the "Bank Flats" on Warwick Road where many Portuguese and Eurasian families lived, the ones who worked for the Hong Kong and Shanghai Bank.

Ricardo. The one next to her in French, who was taller than her. The one who danced with her all night. The one with the birthmark on his left cheek, a streak of discoloration stretching from temple to chin. The one who spoke decent Cantonese. The one who liked brainy girls, or so he said.

It had been a month after learning of Mark's death, the summer right after School Cert, when all anyone cared about was that the awful public exams they crammed for over five long years had *finally* ended. That year, the French nun scheduled to teach at her all-girls' school hadn't showed up, and their principal arranged for the neighboring boys' school to take in her class for French. It had been good for academics, but brilliant for hormones.

During the last slow number, Ricardo held her very tight and said, *Let me take you home.* She panicked, afraid to show him where she lived, knowing she did not belong to his foreign Hong Kong world.

"I can't. My mother's ill," she lied. "It would disturb her."

Ricardo was offended. "I'll drop you at the door already." *Why* were girls so difficult?

How she wanted to say yes. But once she told her address, he'd *never* believe she had an American father, or worse yet, guess the truth. Impossible to explain. Explain? *What* was she even thinking?

That was when he kissed her and she couldn't say no.

Think, Gail told herself, as they bundled into a taxi. "Oxford Road," she blurted, a short ride away which wouldn't cost him much, from where, she reasoned, she could walk home easily once he drove off.

As the flag fell, Ricardo said, "Wow, that's very cool. I can see you all the time, then," wondering if she knew, and pulled her close to kiss her again. She kissed back. Their tongues entwined, his hands roamed. Both wished the ride would never end.

As they turned on Oxford, the driver intruded. "What number, missy?" *These* gwailo *kids* he grumbled to himself. *Absolutely no sense of shame!*

Gail surfaced. "Thirty six." A former classmate, a Chinese girl whose home she'd been to once for a party, lived next door. She remembered the house, which had a side gate that didn't appear locked. Even if it was, she could pretend to fool with it, by which time, he and the taxi would be gone.

They stopped. Ricardo looked at her strangely. "What is it with you, anyway?"

His voice frightened her. "What do you mean?"

"It's okay, you don't have to let me take you home if you don't want."

"But, I …"

"Gail." His voice was dejected. She hadn't seem the type to play games, and he was hurt. "You must know this is *my* house."

Humiliated, Gail rushed out of the taxi and ran home. He tried to follow but she was too fast for him.

Conchita's voice interrupted her memory. "I'm leaving for the groceries now."

Her tea was cold. Gail retreated back into the living room and absently picked up the newspaper.

He loved booze too much, that dad of yours, and food. And he liked sex.

Why couldn't her mother's laughter leave her alone?

Ricardo had said, after their first kiss on the dance floor—Gail's first kiss, ever—*I've been wanting to do that all year.*

Spreading open the morning paper on her coffee table, Gail recalled the reason she took French in secondary school with the non-Chinese—which was what all the French students, mostly Portuguese girls, called themselves—was because Mom insisted. *The nuns will let you,* her mother said. *They let all the foreign girls drop Chinese. Besides, you already know Chinese.* Gail had done what her mother asked, but studied the Chinese curriculum on her own. A sympathetic teacher got her an exception to register for the Chinese exams as well, and Gail aced both language and history with distinction; her only credit subject, a B, was French.

On their way home, Kina said to her father. "Papa, is Auntie Gail your girlfriend now?"

Xavier looked at her. "I don't know, *chérie*." His daughter was growing up fast, probably faster than was good for her. The sudden and overpowering intimacy of being with Gail was not at all what he expected. What had begun as a flirtation was turning into something new and unfamiliar. He wasn't sure it was the right thing, either for him, or Kina.

But the pull was there. Gail was irresistibly virginal. To be only her *second* lover—the shy confession, when he began to undress her, had been sweet, almost girlish—posed a delicious challenge that no man in his right mind could resist. In bed, she *wanted* him to take the lead, and he felt like the only man who had ever touched her. During lovemaking, she never said a word. Her whole body succumbed to the act.

When it came to the women he honored, Xavier Dopoulos was a man who preserved the romance of the past, despite being swept along by the direction, and force, of the future as it inevitably would be.

17

Afterglow becomes women, especially those at midlife, and Gail Szeto was no exception; coupled with power, the effect, radiant. A week later, early on Friday evening Eastern Standard Time, Gordie picked up on the ambient glow surrounding his sister the minute she walked into his home.

He relieved her of luggage. "Welcome to the homestead."

In the background, a CD was on low. Tony Bennett sang to Bill Evans' piano lines.

Having agreed to crash with her brother for the weekend, Gail was now feeling a little ambivalent. There had been a mix up with her reservation, and late that afternoon, the hotel apologetically scrambled to find another room at their sister property in Midtown. When Gail called Gordie to explain she might be late for dinner, he offered, *insisted*, and feeling reckless, she said, *why not?*

Gail cast her eyes around the large, well appointed space. "The Ashberrys," she said. "So this is how you live."

"Just me, mainly, and Dad occasionally, when he came to town. Mother stayed in Connecticut most of the time. It's a condition of being an only child. Your folks either buy you off or leave you alone. Mine did both. Come on, I'll show you around."

The spacious ground floor level, with its beautifully restored wood paneling, opened out to a small back garden. An archway divided the space. The front living room overlooked Gramercy Park through two bay windows and the dining room led to the kitchen and garden. Beside the dining area, a glass door opened onto a side room which comprised a library and music room. The shelves were filled with CDs, LPs and mostly music books.

Upstairs, two large bedrooms opened onto the hallway. A back bedroom had been removed and the bathroom extended. A huge round tub was large enough for the long legged. Bookshelves lined the walls of the hallway.

The easeful elegance of this two-story townhouse reminded Gail of her first rented room in Boston. Gordie was unlocking a window into another world, one that Mark had kept closed to her. Or perhaps—and the idea was new—Mark hadn't. She had chosen the East Coast after two years of college in Hawaii, just as she was now finding her way, however uncertainly, to New York. Her own path, or one set by Mark, Mom, and even Gordie?

In the living room, Gordie opened a sideboard, revealing a superbly stocked bar, one that outclassed any Gail had ever seen. "What can I offer you?" Noting her expression, he added, "We Ashberrys keep our excesses hidden."

She frowned.

"Sorry." He handed her a sherry. "Good trip so far?"

"It's been … I guess the word's 'heady'. I've been promoted without asking for it."

That explained the aura. "Congratulations," he said.

"The problem is I'm not sure I want it." She wanted to say that she felt used, put on display for the board of Shanghai Industrial—and she had performed brilliantly, a high she liked—but couldn't disclose this without betraying the trust of her employers, although perhaps, since Gordie *was* family?

He said, "Gu Kwun would approve, of your getting it, I mean."

"What makes you say that?"

"He told me once, 'Mummy's smarter than her boss, so really, you see, she ought to *be* the boss.' Your son was quite a kid."

She smiled. "He was."

"Hungry?" Gordie preferred not to dwell on things past. "Chinese takeout okay? We need to get an early start tomorrow."

"Well, I suppose," but she wondered what possessed him to

serve her, of all people, Chinese. It seemed unlike him.

He disappeared to the kitchen. A few minutes later, he rolled out a tray bearing an authentic, home cooked spread with her favorite dishes. Gail gazed in astonishment at the imprinted chopsticks which read "Dragon Palace, Boston," the restaurant where she had been a waitress.

She said, "But how …?"

"Simple, I called Hanky Wong, your old boss, and explained who I was. He said to leave the menu to him. They liked you there, didn't they? We organized getting it here this afternoon."

The magnitude overwhelmed and delighted her. "You did this for me? You went through all this trouble? But why?"

He stretched out an arm—lean and long, like hers—and rumpled her hair playfully. "Just eat," he said, adding, emphatically, "*Sis.*"

Later, alone in the guest room—lying in a comfortable, luxurious, *indulgent* bed—Gail did not regret being at Gordie's. Her brother was connection, not only to the Ashberry blood, but to their parallel histories, and Mom and Gu Kwun as well. What she hadn't told Gordie, because she didn't want to admit to it, was her disappointment that she and Xavier wouldn't see each other tomorrow evening as hoped. He hadn't called when he said he would, which probably meant he was too busy.

Her mother's voice harped, always at night. *No bother, Gay-lo,* when she had gone to Mom in tears after Jason deserted her, a rare seeking of comfort and help; she was desperate, because her son couldn't understand why or where his father had gone and cried fiercely, unstoppable, until it frightened her. Her mother comforted him, soothing his fears. Gu Kwun had been four. *The ones we love are never too much trouble.*

In a Cessna Skyhawk early the next morning, seated beside Gordie in the pilot seat, Gail said, "When you said 'the Block' I thought you meant the block in the city your home was on. I didn't expect to be on a runway in Connecticut."

"Block Island is home. Well it was, every summer, till Mother couldn't go any more."

Abruptly, she said, "When I was a child, I dreamt we flew together. You took me to America. It was a recurring dream." She was staring ahead, not looking at him. "I've never told anyone about this until now."

Gordie glanced at her. The revelation caused an unfamiliar sensation, stirring the past in a new way, a past he would rather be over and done with. Her presence now in his life was changing things, perhaps more than he bargained for.

They took off in silence.

Gail had never flown before in a single engine private plane. When she initially prepared to climb on board, her brother told her to "fold up" because the cabin door was only a little more than three feet high. Yet the interior did not feel cramped. There was a spacious elegance and grace about the aircraft, which Gordie called a triumph of minimalist design.

The sky was glorious for flying, sunny and cloudless. Block Island appeared, seemingly out of nowhere, in the middle of the Rhode Island Sound. As they approached the tiny airport, Gail told herself that the dream was over, probably for good.

Later, driving along the empty roads, surrounded by an undulating landscape, Gordie said, suddenly. "Dad taught me to fly here. And cycle, and swim. Mother loved this place. She said it gave her peace."

The house stood on a knoll, alone, at the end of a dirt road, facing the water. It was slate blue. The windows were shuttered. No one had come for a long time. When they stepped inside, the moldy dank made Gail shiver.

"It's a mess," Gordie said, as he opened windows. "I probably should've cleaned first and then brought you here." He had done that once a year, as an adult, for his mother.

Gail looked around, undaunted. "No big deal. We'll clean."

They worked well together. Neither one was given to chatter, focusing entirely on the task at hand. At one point, Gordie asked, "So are you moving to New York?" To which Gail replied, "Probably, there's this man, you see," but hadn't elaborated.

Late afternoon, they sat on the open porch, which wrapped

around three sides of the house. A stepped path, etched into the hill directly below, led to the sea. Gail was barefoot, enjoying a Bloody Mary and cold lobsters. Gordie had acquired from the local fishermen three live ones, which he unflinchingly threw into a huge pot of boiling water. Flailing claws had made the pot cover rattle; Gail held it steady, and waited for the strangled sounds that emanated, like screams, to end.

"So," Gordie said. "Are you going to tell me who 'this man' is?"

The sky was darkening. She pushed at her shades with her wrist, and arranged them on top of her head. "A friend."

"Closer than that, surely?"

"I keep the necessary distance." A tiny piece of flesh eluded her fork. She raised the claw to her lips and sucked.

"You should."

"Why? You don't even know him."

"I know men around women with money." He recalled Jack, his mother's "suitor," from one of her foundations, a man only seven years older than himself. *Predatory.*

"I need sizeable bait, you mean?"

"Hell no …" But she was laughing. "Seriously, Gail. You know what I mean."

"Serious, you?" She threw the empty claw at him, grazing his cheek. Her brother, she was surprised to discover, could make her playful. A bit like Jason.

"Hey! Watch that. Damn. You're worse than Dad." He rubbed his face, upset. "Look, trust me on the money thing."

Then it dawned on her. "Wait, how did you know?"

Her tone, suspicious and demanding, put Gordie on the defensive. "Whoa, relax. Your mother left instructions for Chancellor & Chung to contact me. Just as a by-the-way, nothing more." Then, annoyed by her presumption, he added. "What? Come on Gail, did you really think I *didn't* know?"

"So how long have you …?"

"Since '79."

"What?!"

He liked rattling her, not that he intended to keep her in the dark. Well, not really. "Gail, I don't want your family's money."

"Why not?" The initial shock had abated. Family life was one long, ironic moment. "It probably came from our father anyway." Back in 1968, she had signed the money from the trust left her by Mark over to Gordie, despite her mother's protests.

"It didn't," he asserted flatly. Sucking air between his teeth, his eyes in a kind of entreaty, he said, "Let me start at the beginning."

Easter, 1959. He had been eleven. Right after Dad's fiftieth birthday when his parents held this big party to celebrate. He remembered that trip specifically because he got to miss a few days of school. It was only the third time Dad had brought him to Hong Kong. The first trip was three years earlier.

Gail said. "1956. The year *I* met him."

Deposited with Uncle Jimmy, who let him play with model planes in his office. Afterwards, Dad returned to pick him up, furious. "She insists on my acknowledging the child," he overheard Dad tell Jimmy. "Says it's for future security." Jimmy reassured their father, saying that surely it was understandable, since he couldn't offer marriage.

"That's when Dad flew off the handle and yelled. 'You don't understand! I love that woman, but I won't marry a … a …'," Gordie cut off his narrative.

Gail glanced down at her hands. The nails were growing back in. "Prostitute?"

"I was a kid, Gail. I didn't know. Besides, so what?"

"It's not your fault."

"Neither was your mother's life. Dad was wrong, though. If he loved her, he should have married her. It would have been better all round."

"My mother wasn't Suzie Wong. She wouldn't have been much of a wife."

"He was a coward, and he made *my* mother miserable."

The stinging bitterness in his voice chilled Gail. She had always refrained from asking, had never wanted to know. Did the real Mrs. Ashberry … suffering wasn't unique, not in their unhappy family.

"Mother felt she wasn't attractive enough, blamed herself for his restlessness, even for his infidelities." He spoke absently, quietly, "It was goddamned unfair."

Uncomfortable, Gail prodded. "The money?"

He snapped out of his reverie. "Your mother wound up with a rich Chinese lover, some old guy who never married. It's his fortune."

Gail said, "All these years, I thought she was joking when she said she was 'going fishing for a rich man'." She refrained from completing her mother's commentary, *the older and uglier the better.*

Gordie laughed.

She asked, "So who was he, this rich guy?"

"Can't help you there. I asked Jimmy once, but he didn't know either."

"But Gordie, *why* didn't she ever tell me?"

Gordie gave her a look. It wasn't nasty, but neither was it kind. "Gail, do *you* really have to ask?"

Gail protested. "I don't know what you mean?" But her brother picked up the pot of cracked lobster shells and headed back inside the house.

Around six, Gordie said. "I'm beat."

Gail had just put on her shoes, thinking it was time they should get going. She looked at her brother, surprised at how worn he looked. "Something wrong?"

"No," he lied. "I just need a quick nap, and then we can leave. Do you mind?"

"Go ahead."

He lay on a couch and shut his eyes.

Gail put away the dishes in the kitchen. It settled her, just as working together earlier had, airing out the house, vacuuming away dust and mold gathered over three years of disuse. She had been surprised by his domesticity, and his unwillingness to hire help. *The greatest crime of the wealthy,* he claimed, *is perpetuating indentured servitude.*

Returning to the living room, she flicked through Gordie's CDs—he traveled with a huge selection—and was about to put on the headphones when he murmured, "It's okay, let me listen. I rest better with music."

"Autumn in New York". *Why does it seem so inviting?*

Gail read the sleeve—composed by Vernon Duke—and thought, how atrociously ignorant she was of anything outside work. Surely she had listened to music once, read something other than economic theory or business case studies? The last performance she attended, an opera premiere for Tan Dun's *Marco Polo*, was a couple of years ago, and she went only because Kwok Po couldn't use his ticket and his wife had called when Gail happened to be free.

She glanced at Gordie. He was curled, fetal, looking extraordinarily vulnerable. Among the men in her life—Xavier, Jason, Kwok Po, Vince, or even Ricardo—her half brother was the best looking. A good physique and no disfiguring marks, all his parts perfectly proportional. Plato's dream. Or Hitler's. She shuddered.

Leaning over, she covered him with a blanket, and wondered, what about his love life? One day, she might ask. He carried torches, evidently, like for Jimmy Kho's married daughter.

The tune came to an end. Prysock repeated the refrain. *Dreamers with empty hands. May sigh for exotic lands.*

Gail pulled the blanket up to his shoulders. His hair was in his eyes again. Gently, she removed the offending strands. Her brother, for better or worse.

He opened his eyes and grabbed her by the wrist. A half-dream, at the surface of sleep, of a woman wrapping herself around him.

It's autumn in New York. It's good to live it again.

"Hey," he said quietly.

"You startled me," but it was his grip, like a lock on her wrist, that really surprised her.

Then, she saw that his eyes were wet.

Still clutching, he spoke in a fierce whisper. "They're all gone."

She unlocked his fingers, removing her wrist, and, from some non-habit, from an almost, but not quite maternal instinct, she knelt and gathered him into her arms, hugging him to her chest, stroking his hair. Surprising herself. His whole body trembled, sighed, *heaved,* and then, he began to cry, the tears washing her sweater and arms. "I know," she said, cradling him tightly.

He hung onto her embrace; no woman had held him in a long time. "You're my only family now. I don't want to lose you too." He continued weeping copious tears, for the loss of the certainty that had been Mother. For Fa-Loong, and the chance to play uncle to

Gu Kwun, to pave a future for him in America, one in which he could participate, the way he had longed to years before in Gail's life. He wept from anger at Gail's rejection, during those years in Boston, her *obtuseness,* like Dad's over *everything*, but especially Vietnam—*you run along with those goddamned, privileged kids. No son of* mine *is a coward.* He wept for his own anxieties, finances, *age*—the years speeding by, *stop them! I meant to be good, what happened?* He wept for the lost loves in his life, the loneliness. She bent forward and kissed the top of his head, a full head of hair, the straight silky softness which never would thin, his mother's legacy.

He said. "Don't leave me."

"I won't," she promised.

18

At the bar, Xavier glanced at his watch. It was past two on Sunday morning. As Jim returned, his lap dancer blew him a kiss, a thank you for the generous tip.

Jim pointed at Xavier's drink. "Want another?"

"No. It's time we were leaving." His tooth was bothering him again.

"I'm just getting started."

Xavier pushed his glass back towards the bartender. "Then you'll have to finish up on your own."

"I'll buy you a session with Desirée." Jim motioned towards the woman he had just left. "She's hot."

"Thanks. I prefer the real thing." His partner's "celibacy" never ceased to amaze him, as did his phobia of condoms, which Xavier discovered when he'd once raised the subject in answer to Jim's snide comments about AIDS and the real thing.

"Suit yourself," Jim ordered another drink, adding, "spoilsport."

Xavier zipped up his jacket and strolled out to the moonlit chill. The meat market district was eerily quiet. A few years later, the area would throng with the bright young things of the twenty-first century, exploding into a trendy nightspot. The spillover from nearby Chelsea, already a fashionable area to visit, would further encroach as Chelsea became a desirable place to live, whether or not you were gay. For now, the odd "gentlemen's" club attempted to survive amidst the S&M scene and transvestite trade.

Xavier found solace in the silence. The surroundings felt familiar, like Paris, a much more tolerant city than New York. When he'd lucked into a cheap space in this neighborhood back in 1992, the year after Shelley was put away, Jim had exclaimed, you're bringing your daughter to live where?! Jim, ensconced in his Upper West Side, three-bedroom, mortgage-free apartment, in a building with a doorman on a tree-lined street, was necessarily limited in imagination.

Heading east, he turned south towards the angled corner, where a triangular building intersected cobblestone streets. At the building, a sign above a basement entrance read "The Manhole." Crossing over to the opposite side, he arrived at the doorway on Hudson that was the entrance to his loft.

As he climbed the stairs, Xavier reflected that the gulf between himself and Jim was greater than the Atlantic. All the same, he was glad Ursula had returned before his trip—having gotten into a fight with Marcel—and that Kina did not have to be here with him, in this space that was home for now.

Early Monday afternoon, Xavier finally reached Gail at the New York offices of Northeast Trust.

He said, "The hotel said you checked out. What happened? Didn't we plan to see each other Saturday? Why didn't you call?"

"You said you'd call before Friday if you could make it, so when you didn't, I assumed you were busy. I'm at my brother's. Reservation mix up. But Xavier, why didn't you call my cell phone?"

"I …" He did not want to admit that he had forgotten to bring the number. "I tried. Couldn't get through. Happens sometimes with cells, or maybe you had it off?"

Her phone had been on all weekend. However, she did not press the issue. "I have to go," she said, even though she still had ten minutes. "Meeting with my boss."

"Tonight then?"

"I have to fly out tomorrow."

"We can still have dinner."

"I promised to buy my brother dinner."

"Afterwards?"

"Call me later?"

Although he knew he would, Xavier was irritated. Yet, despite an unease about Gail, her resistance—or game playing—piqued him. And this brother thing, what was that about? One way or another, he would see her somehow, here in New York. When it came to the women he slept with, Xavier did not like to be thwarted.

When Gail entered her boss' office, Josh's visitor rose. He was around fifty, six foot one and athletic. He emanated presence. His wavy dark hair was graying, and he wore glasses. A crease in the middle of his forehead lent his features a perpetual frown, but his blue eyes—intelligent, Gail noted—betrayed intense energy.

Josh said. "Gail Szeto, Jim Fieldman."

They shook hands.

"Jim's going to be working with us on the Shanghai Industrial reorganization," Josh said, adding, "We were at Michigan together."

The meeting, like all the ones with her new boss, Gail was discovering, was short, rushed and destined for interruption. Halfway through, his secretary buzzed, and Josh excused himself temporarily, leaving them in his office.

Jim said, "Is he always like this?"

"You've known him longer than I have," she responded.

He smiled. "So you're based in Hong Kong?"

"At the moment."

"I'll be there next week. We should have lunch and talk."

She handed him a card. "Been in Hong Kong before, or China?"

"A fair amount, mostly on business, although I do have friends in Hong Kong and one real good buddy from here in New York. I've been dealing with Chinese companies for about seven, eight years now." He handed her a card which read "Consultant" next to his name plus New York and cell phone contact information. Nothing else.

Gail found it curiously understated. She turned it over. There were no details in Chinese on the back, which was standard practice for most businesses working with China. "Speak Chinese?" She asked, without looking up.

"My associates do," he replied. "One in Hong Kong, another Beijing."

"What about Shanghai?"

He liked the challenge in her voice. "You didn't let me finish. My Shanghai associate starts next week," but his mind was scrambling for a quick solution.

"That's helpful," she said, thinking that her boss, if he had to do the old boys thing, had at least picked someone who might prove useful. She stared straight ahead at Josh's empty chair. The family portrait behind his desk briefly caught her short, a reminder that mourning was not over, despite her current distractions.

Jim leaned towards her chair, and rested his hand on its arm. "Speak more than a sentence at a time?"

Startled, Gail turned to face him. His eyes glinted. She bit her upper lip and looked away. Josh walked back in.

Afterwards, Jim asked Josh, "What's Gail like?"

"Her? Bit of a cold fish. Smart, though."

Jim said, "Oh yeah?" and then they spoke of other things.

"Hey lady," Perry greeted Gail, who had swung by Legal. "They're keeping you busy this time, aren't they?" They had tried to get together for lunch but to no avail.

Gail said, "The price of something."

"Yup. What do you think Shanghai Industrial's paying? Are they paying?"

"You know?"

Perry grinned. "Counsel always knows." Then, "Can you keep a secret?" She reached out and shut her door. She was glowing.

Gail felt the radiance. Decent sex, perhaps? She traced a finger across her lips. "Zip-locked."

"I'm jumping ship," and Perry explained she was heading to a mutual fund company in Greenwich. "They're not woman-friendly enough here, well, I don't have to tell you that. Besides, I've been in the city all my life. Even though it's great, I'd like Persey to have other advantages as well, like recognizing grass maybe?" She was due to start July 1.

"Promotion?" Gail asked.

"Lateral, pay cut, actually. But there's a point where money makes no difference, right?" Relieved at having unburdened herself, she continued. "What about you? How did it go with Xavier?"

Gail smiled. "It was … good."

"That's not a 'good' smile. Come on, it was great, right? When do you see him again?"

"Tonight. His place."

"Whereabouts?"

"Hudson and something. The lower West, but I'm not sure exactly where it is."

Perry said. "Sounds like the Village. Hey lady, you've got yourself one classy boy there."

Gail flushed slightly, pleased. They talked a bit more about Perry's new job, and Persey, and the neighborhoods of Manhattan.

Steak weighed on Gail's system worse than curry, which ranked a close second. She wished she had ordered fish for dinner, but it seemed absurd at a steak house. Frank's had been Gordie's choice. But the bill! Shockingly expensive. She had paid up graciously though, this price of family.

Outside on Tenth Avenue, Gordie said. "Ready for bed?" He unlocked his Lamborghini, parked at the entrance, surprisingly safe in this still marginal space before the development that overwhelmed, transforming it into just another Manhattan neighborhood.

"I have to meet my friend."

"Not the man?" When she didn't respond, he said, "Where can I drop you?"

She took out a slim pocket diary from her purse and consulted it. "It's on Hudson, in the Village I think. He said I could walk from here," adding, "what time is it, by the way?"

"Too late to be walking," he replied. "Besides, the Village isn't that close. Hop in, I'll take you."

The drive took as long as a walk would have. Gordie headed down Ninth onto Hudson towards downtown. By the time Gail caught sight of a numbered address, four hundred something, they realized they had bypassed Xavier's place in the six hundred's, and circled back up to Fourteenth Street.

When they finally found it, Gordie said. "Sis, this sure ain't the Village."

The numbers on the doorway to the triangular shaped building were barely discernible, and the building itself appeared uninhabited. Gail took one look at it, said, "There must be some mistake," and switched on her cell phone.

Xavier appeared at the front door minutes later. Gail made introductions and then Gordie drove away, a little worried by his sister's taste in men. It didn't square with Fa-Loong's description of the ex-husband, *a decent boy, doctor, you know, but then, my Gay-lo is very choosy,* although these days, Gordie was rethinking everything he thought he knew about all that.

Xavier kissed her and led her up the stairs. "Did you have a good dinner?"

"It was okay." The dark stairwell unnerved her, even though she told herself, it was reasonably wide and clean, unlike the dingy, narrow one of her childhood home. "My brother has, I guess you'd say, expensive tastes," but what she thought was, extravagant.

On the third floor, he opened a large, metal door. "Here's the castle."

The space was a trapezium, with no interior walls. From the door, centered on the baseline of the trapezium, the view narrowed towards the opposite wall where Xavier worked and slept. The only natural light came in on the right, from five ancient sash windows, one of which was broken and permanently closed, masking tape plastered on the glass where it had shattered in a circular spray. The windows on the left were boarded up.

Next to one working window was a draftsman's desk with a

lamp clamped at one end. Xavier's laptop and phone were on it. Besides the workspace was an angled paper screen behind which was his bed, a futon on top of two tatami mats.

Diagonally opposite was a toilet and shower, crude cubicles, installed beside a refrigerator and the two ring burner on a table that made up the kitchen. A couple of chairs completed the table. Beside the entrance was another angled paper screen behind which May slept.

The bare wood floor was paint splattered and scratched, but clean.

No clock, no television, no radio.

Gail laid her purse on the table. "How much time do you spend here?"

He was uncorking a bottle of wine. "Recently, not much." Pointing to May's space. "My roommate is the one who really lives here most of the time, but she's gone for a few days." He added, "It's rather basic, I'm afraid."

It was not even remotely what she expected, but she said, "Oh, it's fine" and took the glass he handed her.

"Come on," he said, leading her to the futon. "Let's get comfortable."

Gail awoke to the hissing from the ancient radiator. The front door was opening, surrendering to keys, one after the other, in three, heavy duty locks. She saw she was naked and pulled the sheet around herself.

A woman's voice in a distinctly Singaporean-Malaysian accent said, "Let me check in case he's home. Don't want to piss him off."

Gail stuck her head around the screen.

The young woman, inclining towards plump, stared at Gail, surprised. Xavier never brought women home. "Where's Xav?" A man's figure remained in the doorway.

"I'm not sure."

May said to her companion, "Hang on, I'll be right out," and then took a dress in its dry cleaning bag from a rack. "Well, see you, I guess. Tell Xav to give me a call, can do?" And left.

A distant ringing sound, and Gail jumped up in search of her cell phone, knocking over the screen. The sheet trailed behind her. It was Gordie. "Hey, are you alright?"

"Oh, hi." She glanced around. "What time ...?"

"Your airport limo's downstairs. You still planning on catching that flight?"

The door opened and Xavier walked in carrying a bag with bagels and coffees. He placed them on the table in front of where she was standing.

Gordie was saying, "I can send your bags along with the driver to get you if you want, or if you need more time, I'll take you to the airport."

Xavier knelt down, raised the sheet up from underneath and took hold of her waist. The cold of his hands made her shiver. He stood up and bit her ear, removing the rest of the sheet, and said, loud enough for Gordie to hear, "Good morning."

"No," Gail said into the phone, tugging the sheet away from Xavier. "I'll come back right away. Tell the driver to wait."

Xavier took the phone and sheet from her and said to Gordie. "Hello, it's Xavier. Tell the driver to go. I'll take care of your sister."

Just before the phone went dead, Gordie heard Xavier say to Gail, "I'm not done with you yet. Take the next flight."

In Gramercy Park, Gordie resisted the temptation to ring back. He recalled his mother, when she had dried her eyes—after the discovery of Dad's Chinese life and the terms of the will—saying, how dare he put you on par with some, some slut's daughter, and he had replied, but Mother, it's not that much money, and her scornful declaration, Gordon Ashberry, this is about blood, not money! You simply don't taint blood.

Xavier waved Gail off in a cab. It was an odd feeling, this goodbye, even though he knew he would see her again within days in Hong Kong. Gail was a remarkably satisfying lover. Her body responded easily to almost anything he did, and they had never once talked about work.

His earlier doubts were dissolving.

He glanced across the street, shielding his eyes from the glare. Shadow puddles said noon. "345"—a brightly colored billboard signaling an address, a realtor's offering—graced a renovated building. When had that gone up? With every departure and return, Xavier was greeted by almost unrecognizable transformations to the neighborhood.

Later, when he met Jim at the Harvard Club, his partner said, "You look pleased with yourself."

"I am," he said. "Ursula's back, I've found a school for Kina and Dahlia will be in the U.S. for half a year and is lending me her apartment, gratis. All I have to do is feed her cat whenever I'm in Shanghai." And, he didn't add, I'm getting some and you're not. "What's up with you?"

"I've got a new contract."

Someone whistling "Autumn in New York" breezed past. Xavier saw Gordie, who waved but did not stop.

Jim said, "Who's he?"

"Just some guy," Xavier replied. "So tell me about this contract," and Jim outlined a job for Shanghai Industrial Bank.

He listened, thinking, another boring job. Most of it comprised training sessions for senior executives, to teach them "how to play ball with Americans" as Jim put it, because the bank wanted to expand overseas. Xavier determined that his role was more like an interpreter or liaison, meaning an overpaid assistant to Jim. There was a secretary, he recalled, one who worked for their CFO, who was a good friend of a woman he'd had a brief but friendly affair with. He must call her, pump for information, find out how the organization ticked. At least, his end on this one was easy, and would not get in the way of Monkey International, the job that really mattered.

What Xavier did not hear mention of was Northeast Trust, because Josh had said to Jim, not a word, not even to your associates, until after the public announcement.

Over the next five days, Xavier called Gail from New York twice. She said she looked forward to his return. Meanwhile, no resolution to Shelley's situation seemed imminent, and the ache in his tooth had abated. Jim's idiosyncrasies aside, even work was calm and organized. Problems, Xavier decided, had a habit of resolving themselves, sooner or later.

19

Xavier's first phone call, in the morning just after Gail had showered and dressed—*take off your blouse, your bra, your panties,* he commanded—flushed her into a sweat. She closed and locked her bedroom door, unable to stop herself as his voice insinuated its way into her thoughts, elicited desire so strong that she wanted to jam the receiver between her legs. When she told him that, he said, *do it, do it, do it*—until she came. Less than half an hour afterwards, the violence of her lust prickled memory, sharp, stinging, like a hand slapping there, and there, and there, like fingers finding every nerve that yielded, and she paused her work, rushed to the bathroom rather than the bedroom so that Conchita wouldn't wonder, and brought herself to another, shuddering climax.

In the days that followed, Gail's thoughts raced between reason and lust in a maddening relay. The aftermath of sex, not unlike that of a battle, pricked her conscience as wounds are dressed and casualties counted, while hindsight instills a desire for foresight.

Surely, she thought, the disparity in their circumstances was obvious from the start?

Who *was* Xavier, really? Attentive when he wanted to be—flowers awaited on her return from New York and he called, *twice*—a lover whose touch induced extreme, *unbearable,* pleasure.

It had been a little embarrassing, returning to Gordie's, the morning after on display in her wrinkled clothes, without makeup—*or* underwear, Xavier wouldn't return those, held onto them, and Gail had no choice but to leave wearing only a slip underneath—legs bare, her nylons having been torn, a habit around Xavier. Her brother hadn't said much, which bothered her. For once, she would have preferred his customary jokes.

Perry emailed *So, did you have a good time?* and Gail replied, *Too good.* Perry quipped, *That's the trouble with deprivation,* and was pleased for Gail, although she couldn't help the twinge of envy, being herself *desperately* deprived.

Gail was not exaggerating. In bed, and even long distance—she was forced to admit the irritating reality that she succumbed to his phone sex—Xavier did everything *too* well. Unlike Jason, he would talk to her when they made love, strangely obscene, although a perfect gentlemen outside the bedroom, and the things he said excited her even though she felt they shouldn't. Jason liked to talk about sex, and about how they had sex, but he did so clinically, taking everything apart as if he were dissecting a cadaver.

But the greatest surprise to Gail was that despite her initial shock at Xavier's circumstances, she *hadn't* been uncomfortable at his place. It was a little like life with her mother. They were all a part of the same *demimonde,* the *déclassé* and *déraciné*—those French words she'd looked up as a girl, in search of a *raison d'être*—and with Xavier, there was comfort in stripping off the tedious pretense of respectability. A little like family, a little like home.

Mom and her artist lover, the painter, when her body was *not* for sale. Could *he* have been the rich lover?

I know men around women with money.

Gordie was wrong. He had to be. After all, Xavier didn't know about the money.

The following Monday, a packet of legal documents for Gail's signature arrived by courier from Chancellor & Chung. The card, gold embossed, in an unsealed envelope of thick, cream colored paper, fell out first. An invitation to their cocktail reception, at five-thirty p.m., today, to show off their new offices. Go, she told herself. Chances were there would be people she knew. It would be good to do a little business socializing, which she hadn't done in awhile. Contacts never hurt.

Conchita entered the living room, holding up a gift-wrapped package the size of a small book. "I found this in your mother's room."

Curious, Gail unwrapped it right away. A Chinese version of *The Little Prince,* in simplified characters, the written language used on the Mainland. She began to cry, tears streaming, unstoppable. "My mother," she began, "She actually got a copy."

Concerned, Conchita approached, "Ma'am?"

Gail looked up. "The book. My mother really got me a copy." And then, snapping to, she roughly dried her face with the back of her hand. "It's nothing, Conchita, you can go back to work now," her tone dismissive and unconsciously rude.

Conchita did not move. "No, ma'am, I cannot just go back to work, not even if you order me to. There's something *wrong* with you ma'am. I think you need to get help from someone. A doctor maybe, or a priest."

Gail glared at her employee. "How dare you! How dare you talk to me like that!"

Ordinarily, Conchita would have said something to calm the flare-ups. But this time, she stood her ground. "You can shout at me all you want, but I'm right and you're wrong. You're only angry because you're sad, because of everything you've suffered in the last few years. God is testing you. Yet you never stop, never try to understand why you need to be tested. You can't live like this, Ms. Szeto. In the end, you'll only be very unhappy." She turned around abruptly and went to the kitchen.

Gail realized she was trembling. *What was wrong with her?* And what did Conchita mean by a test? She glanced at her wrist. Her watch. Gone. Irreplaceable like everything else. She took a deep breath. There was no reason to shout at Conchita.

On the book cover, the boy with spiky yellow hair stood on his planet, gazing at the galaxy. The past poked at her, insistent. *See, see, even the book came back. Just like your father. And mother.*

They'll always be there whether you want them or not. Always. For a very brief moment, she almost wanted to destroy it the way she had her original English version, a present when she was six or seven. How proudly her mother had presented it! *Here, Gay-lo, a very special present from your father. He said that the writer is a fighter pilot, like him.* Gail had torn it up deliberately in front of her mother, pulling out a page at a time, ripping each one to shreds. Fa-Loong watched in silence. When all the pages became a pile on the floor, she slapped Gail hard across the face. *Stupid girl! Ungrateful child! You know nothing.* Gail did not cry and glared mutely at her mother. *What did you mean by destroying such a precious gift? Other children would be overjoyed if their fathers brought them an English book from America.* Gail sulked all that night, did not say a word, refused to eat dinner. Right before she went to bed, she finally declared: *If you really loved me,* you *would have given me a Chinese book. I have no father.*

Meanwhile, in the kitchen, Conchita, shaken, was trying to decide whether or not to give notice.

Do something, Gail told herself. Anything. When in doubt, work. Her son's voice interrupted: *Janie doesn't read real Chinese.* When she had pressed him to explain, she understood that Janie was learning the simplified characters in her Putonghua class.

On an impulse, she flicked through her Rolodex and found Rick's card. Enrico Hammond. Only afterwards, when she reflected on how pleased he sounded and how quickly he agreed to meet her this evening did she recall his previous invitation, and then wondered, was Conchita right, was this a test she was failing miserably, regularly, with little hope of ever passing, no matter how hard she tried?

Chancellor & Chung's new office had not moved from Exchange Square, but was twice as large as their previous space. They were profiting in this downturn, Gail thought, as she shook hands with Benny Chung, and probably getting a deal on the rental as well. Everyone re-negotiated leases now.

"Ms. Szeto," Benny said, "we're so delighted you made it. When we hadn't heard, we thought you might be out of town."

She raised her eyebrows. "I only just received your invitation today."

"Really?" He glowered. Some secretary was already in trouble. "My apologies. Please, come have a drink." He motioned to a waiter with a champagne tray, and then excused himself.

The reception was well attended. "Thank you. It's getting easier," she responded several times to acquaintances who had heard about her personal tragedy. The civility was soothing, as was the interest in her move to New York.

Around six-thirty, she wandered towards the table of lavish hors d'oeuvres, and dug into the yellowtail sushi. From behind her, a soft spoken, oddly familiar, Midwestern voice said. "So you do speak more than a sentence at a time."

John Haight breezed past as she turned, saying, "Ah, you've met Jim Fieldman?" and then flitted off.

Jim had been watching her for the past half-hour, waiting to see if she'd notice him. "You know a lot of people here, don't you?"

Nonplussed she responded. "And how do you know these guys?"

"We've done a little business. You?"

"They're my lawyers."

"Oh, really?" *Which Szeto is she,* he wondered, but was unable to place her in the roster of wealthy Chinese families. "By the way, have we met before? [illegible] I mean."

"I don't think so. Why?"

"Your name's familiar." When she didn't respond, he said, "I was going to give you a call in the morning. About lunch. Unless," he hesitated, did not want to appear pushy, "you wouldn't happen to be free for dinner tonight?"

In the doorway, Rick Hammond caught Gail's eye. "Sorry no, I have to meet someone," and waved. "Give me a call tomorrow."

As Jim watched her walk away, he noted, *nice legs,* and then wondered if she and the man she was meeting were romantically involved.

Over coffee, Rick said. "It was really nice of you to do this. Janie will be pleased to have a Chinese version." He leafed through the book. "She likes *The Little Prince*, says he's like Gu Kwun."

"Gu… my mother would have wanted her to have it, I think."

"How are you holding up?"

"It gets easier, not better." And then, "How's Janie doing? I mean, since you and your wife broke up."

"Not so good." He paused. Then, abruptly, "I have custody, you know."

Uncomfortable, Gail glanced down at her coffee.

Rick continued. "You'll appreciate this. My wife had been having an affair for over a year." Seeing Gail's startled expression, he said, "Gu Kwun told us. I hope you don't mind my bringing it up."

They looked at each other awkwardly.

He added. "Janie still cries a lot, although she pretends she doesn't. But I've checked her pillow and it's often wet." He glanced away. "My wi… her mother doesn't have a lot of time to see her."

"That's …" She was about to say "unusual" but said, instead, "That must be hard."

"Not really. Her mo… my wife was, is not exactly the parental type."

"Well," Gail began, finishing off her coffee. She needed to escape the encroachment of this intimacy.

He spoke quickly, "How did you handle it with your son?"

She was about to say, *I told him the truth,* but her mother's voice, murmuring *ngaahnggeng ngaam* arrested her. "I didn't, handle it that is, not well."

"What would you have done differently?"

Perhaps it was his journalist manner—the probing interviewer, even though all he needed was to share—but Gail was moved, or induced, to talk.

"I suppose," she began, "if I could relive it all again, I would have made sure Gu Kwun spent time with his father. He didn't, you know. I wouldn't let him. I think that's why he liked being with you and Janie so much."

Rick reached across the table and squeezed her hand. She did not pull away and continued, "He told me once that 'Mr. Hammond really loves Janie' which I didn't fully appreciate at the time. I guess I do now."

He let go of her hand, exhaled, "Thank you for that."

She said, "It gets better."

"Listen," he finished off his coffee. "I'd like to talk more. Want to get some dinner?"

"Oh …" she was about to say, *I'm with someone,* but then thought *why shouldn't I?* But … "Sorry, I have work tonight."

"Another night?"

"Sure."

As she left, Rick thought it a shame, but promised himself to call again. He wasn't sure he really liked Gail—she was cold, even when talking about the personal—although she was stunningly attractive. Her eyes, frank and direct. Something Gu Kwun said still piqued. *Conchita says Mummy needs a boyfriend, Mr. Hammond, do you know anyone?* which used to make him laugh. Now, it seemed unbearably sad and he was struck, once again, by the inexplicable reality of Gu Kwun, a child who was perhaps too good to have been true.

The encounter with Rick Hammond nagged at Gail. Janie, apparently, was not as unconditionally loved as she had presumed. *Janie still sometimes cried over Gu Kwun, and now she cries over your mother* Rick had said, and Gail, feeling the sting of recognition remarked, *[illegible] take time to dry*

At home, there was an email from Xavier, saying he'd been delayed a day and was arriving tonight and would call in the morning, but she wondered, why hadn't he simply *called* instead? By mid-morning Tuesday, Xavier still hadn't called. Jim Fieldman, however, did, and booked dinner Thursday. Minutes later, Josh rang, telling her to go to Shanghai for a series of meetings with Jim, and ended with, "Make sure Fieldman doesn't cut any side deals I don't know about." So much for old boys. Apparently, these American boys *did* only play hard ball, something Josh said *ad nauseam*.

By early Wednesday afternoon, Gail was tempted to ring Xavier. Instead, she rang the third number on his card, in Oslo. A Norwegian recording. Giving up, she called Rick Hammond.

"Well, hello," he said, pleased. "I was hoping you'd call."

Gail did not immediately register his meaning. "Could I ask for a favor?"

"Sure."

"Is there any way you'd be able to find out if someone were jailed in Malaysia, supposedly for political reasons? It's been a few years, though, and it's not high profile."

He picked up a pencil. "Maybe. There's someone at the *Far Eastern Economic Review* I could ask who might know. What's his name?"

"Her. I only have a first name though," and she named Shelley, describing her circumstance as Xavier had briefly outlined it. "She has a young daughter, apparently, and a sister named Ursula."

Rick finished off his note taking. "No promises, but I'll give it a shot. Why do you want to know this?"

"It's ..." she was about to say "personal" but then thought better of it, "to do with a party on a deal. Normally, we'd handle our own due diligence, but this was a little out of my experience. Confidential, of course."

"Of course." He hesitated. Then, "Could we have dinner Saturday if you're free? A date, I mean."

Gail stumbled, searching for the right response, "Oh, that's very kind but ... I'm afraid, business trip," which was more or less true, although she didn't have to leave till Sunday, but the words she meant to say, *That's very kind, but you should know, I'm with someone*, didn't seem right somehow.

"Too bad," he said.

Afterwards, Rick shrugged it off, *Okay, but at least I tried*, suspecting a polite brush off. Gu Kwun had told him once that his mother *never* traveled on Saturdays because "Sundays were imposition enough." The boy had been accurate and meticulous, *honest*, as he often bragged, "like my father, he's a doctor, you know, but he doesn't live with us. Doctors are special. They're not allowed to tell lies or make mistakes," which pretty well broke Rick Hammond's heart.

Afterwards, Gail regretted the lie. Unnecessary, surely? She *was* flattered, but had no time to reflect further, because Jim rang asking if he could switch their meeting to tonight instead, to which she said "no problem." These days, work filled in the missing space of evenings, and was even reassuring.

At six, just as Gail was about to leave to meet Jim for drinks, Josh rang—*didn't her boss sleep?*—and told her the Shanghai meeting was moved to Sunday, which meant flying out Saturday. "No problem," to which he responded, *Good girl, knew I could count on you,* an overused phrase that irked Gail, but this time she countered, "not 'girl' if you don't mind?" A long, three-second silence followed. Then, "Yes sir." It was the first time Gail had heard him laugh.

Dinner proved more relaxing than Gail anticipated. Jim seemed to have things under control, which impressed her.

Afterwards, Jim offered to drop her because "we're going the same way."

"How do you know where I live?"

"The office told me. You're working from home now, aren't you?"

"Aren't you at a hotel?"

He hailed a taxi and held the open door. "I'm living in Hong Kong temporarily. Go on in. I'll explain."

Through the ride they sat with a comfortable space between them.

Jim said, "I can't help feeling I know your name from somewhere."

"I don't think so," she said. "By the way, about Sunday ..."

He interrupted. "You're not related to the Szeto shipping family, by any chance?"

"No," but his probing amused, even pleased her. Most business associates only noted her Harvard MBA and job titles. No one had ever expressed such interest in her potential social importance.

"Well, I'm glad we'll be working together. You're an interesting person."

"So are you."

He leaned back. "Nice of you to say so."

At her building Jim stepped out of the taxi and shook her hand. She caught a whiff of something familiar in his cologne or aftershave. When she walked off this time, he observed, *great ass as well.*

There was no message from Xavier when she returned. She went to bed disappointed and slightly piqued.

The conversation with Rick Hammond troubled her. Perhaps she ought to call, to tell him *Don't bother the deal's fallen through*, or some such excuse. But then, wouldn't that raise a journalist's suspicion and in the end she did nothing.

Gordie, Josh, Rick. All these men, American men. Once upon a time, American men weren't real. They wore uniforms on shore leave, R&R during Vietnam, when she shut out their catcalls, wishing they would vanish. Things were worse if she were around Number Four *A-Yi*, the blonde Chinese hooker who encouraged them, and she learned to avoid being seen with any of the *A-Yi's*, and even Mom, who didn't service foreign men—*no money, just honey that's the* gwailoes *for you*—when the U.S. Navy was on the prowl.

Her mother's life suddenly seemed unbearably sad.

She closed her eyes. The fragrance, familiar, recalled. *Old Spice*. Just like, and now she couldn't be sure if it was Jim or her father or even the right scent … Jim Fieldman, *hadn't that been, back in Harvard, the voice sounded like*, but no, didn't Josh say they'd been at Michigan so probably not, she decided.

On Gail's thirtieth birthday, Kwok Po had said, *Wonder Woman, you had your share of admirers back in Harvard*. This was after the incident between them.

She said. "Really? Who?" Among their mostly male MBA classmates, no one had ever tried to date her. It had been that way all through college and remained so all through work life in Boston, until she met Jason, the tall medical student from Hong Kong who did fall in love with her—an older woman for whom school was still the best time of her life—and removed her off that shelf for awhile.

Kwok Po continued, "You intimidate them, *leikhneuih*. They called you Wonder Woman because you were so smart."

"Great. She ran around in garish underwear and had a fish and a bird for boyfriends."

"She did?"

"In the comic books." Her father had brought these as gifts which she pretended to find boring, but Gail had read them, thought she'd never admit it to Mom. Residual images lingered. "One lover had bird claws and wings, the other a fish tail. I wondered how they did it."

He laughed and invoked hyperbolic Chinese menu language. "Between the phoenix and the dragon, we have our fill." Chicken and fish were too mundane, too obvious for those who knew.

Men, Gail had decided at the time, found her funny. Chinese ha-ha, American peculiar. But romantic, never.

Part Three

Hong Kong to Shanghai Shanghai Hong Kong
(or HKG–SHA RT)

20

On Thursday morning, Xavier called Gail and apologized profusely, offering work pressures as the reason for his silence. Her response, cool, was that the weekend was out because of Shanghai.

He said. "It's not out, I'll be there too. Where will you be staying?" and, hoping to improve things, added, "It's a happy coincidence, don't you think?"

"Don't know where yet. I'll call," and then she hurriedly rang off.

Merde, he'd blown it. Damn Jim. He was partly to blame with his dawn to dusk sessions, barely stopping to eat, occupying all of Tuesday and most of Wednesday as well.

Xavier had returned a day late because working with Jim in New York made him miss his flight, and there were no seats available till the next day. Jim, meanwhile, got to Hong Kong before him, and then had the temerity to be pissed off, saying, *You could have left, Xav, all you had to do was say so.* And so it went.

And then there was last night.

A man past fifty must accept certain things about himself. Too late for wholesale transformation, unless he is at odds with who he has been, and desires to renounce his former self. Xavier was not completely at odds. He hadn't been when he married Shelley, and he wasn't now that Gail had entered his life. So when he bumped into *Ma'mselle C'est Moi* Wednesday at twilight, high on something, arm in arm with a vivacious Latino girlfriend, both wanting to "play *à trois*," he did, too hard, till much too late, reveling in their young bodies, in their lascivious abandon, in their *je ne sais who gives a fuck*. Regression, perhaps, to life before Shelley, before Jim, before parents growing old, when money was enough for what he needed and the work day ended at five, in time for trysts and other pleasures. A visitation to another era, if only for a night, when Xavier Dopoulos was his own man, and made no apologies for whom he had chosen to be.

It was Friday morning. Xavier and Jim were at McDonalds.

Xavier glared at his partner. "You want me to move to Shanghai *right now*?"

Jim shrugged. "What's the big deal? You said Dahlia's place was available. And Ursula's back, so your daughter's okay, right?"

"But …"

"Xav, this Shanghai Industrial contract is big." For Jim, it was a footing into Shanghai's financial world in a way that Monkey International was not.

"You say that about everything. From my vantage point, they're all the same. And another thing, Jim, no more McDonalds."

Jim said, "The coffee's good," and took a sip. "Okay, what's the real issue, Xav?"

The real issue, although Xavier could hardly say so, was that he was fed up of Jim calling the shots and controlling his life. "Forget it," he said. "Bad week. Fill me in on the schedule."

Jim said, "You're looking ragged. Getting any exercise, and I don't mean the bedroom variety."

"Look, do you want me on this job or not?" Not given to threats, Xavier was upset that he had to speak this way, but there were limits to his patience.

Unperturbed, his partner continued. "Is it the money?"

"No, forget it." If there was one thing he would *not* do was to put himself into an even more compromised position. Too much of his income depended on Jim. Time for a change. Monkey International was his trump card. Also, he'd secure introductions through Gail, sooner or later.

Jim persisted. "You get a fair cut."

Xavier's tooth flared up in pain and he raised his voice. "I said, forget it."

"Alright, alright. Take it easy," and they resumed their discussion of the work at hand. Xavier pressed his cheek but it did not help the ache, which was sharper now than it had been before.

At the bar of the American Club that evening, Jim said, "Sorry about killing your weekend."

Gail sipped her wine. "Why? It's not your fault."

"It is, I'm afraid. I opened my big mouth and made some comment to Shanghai Industrial's CFO about the tight schedule. He went into a flap and pushed everything forward to Sunday. So you see," he said, sheepishly, "I'm to blame."

"It's just work. By the way, will I meet your associates? They'll both be in Shanghai, right?"

"You deal with me," he said, sharply. Then, softening. "Client privileges. Besides, they just do grunt work. You shouldn't have to concern yourself with them." He was thinking that it was good timing, pulling in Tony Dong when he did since Xav was becoming increasingly undependable. "Besides," he added, "my associates can't be told the whole story, not yet. Josh would have a coronary."

She laughed. "He doesn't stop, does he?"

"Not as long as I've known him." He drank up. "I have to meet my buddy tonight, but let's have dinner tomorrow in Shanghai. How's that?"

"Plans, I'm afraid."

"Oh, family in Shanghai by any chance?"

"Just a friend."

"Well," he signaled for the bill. "Don't want to keep Vince waiting."

She said, "Vince?" The double coincidence of names was unlikely. "Not da Luca, by any chance? Photographer?"

Two lights clicked simultaneously.

He said, "You're not *that* Gail Szeto?"

"Looks like I am, doesn't it?"

They looked at each other through the lens of history, revised.

The waiter handed Jim the bill. He signed without taking his eyes off her.

Gail said, "I recognized the name, you know. But Josh said Michigan."

"Undergrad," Jim said, still staring. "I was at Harvard Med School."

She didn't know whether to laugh or blush. "Say hi to Vince for me."

Jim took in all of her, unable as he was to stop staring, pissed off at his midlife memory abandoning him, and worse, his own *obtuseness!* Recovering, he said, "I'll tell him he wasn't wrong."

At home afterwards, Gail emailed Perry. *I met my blind date.*

In New York, Perry was glad it was Friday. She emailed back. *Explain?* Minutes later, her phone rang.

Gail said, "These things don't happen to me," and explained about the man who had said, *There's this friend in New York you ought to meet,* and how they missed connecting a couple of times, despite Vince's valiant efforts, once in Hong Kong and the other time, New York, work getting in the way for both parties.

Not one, but *two* men! This, Perry thought, was beyond envy, was ridiculously, outrageously sublime. First, though, the important details. "So, what's he like?"

"Intelligent."

"That's a start. Cute?" although what Perry wanted to ask was, *sexy,* but you didn't talk that way to Gail if you wanted answers, she suspected.

"He's ..." Cute didn't seem right somehow, although he was sort of handsome. "... not bad."

"That's *it,* 'not bad'? What? Is he missing parts?"

"Okay," she conceded, laughing, "He is reasonably attractive."

"What's it like, being around him?"

"Comfortable. He's straightforward, has a nice manner and isn't pushy. The funny thing is, he used to have this radio program in Boston, 'Psycho on Call.' It was hilarious. I used to listen to it quite often, never dreaming I'd meet him." She hesitated, then confessed, "I always thought he had a really nice voice."

"Gail, it's fate. You guys were meant to be."

"Don't be silly," she said, "It's just a coincidence."

"The point is, lady, *would* you go out with him?"

"Yes." It caught Gail off-guard, how easily that came out, and she added, quickly, "but of course I won't. We're working together. Besides, there's Xavier."

"Oh, *of course*." But Perry was cynical. Xavier, she thought, had better be really, *really* special, because she was sorely tempted to tell Gail to give this one a shot. *It takes a man to target the* right *man for a woman.* Peter, her husband, had come to her that way.

In an eighth-floor room of the Portman Shangri-La in Shanghai, Xavier propped himself up on a pillow. He admired Gail's naked back as she headed towards the bathroom. Things could be worse, he decided, than being with a woman who actually *preferred* room service and whose employer paid for luxury hotels.

He said, "I'm really sorry about not being in touch sooner. It won't happen again."

"I hope not," she said from the bathroom. An unexpected period caught her by surprise. The sheets were a mess. Unlike Jason, however, Xavier seemed undisturbed by this. She returned and dabbed the bedclothes with a damp towel.

Xavier waited through her ministrations, and refrained from saying how pointless they were. For someone so ... *lascivious* in bed, it was amazing how quickly she reverted to being fastidious. When she'd *finally* finished removing the tiny spots, and had settled back in, he asked, "Will you really move to New York?"

"It looks like it," she murmured, though she still found difficulty believing the move would happen.

"I have to relocate to Shanghai temporarily." He put his arm around her and sighed. "Actually, I'm already stuck here. My partner's being difficult about this new contract we've picked up. I mean, I could just as easily do it from Hong Kong."

She said, "Don't worry, it's a short flight for me to come visit."

He leaned his face into her shoulder. "I'm counting on you to do that. I will have a nice apartment for us to stay in, by the way.

It's in the old French concession and overlooks a park, the *Fu Xing Gong Yuan*."

They sat in silence for awhile.

Gail said, "Xavier, what do you want with me?"

Here it was, he thought, the relationship discussion he dreaded. Trying to keep things light, he kissed her cheek and said, "Whatever you want from me."

"I can help you with Kina. After all, it's not like Shelley …" She was trying to find out, to understand more about the whole situation. All he would tell her was that Shelley wouldn't be freed in the near future.

He evaded the unspoken request. "That's kind. She likes you, you know."

That made her happy. "She's a wonderful child," and then, "I so miss …"

He took her in his arms. She cried silently for a few minutes.

Drying her eyes, she said, "I'm sorry, it's just that …"

"Gail, don't apologize. You don't ever have to apologize for life."

She felt herself immersing, folding her body into his arms, wanting to climb inside him. His fingers forked through the hair, pushing it over her forehead and he kissed her hairline. It was curiously comforting, intimate, and just for awhile, the emptiness of all those long, empty nights fell away, disappeared, and she wasn't alone anymore. It almost didn't matter who Xavier was, whether or not love entered into this, or even if their relationship had a future. The present was a safe house for now.

He leaned over and they kissed. When she felt his hand roving over her stomach, down between her legs, the slight tug at her tampon string—*so slight, undemanding*—she ran her hand over his penis which was hard, readied, and rolled her thigh partly over his to say, *yes*. She did not resist when he pulled, climbed over her, entered.

Just shortly after midnight, she said, "You can't stay tonight."

He was just getting comfortable. "Why not?"

"Breakfast meeting."

"So why can't I stay?"

"Xavier, I try not to confuse business with pleasure."

He tickled her. Gail, to his surprise, could be childishly playful during and after sex. "Why not? I do."

She squirmed and remained serious. "That's your prerogative."

"Come on Gail, it's late. Be reasonable. We'll get up early and I'll leave so you can do your thing."

"My … colleague is on the same floor," she said, because "associate" might not carry as much weight. "It wouldn't look good if he saw you leaving my room." She and Jim had been on the same flight, although they hadn't realized till after arrival, and checked in at the same time that afternoon.

"But this is your private business. Why care?"

"Because it *is* private and I want to keep it that way."

Xavier knew when he'd lost. He began to get dressed. "Alright, *Ms.* Northeast Trust. But this is not a very nice way to make a living."

Three doors away from Gail's room, Jim's imagination was running riot. Turning in early was a mistake, and he was still kicking himself for missing the opportunity of talking to Gail onboard the flight, *especially* since there had been no one seated beside him. It was impossible to sleep.

For a man in crisis—particularly a cuckold—the salve of work is readily surpassed by a victory for the libido. The spiritual path at midlife is tempting, but it is a rare man who completes the ascent. Jim Fieldman, on the occasions he hunted, was a man who seldom took aim. When he fired, he did so with a deadly accuracy, and to date, had never missed.

21

Gail returned to Hong Kong Sunday night in a thoughtful mood. Xavier remained in Shanghai and they agreed she would fly up the following weekend. Both were privately relieved at this arrangement. Meanwhile, Jim returned to Hong Kong Monday night, which made Xavier even more determined to look for alternatives to this increasingly presumptuous partner.

From the round of meetings, it was clear to Gail that this "joint venture" was an easy way for Shanghai Industrial to list themselves on the New York Stock Exchange and eventually swallow up Northeast. They were the larger entity—a bank backed by the Central Government—and already had an international presence through other subsidiaries, principally in real estate. *Capital markets,* their CFO had said to Gail, isn't *that* the American dream? He was delighted that Gail was Shanghainese and spoke the dialect as well as Putonghua.

Of course, he had also said to Gail, in Shanghainese, at the end of their meeting, *have you ever thought of returning home?* Gail, who understood his meaning perfectly, replied, *Everyone considers it, perhaps some day.* And he replied, *The day, you will recall, ought to be seized. When your day dawns, call me.* The reference to Mao's "seize the day" had not been lost on Gail.

Jim, who had been standing right beside them, hadn't a clue.

On Monday afternoon, Gail went to an appointment with Chancellor & Chung, having spent the morning trying to decipher a muddled, half-finished report one of the analysts was working on the morning of the layoff.

John Haight took their meeting alone, and apologized for Benny's absence.

He said, "Family crisis. His son fell off a swing at school." Haight, who wasn't married, considered children a convenient, and annoying, excuse. "Thanks for coming the other evening," he said. "By the way, I see you know our friend Jim?"

Gail looked at her wrist. She'd forgotten to wear a watch. She was reminded, yet again, that she needed to purchase a replacement for the Seiko soon. "Yes, but not very well. Anyway, what do you have?"

"Yes," he shuffled through papers, trying to find the right ones. "Sorry, but Benny didn't give me much notice … here we are. Nothing to the probate, you just have to wait for the wheels of government bureaucracy. But on that Shanghai Commercial account, we pulled up the transactions. They were mostly what you guessed, automatic dividend deposits. However, there were two large withdrawals," and he pointed to the lines on the printout.

She frowned. One amount, in 1993 was for a million and the second in 1997 for five. The combined total was almost U.S.$750,000.

He continued, "The first withdrawal was in cash, if you can believe it. So we don't know who that went to. The second was telexed to a Bermuda bank account, so we also can't tell you the recipient. It's not your mother's account." He paused. "Did she have reason to pay out such large sums?"

"Not that I'm aware." The situation suddenly struck her as comical and she smiled. "For all I know, she might have offshore accounts with millions more we don't know about."

He laughed. It was nice to see her loosen up. "Your mother was an amazing woman."

"That she was. Well, I guess this will just have to remain a mystery, won't it? Thanks for checking," and she stood up to leave.

"Ms. Szeto, there's something else." He hesitated, knowing it was now or never, since she was really Benny's client. "This is strictly between us, but you know my brother, the one at Merrill? He knows your half brother."

Gail sat back down. "Does he?"

"They were at Yale together. In fact, to be totally honest, our family knows Gordie well. Your brother was the one who arranged the green card and set your mother up with us. My brother is a lawyer and handled your brother's case that time, when he was almost bankrupted by that shady partner of his."

"Really?" Then, "Why are you telling me this?"

"Benny didn't want me to, but … I thought you had the right to know. She *was* your mother, after all." He studied her cautiously. "You won't say …?"

She looked him in the eye. "No," and smiling, "client's privilege, right?"

Afterwards, John Haight breathed easier. Both Benny and his brother would *kill* him if they knew, but in John's book, unlike in theirs, there was more to life than law.

Mystery history!

Death can be a way of finding out who we are. Perhaps Number One *A-Yi* knew something, might tell her a little more. Gail found the cell phone number and rang.

"*Gay-lo!* I would love to have tea. You want me to come right now?"

Gail was taken aback my her enthusiasm. "Oh no, I meant, whenever it's convenient for you."

"For my *Daijeih's* girl, everything else can wait. I'll come now. Where do you want to meet?"

Within the hour, *A-Yi* arrived at Gail's home. Gail had protested at her coming such a distance, offering to pick her up or meet somewhere in town. But her offers were dismissed by the familiar, rasping tones.

A-Yi said, "So this is where *Daijeih* lived. *Gay-lo,* I'm so proud of you. Look at how far you've come, how much you've done for yourself," and she held both Gail's arms and squeezed them before sitting on the sofa.

"I saw the lawyers today," Gail said, "Maybe six months, and

I can give you the money Mom left."

"No hurry, no hurry." She accepted the tea Gail served. Her hand trembled.

"Are you cold? I can turn on the heater." For an elderly person, the damp, early spring afternoon might prove chilly, and Gail wanted her guest to be comfortable.

"No, no, too much trouble."

"No trouble, *A-Yi,* really," and Gail moved the space heater closer to the sofa.

A-Yi was trembling all over. She dabbed her lips with a tissue, imprinting on it a scarlet mouth. "*Gay-lo,* don't get angry at me."

Gail sat down next to her, startled. "Angry? Why would I be angry?"

"I need to confess something." She placed the teacup on the coffee table and looked as if she were about to cry.

The sensation—*I intimidate people*—worried Gail. Gently, she put an arm around her aunt. "*Wei*, my *A-Yi,* what's the matter?"

The possessive in that endearment touched the old woman. She began to sniffle. "Oh, this is all my fault. Now, I have no face left at all. *Gay-lo,* don't think badly of me, please. All because of my gambling. But this time, I'm going to do the right thing."

It transpired that she had been badly in debt about five years earlier, and had begged Gail's mother for a loan. "She gave me everything she was going to leave me, saying what good was holding onto it? So you see, that isn't my money. I don't have any right to claim it, but of course, you wouldn't have known."

Gail hugged the frail figure. *Sor muih, sor muih.* From years ago, her aunt's teasing voice, calling her a "silly girlie" because of something she said or did. That voice had been her lifeline more than once, the one person she could count on when she was upset with Mom. Unlike her mother, Number One *A-Yi* had never been a prostitute, only a dance hall girl. *Forgive your mother, Gay-lo, A-Yi* always told her. *She can't help herself. You'll understand some day,* and Gail would be a little consoled, knowing that somewhere, someone understood the pain in her heart about a mother who sold her body time and again.

"It's okay *A-Yi,*" she said, rocking her, "I don't care about the money. If you need it, you can have it. Mom wouldn't mind.

You know she wouldn't."

A-Yi dried her eyes. "No *Gay-lo,* you don't understand. She *would* mind. The money belongs to your brother."

"What?"

The old lady smiled, relieved by truth. Although she had never met Gordie or Mark, their history was no mystery to her. Using her lipstick mirror to dab at the smeared mascara, she said, "*Daijeih* said, 'The boy's been like a son to me. So you tell *Gay-lo* to give him something.' You can give however much you want. Your mother said the amount was entirely up to you." Then, cautiously. "You're not angry, are you? I know you don't like your brother."

Like a son.

"No," she said, "I'm not angry, but *A-Yi,* why didn't she say so in her will?"

A-Yi clicked, impatient, invoking the privilege of age. "*Ai-ya, Gay-lo,* silly girl. That would be the *gwailo* way! Surely I shouldn't have to tell you this. Your mother wasn't *gwai*. Naturally, she would only do things the *Chinese* way."

They talked till the sky turned dark.

Time, flying, as mysteries unraveled and rewound around Gail. The withdrawal in 1993 had obviously been for *A-Yi,* who knew about the rich Shanghainese lover, one who called Gail's mother whenever he needed a woman, and eventually supported her as his mistress. They had first met in the late sixties and developed an exclusive relationship during the years Gail lived in the U.S. *Daijeih said he was so old he could barely … you know, but no, never met him. Your mother always went to his place. He gave her money, taught her to trade stocks. Daijeih had a lucky streak. By the time he died, she had already made quite a lot and then his fortune made her rich. That was just before she moved in with you here. She kept it a secret, to be a gift for you one day,* "so that my daughter can be a lady of leisure," *Daijeih said.*

But the other withdrawal still baffled Gail.

That evening, she was fifteen minutes late to dinner with the old girls.

When she arrived, Barbara Chu was the only one at the

Banker's Club table for six, booked under another classmate's name. Tonight's gathering was a small one, comprising only the "money girls" as they called themselves, the ones in finance and banking.

Barbara said, "As usual, no one's on time, but how come you're late?"

"Lost track of time. It's nice not to arrive first for a change." Gail laughed.

Barbara was pleased to see her friend in a good mood. "How are things?"

"Getting better," and then she told Barbara about New York, the likelihood of moving, at which point three of the others arrived at the same time and Gail repeated her story, and told them of the incredible inheritance, *over four million U.S.* She allowed them to assume it was family money, saying, *Old folks really surprise you. I knew Mom had some investments, but had no idea it was so much.*

Among these women—private bankers, accountants, controllers—money was a matter of daily routine. Advice on money management slid around their words with ease. Everyone congratulated Gail on her good fortune; Barbara privately hoped her friend would take a break from work.

The conversation turned, as always, raucous—especially at dinners, less sedate than lunches—laughter-filled, as they launched into memories of school days, netball and basketball matches won and lost, girl guide excursions and campfires in the rain, Bunsen burners in science lab singeing the eyebrows off a hapless classmate.

"Shhhh, simmer down, *girls,*" loudly from Barbara as a man known to all of them approached their table.

Tang Kwok Po stopped beside Gail. "So many first class seats of power, all at one table. This could be dangerous."

Barbara, whose firm handled Kwok Po's company's accounting, said, "Then you better not come too close," and everyone laughed.

He said, "Well, good night ladies. Gail, good to see you. Let's do lunch."

Afterwards, someone asked. "His wife's a *gwaipo,* right? Gail, did they meet at Harvard?" Barbara gave her classmate a nasty look, but the woman paid no attention. But then, they all did tend to forget that Gail Szeto was part American, and thought of her as one of them, just another Chinese "old girl," her Caucasian blood invisible to them all.

Time, rewinding, as history caught up with Gail into the night.

After dinner, Barbara had given her a hug—out of the blue—and said, "Take care of yourself, okay? You've still got a long life ahead. Remember, you always were our best offense." In competition, their strategy had been simple. Barbara saved while Gail scored.

What, wondered Gail, would Kwok Po, Barbara and the other old girls say if she had announced to her respectable Hong Kong world, "You know, my mother was a prostitute and dance hall girl," stripping away the secrecy, the mystery of her not-real Chinese self?

Somewhere, music played.

I worry and wonder ...

The waltz drifted over Gail's memory, a half-remembered tune—the *A-Yi's* clacking *mahjeuk* tiles in her home; dresses and makeup strewn around their living room; Mom pouring endless glasses of tea for everyone; bowls of melon seeds, deftly snapped between the front teeth of these "girls," the shells discarded in piles of red, white and black—in a raucous scene not unlike the gathering of classmates from her elite girls' school.

In time to the melody, Connie Francis crooned, *I worry and wonder.*

Against the album's cherry pink background, Connie glanced over a half bare shoulder, smiling seductively. Gail had brought that cover to her mother's hairdresser the day she was ready to crop off *all that hair,* willing, at last, to accept her mother's suggestion, murmured frequently through Gail's teenage years, *my daughter, your hair's too thick to wear long.* Cut it like this, Gail told him, pointing to Connie's wavy, stylish do. *Good choice,* he said, *Just right for you.* She had watched the falling locks, unafraid, and emerged, as radiant and sleek as her mother had promised she would be.

Somewhere, the music played on.

Your lips may be near.

Gail was seven. *One two three, one two three. That's right. You've got it.*

They waltzed together, mother and daughter, singing, playing.

Mom, I like this song.

Everyone likes it. It's catchy.

Does Uncle Mark like it too?

I think so, but I'm not sure.

Why aren't you sure, Mom?

Gay-lo, Gay-lo, you ask too many questions! How can I answer them all? Maybe he does, maybe he doesn't. Who knows for sure how anyone else feels?

The child placed one hand over her heart, excited by the rhythm of the dance, by her mother's glamorous face and smile, by the touch of her mother's hand. Do you know how I feel? Do you? Do you?

Sometimes, sometimes, I do.

Connie sang, her voice fading away. *So please won't you tell?*

The child said, I love you, Mom.

Her mother bent down and kissed her cheek. *I know, Gay-lo. I know.*

When Xavier called, shortly past midnight, Gail was already asleep. She had left the cell phone on the dining room table instead of bringing it into the bedroom as was her habit, and did not hear the ring. It did however awaken Conchita, who came out of her room to answer it.

She said, "Do you want me to wake her? She doesn't mind."

"No, never mind," Xavier replied. "Let her sleep. The lady needs her rest," but he accepted Conchita's offer to leave a voicemail, which he did—a love message—to be retrieved by Gail in the morning.

22

Gail had just begun listening to Xavier's message when Jim called. She meant to save the message for later, but hit the wrong button by accident and erased it instead.

Jim said, "Long weekend, wasn't it?"

"Sure was."

He gave her a quick update. Gail tried to concentrate, but she kept hearing Xavier's voice—*bonjour my love*—before its abrupt end.

Jim was saying, "…and by the way, would you have dinner with me tonight?"

"Oh, I, oh sure, what time?"

Later, an email from Perry teased—*so did your blind date try to ask you out?*—and only then did her second morning error dawn upon Gail.

Time slipped away. Gail's focus shifted between work and personal affairs; the contents of those two, formerly neat compartments became messy with the balance of priorities. The CFO of Shanghai Industrial—*was Ms. Szeto free to meet their Hong Kong staff for dinner Friday?*—but then the message, *no, change that to next week, we'll reconfirm later.* In the afternoon she tried, in between the explosion of work, to reach Xavier on his cell but a recording said, each time, *This customer's line is currently not accepting calls,* and then she remembered, his line didn't work on the Mainland but that he said he would call with the number for Dahlia's. The number, she realized in frustration, was probably on the erased message, lost in memory.

Around four, Rick Hammond called.

Gail said, sharply, "Yes?"

"Is this a bad time?"

"Oh, sorry. Thought you were my boss."

"I have the information on that woman." What he had learned was minimal. The closest 'Shelley' was a Sha-lei Jamal, a former member of an extremist Islamic party, not Chinese, in jail for embezzling, and Gail knew, *wrong person*.

"Anyway, thanks for trying," she said.

"So mind if I ask a favor in return?"

"Well." Uncertainly. He *was* interested, and persistent.

"You can say no."

"Shoot."

"Would you let my colleague interview you? She's doing a piece on the crisis."

"Oh, that." She was relieved. "I'll have to clear it with PR, but yes, ask the writer to give me a ring."

"Okay, thanks." But afterwards Rick thought she sounded slightly disappointed. So maybe he *did* have a chance after all.

By evening, Gail was exhausted.

Between work and Xavier—it *was* about him, this unbearable turmoil, not to mention the physical aches of joints and crevices—she was off balance, precarious, stumbling on rocky ground over a new time terrain, intervals without a steady, predictable rhythm. It was like being on the dance floor at the Copacabana with Jason, the pair of them learning the samba, when a Hispanic couple had tried to show her the hip sway—*the dance is not only in the steps,* they said, *you must* feel *the beat, we call it the* "clave"—but it eluded her even though her feet found their way.

Conchita, who had been waiting for the right moment to speak, said, "We have to talk about my departure." Having eliminated "Ms. Szeto" and "ma'am," she was still not comfortable using Gail's first name, and consequently called her nothing.

Gail said, "Departure?"

"Easter's the twelfth, remember? That's this Sunday. I leave the day after tomorrow."

The look on Gail's face showed she'd completely forgotten.

Conchita said, "When do you move to New York?" The question was rhetorical. She was aware that Gail had made nothing resembling arrangements to move, and when she'd offered a couple of times to help, Gail responded *I can't deal with it right now.*

"I'm not … I don't know." Guiltily, she recalled Dick's last email, a not-so-gentle reminder that she *still* hadn't sent back her signed contract.

Conchita continued, "Bonny from downstairs will come do your cleaning once a week. I'll show her what to do tomorrow. And the temp agency is sending a secretary in the morning, so I can hand over the work."

"Oh." What Gail wanted to say, what she *felt*, was panic, that the last of all that was familiar in the person of Conchita was disappearing as well. She was in a state, unable to think straight, and simply said, "Thank you very much for making the arrangements."

That evening on the stairwell, Conchita told Bonny. "She hasn't changed, not really. Maybe a little less bad tempered, but as impersonal as ever. I hope the man she's seeing softens her up, *di ba?* She needs that, badly." She reflected a moment. "Do you suppose something real terrible happened to her when she was young?"

As Gail approached his table at the American Club bar, Jim Fieldman was surprised to discover that he was nervous. He heard his buddy Vince say, *She's your type,* adding with a laugh, *you're the leg man,* and he shifted his glance up towards her face.

Gail was thinking of Perry's comment, *Psychiatrist, huh? He'll mess with your head.* She had almost cancelled, but decided that, unlike with Rick Hammond, she must confront this, tell him about her involvement with someone else. As it was, too many loose ends dangled, threatening to tangle into an impossible knot.

They stood facing each other uncomfortably.

He spoke first. "We should sit."

That made her smile. "It's a start."

He began, "So …"

"Well," she said, simultaneously.

Gail said, "You first."

"Okay. What about we *don't* call this a date?"

"That's good. So what is it?"

"Getting acquainted. For all I know, you're seeing someone."

"I am, as a matter of fact."

"Besides," he continued, "we're working together, at least for the moment."

"My sentiments exactly."

"But is it okay if I call you socially? I promise I'll keep things casual. Just for drinks, a meal, maybe with a group, or Vince, since you know each other. You know, that kind of thing. I'd like us to be friends." He paused uncertainly, and then added. "I'm not involved with anyone, by the way. Just so you know."

Perhaps if Xavier had not relocated so abruptly to Shanghai, or if the previous encounter with Vince had not turned out well in the end, or if Jim were not "Psycho on Call," and hence a chapter in her happier history, she might have said, *It's probably not a good idea.* Gail's loyalties—to work, husband, family—and actions had always been clear cut, along the straight and narrow. Perhaps a lifetime of covering up her origins demanded an alternative, unmarred reality. But Conchita was wrong. Gail *had* changed; she was now less afraid of the crooked path.

Gail said, "I'd like that," and flashed him a smile, the same sort of smile that used to make *A-Yi* say, *Gay-lo, you can be such a sweet girl when you want to be.*

Jim was visibly relieved. "Good. Do you like Italian?"

And then they spoke of the merger, and Boston, and the pitfalls of Harvard for those, like themselves, who had arrived as older graduate students, returning to university after working; what it had been like to be able to attend only on scholarships and while working. They avoided intimate confessions. He said nothing about wife or family beyond giving a sketchy chronology; she did not speak of Jason or Gordie, except in brief, but told of the deaths of her mother and son because there was no reason to hide these facts of her present situation.

When they parted company at eleven, Gail no longer felt under as much pressure by the circumstances of their connection.

Jim was buoyed by her response to his question, casually slipped in between the pasta and pastry, in much the way she asked *Did you know Josh before Michigan,* Jim's question—*have you been seeing this guy long?* A month or so, she had told him. A month, he reassured himself, was barely a blink of the eye in eternity. As long as he was patient and his aim was true.

In New York at Northeast Trust's personnel section, Dick was trying to nail down Gail's exact start date. Her delaying tactics over the contract did not fool him. Perry Martin had just handed in her resignation, so she was now useless as an information source. Gail's *obvious* move would be to Shanghai Industrial, although Rabinowitz had shouted that one down when Dick suggested the possibility.

Give it another week, he told himself. After that, it would be time to say something, even at the risk of incurring his boss's wrath. If he was right, Gail might easily become *their* boss. The idea tickled him. Dick was himself months away from retirement. The future of Northeast Trust was now the comedy, and not the tragedy, of his life.

When it came to human resources, Dick considered Rabinowitz clueless. With that man, everything was *ready, fire,* and then, *aim.*

In Shanghai that night, Xavier strolled along the Bund. The air was warm but not stultifying. Along the water's edge, people thronged to catch a bit of the breeze. A young boy, who looked about nine years old, ran headlong into him, almost knocking him down. Xavier caught his balance, and was about to say something, but the boy laughed and ran away.

He moved out of this flow of humanity, and stopped to lean against the railing. Too many people, everywhere! Why was he in

Shanghai? Why was he killing himself to keep this contract, to remain here? He didn't even like the city. *Fuck Jim.*

Meanwhile, May wanted to move out of their New York loft because she had found a girlfriend to share an apartment. *I need my own room, Xav, with a door, know what I mean?*

In Oslo, the group was accusing Xavier of sabotaging its efforts, accusations based, said the spokeswoman, on what Shelley had told them about his lack of interest.

His cell phone shifted against his waist, a bulky reminder. He ought to call Gail, although he wondered why *she* hadn't returned his call. *Bonjour my love,* it began, *I whisper to your sleeping self, dreaming of when we'll lie together again. We'll speak at sunrise to make the day go well. I live to hear your* cri de coeur, *your love cry.*

The meetings yesterday with Shanghai Industrial were long and pointless. Xavier was especially annoyed by Tony Dong, the new "associate" Jim had sprung on him without warning. Besides, Shanghai Industrial cut into the time he could have spent on Monkey International. Jim had promised them a report by next Monday, which was unnecessarily early. With this job, Xavier was knowledgeable and management liked him. The client had been his contact, through Dahlia; his mistake was to involve Jim in the first place, whose contribution was too negligible to warrant his percentage. He needed to lock this one up for himself and cut Jim out of future contracts. It meant paying attention, something Xavier did well when he chose to.

The weekend loomed like a storm cloud—Gail—and then of course, he had to break his promise to Kina about Easter. She cried tonight when they spoke, and then pouted and threw a tantrum, which made Ursula threaten to leave again. Ursula had latched onto a friend of Marcel's and was feeling confident.

On top of everything, a prominent government minister had suddenly decided to back Shelley, exerting influence to get her released. The lawyer said, *May 1, guaranteed, you watch. It's now moved past politics to a compassionate family issue,* because the minister's goal was to reunite mother and child by "forgiving" Shelley.

Xavier wished he were in Paris.

It was almost spring. Crêpe vendors would be out and the painters along the quays, while girls and women perfumed the air, no longer repressed by the coats of winter. He and Kina would walk along the Seine where beautiful ladies played with her, charmed by her manners, while flirting with him. Life was redolent with romance. Even his parents aged more gracefully during a Parisian spring.

To be there with Kina! In their modest, but comfortably furnished *appartement* in the seventeenth *arrondisement,* the one asset he owned. It housed an eighteenth-century china cabinet that had belonged to his French grandmother, his wine collection and a few other personal treasures. Never rented to anyone, he preferred to leave it empty but ready for their return so that somewhere in the world, one space would always be home.

To be away from these other cities which he did not love, but in which he must live.

Momentarily lost in a safer place, Xavier was not aware of a young Chinese woman approaching, until she was virtually in front of him. She asked in hesitant English, "Excuse me, do you have the time?" smiling in a fetchingly sweet way.

"Of course." He told her the time in Mandarin.

She made as if to walk away, then stopped, glancing coyly back at him. *"Tu parles Français, peut-être?"*

Puzzled, he replied. *"Mais oui, pourquoi?"*

"Parce que ..." She spoke excitedly, stumbling over her French. *"Je veux pratiquer, si tu veux?"*

"Vous ... tu es étudiante?" Although he judged her to be thrity-ish, she still could be a "student" of languages. She wasn't a hooker, though. Had she been, he would have avoided the familiar "you."

This time, her smile was neither coy nor pretty, just easy, very easy. *"Quelquefois."*

Xavier glanced over the rest of her. Buxom, slightly plump, dressed in a too-tight skirt and sweater designed for curves. He was about to wish her well and walk away—guilt perhaps, even though he wasn't in love, *not* with Gail, but he tried to respect what they had, wanting, really, *not* to cheat on her—yet wouldn't, didn't most men yield, didn't most people need tensions pushed aside for awhile when opportunity arose?

He said, *"Café?"*

"Si tu veux," she replied, and offered him her hand.

The pain in his head dissolved. It suddenly didn't seem so bad being in Shanghai.

That night, he did not call Gail.

23

On Tuesday, around ten at night in Gramercy Park, Gordie vacuumed, dragging the machine furiously over the ground floor of his home, after which he did the same around the entire upstairs.

For the past week, he had been unable to get Gail off his mind.

He had wanted a sister, and suddenly, there she was, but he hadn't counted on such powerful emotions taking over, reducing him to tears, reawakening the way he felt when Mother died, an unendurable mourning jagged with fury. But after all that, Gail had taken off with some continental clown, barely a cut above Eurotrash, just when he thought she was ready to become a real Ashberry at last, a part of him. There were *dozens* of men he could introduce her to, far superior to Xavier.

What he really wanted was to be the big brother, to look out for her.

To obey Dad's final command. *Take care of Gail. I couldn't.*

Instead, he didn't even have the guts to tell her about the debt.

His latest Indonesian-Chinese deal was unraveling. What had possessed him to take that one on? Why this lust for risk? *When* would he learn?

As often as he had ragged on Mother about her charities, at least those funds helped people in need, as opposed to lining the pockets of corrupt officials as his cash was undoubtedly doing.

And how on earth could he pay back his sister's money if he couldn't bring himself to tell her he owed it?

Gordie switched off the vacuum and returned it to the hall closet. The dining table gleamed with a new coat of wax. There wasn't a streak left on the mirror above the sideboard. What dust remained floated in the air, and no longer lurked on shelves or skirting boards.

Time to face the music. He hit Gail's speed dial code.

Gail said, "I'm so glad you called. You won't believe what my mother's done," and she told him about the inheritance that was his. "I wanted to tell you right away, but it's been frantic."

She offered him half a million U.S., less than what he owed, but her generosity still stunned him. "Sis, I can't take that."

"But why not?" It was annoying how hard it was to *give* her mother's money away.

"It isn't right. Besides, you only have that woman's word for it. Surely your mother would have wanted you to benefit."

"Gordie, I couldn't spend all that if I lived to be a hundred and fifty. In fact, I was going to ask you about setting up a foundation or something. You used to help your mother with those, didn't you?" One of the old girls had suggested it, and the idea appealed to Gail.

The trouble with the women in his life and money, Gordie decided, was that they didn't know how to splurge. Mother had been the same, although she was better than Gail. He replied, "Yes, I did. Whatever you need, I'll be glad to help."

They talked briefly and then Gail had to go. He did not mention the loan.

The truth was, Gordie couldn't, at least not yet, maybe even never.

Contrary to what everyone believed, Gordie had known about Gail since he was sixteen. He had half-guessed and charmed the story out of Jimmy Kho. To confirm it for himself, he followed her to school once, sneaking out early on a morning while his father was sleeping off a hangover.

Gail had emerged from the shop house at around seven and

walked quickly towards the end of her street to the corner of Prince Edward Road. As a girl, her resemblance to their father was uncanny, although over time, her features became more Chinese. She turned right—headed away from the airport which was on the south side across Prince Edward—and broke into a stride. Even at twelve she was a lanky, long-legged athlete. Back then, flyovers had not yet turned the road into a multi-lane, dual-level stretch of highways that converged into each other, and Gordie kept his distance so that she wouldn't see him and be scared.

As they crossed street after street, he glanced at the names flashing by, trying to remember them so that he could trace his way back. The Chinese transliterated ones were difficult—Nga Tsin Long, Hau Wong—but *Siji Sekh* had a real English name, Lion Rock, as did *Lyuhnhahp,* Junction. When she turned on Grampian, the scenery changed from older, shabbier blocks to something resembling a posh Connecticut suburb, except that the houses were much too close together. Gail slowed her pace around these, gazing at the homes, and he watched, intrigued by her behavior. She appeared to be studying them, memorizing their shapes, drinking in the tree-lined streets as if these led to paradise. This was Kowloon Tong, as he later learned, where the flight path prohibited high rises.

That morning, she stopped on Sau Chuk Yuen, and fingered a vine of morning glories creeping down the side of a wall. Realizing he was too close, Gordie stepped back, flattening himself against the solid gate of a house in the process. His sudden movement caused a clanging thud of body against metal. It startled Gail, and she looked back. Seeing nothing, she continued on her way. Gordie turned around at that point and did not follow her anymore.

That day, Gordie had made up his mind to study Chinese so that he could one day speak to this half sister of his in her own tongue. When he began his course in Mandarin at Yale, Mother had said, *but darling, why don't you learn a useful language, like French, perhaps? No one speaks Chinese.* The Flying Tigers, Mother said, had been *one of those silly things your father felt compelled to do,* why *I'll never know. He doesn't even like China.*

Talking to her brother put Gail in a good mood. The offer she had made of Mom's money was impulsive. She hadn't thought much about the amount at all, which was four times *A-Yi's* legacy and represented roughly twelve percent of the total inheritance. Money, like men, recently kept appearing out of nowhere. It made her want to be reckless, to do something wild, even foolhardy.

An idea struck her, and she thought about calling Rick for help. She shouldn't, she knew. He was *so* obliging though, and straightforward. Why couldn't she be attracted to someone like him? Was it because he just wasn't needy enough, like Xavier or even Jason?

In the background, Conchita was explaining to the temp what was what. The door buzzer sounded and Conchita said, Jim Fieldman, a name she had come to recognize, was on his way up. Gail quickly touched up her lipstick.

Jim stood by the door. "I hope you don't mind my dropping in unannounced, but I was on my way to town, and this is the office after all, even though it's your home, and I had some papers for you, so I thought it best to deliver them. Personally." He sounded like a car with bad brakes.

"Thanks. Come in." She took the papers and closed the door. "Can I offer you coffee, or tea?" Then, remembering his voice over Boston's airwaves, and the wise-and-not-so-wise cracks which were his signature, she added, "Don't you *dare* say it."

He relaxed and smiled. "I know I'm corny, but I'm not *that* bad." Then. "Thanks for last night. I enjoyed myself."

"Me too."

Each waited for the other to speak.

Gail said, "By the way, you wouldn't know how to trace the owner of an offshore bank account, would you? In Bermuda?" It was instinct, perhaps, or her new found license for recklessness that made her ask.

"Isn't that *your* specialty?"

"*Mr.* Fieldman, at Northeast Trust, we *securitize* assets. That doesn't mean we make a practice of ferreting them out."

He liked the laughter in her voice. "I know someone, but he can be expensive. It's not exactly standard, you know." He meant, not altogether kosher, but didn't want to insult her. "This is due diligence for …?"

"It's personal."

Now, Jim was intrigued. "Is it?"

She stopped short, wishing now she had not begun this, thinking it was ridiculous since what did it matter how her mother spent her money. "Look, forget it, I was just, I mean …" but she saw the hint of a tease in his smile, a dare almost, and she smiled back. "Isn't it always personal?"

Afterwards, she scolded herself, *bad girl, such provocative, unadulterated flirting*. But it wasn't hurting anyone, she reasoned, and it made her feel sexy, *strong*, and very much like a woman whom men would laugh with, and never, at.

A woman … like Mom. The idea, which once would have shocked Gail, didn't. Instead, she wondered what her mother would say about all these men around her now.

Gay-lo, I know more about men than you ever will.

The night her mother said that had been Gail's thirty-ninth birthday. She hadn't moved in with Gail yet, and insisted her daughter come visit to get a present. It was a pretence, Gail knew, because they didn't observe birthdays.

What her mother really wanted was to tell her, "My daughter, your husband is cheating on you."

At first, Gail thought she misheard. "Cheating, who?"

"Jason must have a mistress."

"That's absurd!"

"*Gay-lo,* trust me, I know men. I have a nose for these things, like sniffing out cum I'm not supposed to smell, understand? I know more about men than you ever will."

"You can't possibly know," she countered, "You have no proof. Your so-called instinct doesn't prove anything. How can you accuse him like that?"

Her mother sighed, "He does. *A-Yi* saw him with …" she paused, as if unwilling to say more. Then. "Listen to me *Gay-lo.* We … we girls you know, we know about certain places, the ones men go to? Not the kind of places you go."

Gail exploded, "I don't believe you!" and then she screamed words she never used. "Fuck you 'chicken woman.' Just because you can't find your own prick, you *deliberately* want to wreck my life!"

Her mother remained calm. "I'm telling you because I love you."

"You don't love me, you never have. You've never loved anyone. You're a selfish, self-centered, conniving *bitch!*"

Her mother admonished. "Daughter, your language. Don't be like me. You're an educated lady."

"And you're *definitely* no lady. No wonder my father wouldn't marry you." Then, her parting shot, drawing upon the coarse chatter she had heard as a girl, the very vulgarity she had left home to escape. She spat at Mom the ultimate, the worst, the most common, low-class insult of the streets—*fuck my mother's smelly cunt*—doubling the shame and hate by the possessive she used.

Gail had apologized the next day, thoroughly ashamed, but Mom seemed unconcerned, only saying, *you really must learn to control that temper of yours, you're not a child anymore*. Months later, when Jason confessed his affair, Gail wept in the arms of her mother. *Never mind, Fa-Loong* consoled, *he's just a man. Trust me, Gay-lo, there are always plenty of others.*

When Xavier called Gail later in the morning, having not heard from her, he was astonished that firstly, she had *erased* his message and then, hadn't even tried all that hard to get in touch.

"But why," he demanded, "didn't you email, or something?"

"I assumed you'd call."

"Gail, I've told you I have this impossible situation here. Work's ridiculous, there's all this pressure. It would have been *nice* if you'd taken some initiative and helped me out by making some attempt to communicate."

Unsympathetic, Gail said, "Xavier, we all work in ridiculous situations. Do you hear me complain?" She was tempted to add, *I don't recall you helping* me *out.*

Conchita, with Bonny's help, was bringing luggage out of her room and placing the bags next to the front door. Gail signaled her to wait, lip-synched "Xavier" and rolled her hand to indicate that he *did* go on.

He calmed down. "Okay, never mind, I forgive you, but you

must promise to make it up to me this weekend. You're still flying in Friday night, aren't you?"

"As of now, yes."

He softened and his voice undulated. "I'll look forward to it, especially when my tongue ..."

She interrupted. "Xavier, got to run. Conchita's leaving and I'm due for lunch with our consultant," and, adding a hurried "see you," she hung up, abruptly.

Conchita registered the conversation, as she had the presence of Jim Fieldman, who seemed to call a lot recently. Picking up her suitcases, she thanked Gail for the extra, surprise bonus—amazingly generous, three times what she expected—and wished her well. Gail actually gave her a hug at the door and then excused herself to run to lunch with Jim. As the lift door closed, Conchita said to Bonny. "I never thought I'd say this, but I wish I weren't leaving. After all those tough, terrible things, the Lord's going to let the lady have a little fun. And you know what? It's about time, man."

24

Shortly after speaking with Gail, Xavier's doorbell sounded. He was shocked to see the *étudiante*.

She held out a bag of oranges. *"Pour toi."*

"Why?" He did not take them and did not invite her in.

"Last night …" she began, in Chinese.

He interrupted, also in Chinese. "Was yesterday. We agreed."

She placed a hand on the door jamb and pretended to peer into the apartment. "Your wife is back?"

He raised his hand to block her vision. "That's not your business."

Before he could stop her, she slid her hand around his crotch and between his legs, dropping the oranges at his feet. "You know my number, so I expect your call," and left.

Unnerved, Xavier closed the door, leaving the bag outside.

It had been a mistake, bringing her to the apartment. Dahlia's womanly presence was evident. He had lied and said his wife was out of town.

As a rule, he did not bring women like her to where he stayed, unless it was a hotel room. For one thing, there was Kina; besides, he guarded home, wherever it might be for the moment, as a safe haven, a fortress. Last night, he had taken her to a café where she had been horribly, *delightfully* vulgar with her hands, and feet, under the table. So, he had been careless.

He assumed she would be another *Ma'mselle C'est Moi*—a free spirit, the bad girl who disappears once the party's over—but as soon as they were alone, she became intense, *needy, desperate,* saying how ugly and shameful she was while offering herself, asking, *Do you think I'm a nice girl,* and he stopped short of intercourse, which upset her. This, after first telling him at the café that she *preferred* married men.

Surely now she'd get the message and wouldn't dare come back.

Xavier tried to focus on work, but couldn't. The phone call with Gail peeved him. *What* was her problem? The mention of a consultant disturbed him. He must raise the possibility of doing work for her company, or at least, getting introductions, although given his current workload with Jim, he didn't see how he had the time.

In the evening, an odd email came through from Jim.

Any chance I could crash occasionally with you at Dahlia's? No big deal if not.

Now what? As project director, Jim's hotel expenses were covered by Shanghai Industrial. Xavier was the "local liaison." A wrinkle in the budget? Somehow, he couldn't imagine Jim making a personal request. He held off replying because it was simply too puzzling. Besides, this Shanghai Industrial job required an incredible amount of research, most of which he suspected they wouldn't use, setting him back on his other big project.

Xavier stayed up till two in the morning, trying to complete as much of the Monkey International report as possible. He *must* edge Jim out of this one. Their key director had said to him, only yesterday—*why do you work with the American anyway? He doesn't know a thing about China*—and mentioned a new contract, a big one, but made it clear that they didn't want Jim involved.

His tooth throbbed. Ignoring it, he focused on the pages of charts in the draft.

Thursday night, at eleven, Kina called, crying, saying that Auntie Ursula had hit her. Knowing his daughter, Xavier insisted on speaking to Ursula first, but all Kina would tell him was that she was "out."

"But *chérie,*" he demanded. "Where did she go at this hour?"

"I don't know, Papa. My face hurts."

"What time did she leave?"

"I don't know."

"Was she alone, or with Marcel or someone else?"

"I don't know."

"Come, Kina, you must know something."

He had stayed up late, worried sick, and told Kina to lock the door, leave a message for Ursula to call when she returned and to stop crying and go to bed. By two, Ursula hadn't called, so he did, but the phone rang and no one answered. His daughter could sleep through even a loud explosion, he knew, as she had once done in Paris when a gas main in their neighborhood blew up. He nodded off around three-thirty. At four, Ursula called. Her speech was slurred.

Xavier said, "Ursula, you've been drinking."

"So what?"

"There's a child you're responsible for. Doesn't that mean anything to you?"

"She's fine. Besides, she's *your* responsibility. If she means so much, you come back here and take care of her yourself. Better yet, bring her with you to Shanghai."

"Be reasonable, you know that's impossible. What about school, her meals? You know I'm inundated."

"Xav, don't give me all that crap. Listen, get back here tomorrow. I'm clearing out by four, and this time, I'm not coming back no matter what," and hung up. She would not answer even though Xavier rang back twice, letting the phone ring up to five minutes, if not longer, each time.

By noon on Friday, Ursula had disappeared. *Hold on,* he told Kina, *and don't open the door to anyone until Auntie Gail gets there,* and then he rang Gail's office number. She was out at lunch with an associate, the temp said as instructed, and promised she would get Ms. Szeto to return his call as soon as she returned. Not recognizing his name, she would not give out Gail's cell phone number.

While waiting, he called Kina every half hour. She assured him she was coloring pictures and being a good girl. Meanwhile, he rang the airlines, and booked the latest flight to Hong Kong that evening, just in case.

When Gail finally returned his call, it was almost three. He explained, apologizing repeatedly, and asked would she please get Kina and bring her along to Shanghai?

He needn't have apologized. Gail said, without hesitation. "I'll take care of everything, no problem," and he could almost hear her mind ticking through arrangements with a frightening efficiency. Her parting remark. "Xavier, *why* in heaven's name didn't you call me right away, on my mobile?"

Afterwards, Xavier cursed his stupidity when he realized Gail's cell phone number was stuck up on his computer all the time, right there, in front of his face.

In Hong Kong, as Gail crept her way in the queue to the Cross Harbor Tunnel, she thought it might be best to leave her car somewhere in Kowloon before catching their flight. The line of cars extended all the way to Wanchai North, and Gail wished she had taken the Eastern tunnel—a longer distance but less traffic—and wondered why she hadn't.

By the time she arrived at Xavier's place on Observatory Road, it was almost six-thirty, even though she'd set out shortly before four. Kina was poised and calm when she opened the door. Gail rang Xavier to say that there was no way they'd make it tonight, but that they'd be on a flight first thing in the morning.

His relief was palpable as Gail reassured him. "Please, don't worry anymore, she's in good hands." To Kina. "You can stay with me tonight, would you like that, darling?" in a mother's voice. And Xavier heard Kina's reply. "Oh yes, Auntie Gail, you're *so* very kind to me. I think I love you, do you love me too?" which both troubled and pleased him, a conflict of feelings he did not comprehend. He told Gail he would ring around nine.

"Don't," Gail started to say, as Kina put her hand on the door handle, but it was too late and the door opened to Gu Kwun's room.

Seeing the child sized bed, Kina smiled. "Is this room for me?"

Gail came over and stood in the doorway. "It belonged to Gu … to my little boy."

Kina walked in and looked into the wardrobe. It was empty. Seeing the toy box, she opened it. The only thing left in there was a half-completed model plane. "Where's your little boy? Can I play with him?"

Gail felt her throat tighten, and cleared it.

Kina said, "Has he gone away?"

"Yes, I'm afraid he has."

"Did he go very far?"

"Yes."

"When will he come back?"

Unable to hold back, Gail began to cry. Kina looked up at her curiously. She went to Gail and touched her hand. Closing the door, she led Gail back into the dining room.

Gail dried her eyes. "Are you hungry, sweetheart?"

"Oui."

"Would you like to come to the kitchen and help me prepare something?"

The child pulled out a chair and sat herself at the dining table. "Oh no, Auntie Gail. Papa does that."

"Well …" and Gail realized she was at a bit of a loss in Conchita's absence. Most of her life, Gail had rarely cooked. With her mother, food had been delivered, prepared, from neighborhood restaurants, which was one reason Gail chose to be a waitress when she first arrived in the States, so that meals were covered. During the early years of her marriage in Boston, Jason cooked, unwilling as he was to eat her attempts to make food, or they ordered take out. Once she returned to Hong Kong, she always had a domestic helper. Giving up on the first idea, she said, "Would you like me to take you to a restaurant?"

Kina said, "Is this a special day? Papa and I only eat in restaurants on special days."

"I suppose it is. Come on, let's go."

In the car, Kina chattered nonstop, talking about nothing in particular, slipping in and out of various languages, not all of which Gail recognized. She did this unconsciously, as if no single tongue was hers. As she spoke, she kicked the base of the glove compartment rhythmically.

Gail said, "Kina, stop that."

"Stop what, Auntie Gail?" She continued kicking.

"That kicking. You'll break something."

She did not stop. "What will I break?"

Gail said, "Stop it, *now*."

She persisted. "But why?"

"Because I told you to. Now stop before I spank you." She had had no compunction about spanking her son, who had been far more obedient than Kina.

At that, the girl burst into tears and undid her seat belt. They were on the highway. Kina tried to unlock her door, but the child lock resisted her efforts.

As soon as she could, Gail drove off the highway onto a side street and stopped the car. She was shaking. "Kina," she admonished sternly. "That was a bad thing to do. It's very dangerous. You must promise me never to do that again."

Kina was whimpering. She curled her body into a ball against the passenger door and refused to turn around.

Gail's voice rose. "Behave yourself."

The child put her hands over her ears and shrieked, in French. "Don't hit me, don't hit me," but Gail could not understand what she said. Eventually, Gail managed to calm her, and they went to the restaurant where Kina sulked and refused to speak or eat, no matter how much Gail coaxed. Gail did not lose her temper, ate quickly, and brought the child and her food home where Kina went into Gail's mother's room, climbed into bed and fell asleep without another word. Gail shut the door.

Five minutes later, at nine, Xavier called.

Gail said, "Oh Xavier, Kina is …" She was going to point out how undisciplined she was and suggest to Xavier some ways to improve her.

He didn't let her finish. "How's my girl doing? Can I talk to her?"

"She's sleeping. It's been exhausting."

"Poor baby, such a difficult day for her. You've been so kind about this, I can't begin to tell you how grateful I am. Kina adores you, you know. I'm sure you've been wonderful."

Gail had meant, exhausting for herself, not the child, but Xavier's gratitude mollified her. Besides, she didn't want him to think she could not handle Kina. She said, "It was terrible, what Ursula did."

"Ah, she's like that, not responsible like you."

"I always try … tried to be a good parent."

"You are." He stifled a yawn, worn out by the last few days. "But I'm sorry to ruin our weekend like this, my love."

"It's not your fault."

They talked briefly. Xavier explained, apologetically, that he would have to do some work while she was in Shanghai, and asked if she could stay a few more days. She could not, but told him she didn't mind about the work one bit.

Afterwards, Gail wondered, was it possible that Xavier was falling in love with her? He was willing to depend on her, and called her "my love," which he never had before. Surely, a first, tiny hint, and this pleased Gail, more than even she expected.

25

In the morning, Kina was cheerful, the night before seemingly obliterated from her consciousness. She asked for her dinner and Gail gave it to her, albeit reluctantly, because it upset her sense of order. The child ate it all, and was excited by the trip. On the way to the airport, through check-in, even at the lounge, she was obedient and quiet. Gail was impressed by her improved behavior and told Kina she was being a very good girl indeed, and that Dad would be proud of her. Kina corrected Gail. "Not 'Dad', *Papa*."

When they boarded the plane, Kina stopped at the entrance to business class. Gail had used her surplus mileage, which was considerable, to buy Kina's ticket.

Gail said, "Darling, our seats are over there." She pointed to the last row in the business class cabin. "Come now, we mustn't keep all the passengers waiting."

Kina pointed towards economy. "Papa and I sit there." She stared at Gail stubbornly, the certainty of her voice brooked no argument.

The flight attendant said to Gail, "Please, you're blocking the path. Could you take your seats?"

Kina broke loose suddenly and ran down to the back of the plane, twisting her way between people's legs to get past. Gail tried to go after her, but the line of passengers blocked the aisle. The flight attendant glared at Gail with a look that said,

Honestly, some parents have absolutely no control.

For the next ten minutes, Gail peered around the cabin in frustration, trying to enlist help from the flight attendants, but the confusion of boarding prevented this. Eventually, a Vietnamese woman came to the front, holding Kina's hand. They were talking in Mandarin and French. When Kina saw Gail's angry look, she hid behind the woman. However, she went to her seat without further protest.

The Vietnamese woman waved good bye to Kina, and then, turning to Gail, said to her in Chinese, keeping her voice low, "I just wanted to say how terribly sorry I am for you, to lose a husband that way. You must understand though, your daughter doesn't mean to be naughty. Surely you can appreciate how horrible it was for her, finding the body," and then, shuddering at the idea of the father being murdered, which Kina had described in graphic detail, she walked quickly away before Gail could say a word.

Kina appeared to be asleep when Gail returned to the seat, and did not open her eyes until the flight landed in Shanghai.

By the time they arrived at the apartment block, Gail was in the worst mood. Kina would not speak to her the entire trip, and refused to respond to Gail's scolding about not telling lies. The taxi driver had taken them the long way. Gail protested, repeating loudly, *Fu Xing Gong Yuan,* but the driver acted as if he didn't understand, even when she spoke Shanghainese.

Kina squealed with delight the minute she saw Xavier, who picked her up and kissed her. He leaned to kiss Gail as well but she jerked her head away.

He put his daughter down. "Can you let me talk to Auntie Gail alone?"

"Oui, Papa." And she took her bags into the room she knew would be hers and shut the door.

Xavier tried to embrace Gail, who resisted. "What happened?"

"We must talk seriously." She stalked towards the dining table and sat. The table top was covered with sections of the Monkey International report.

He remained standing. "What about?"

"Kina tells the most disgraceful lies," and she related the incident on the plane. To her horror, Xavier burst out laughing, doubling over. Restraining her temper, she said, "*What* are you laughing at? This is serious."

That made him laugh even harder and he could not speak for several more minutes. "Oh, Gail, you should see your face." He tried to stop himself, but another guffaw erupted. "I'm sorry," he said, finally calming down. "Okay, I'll be serious."

Gail was furious. "There isn't anything funny about this whatsoever."

"She's a child. She tells a few stories, I know, but you must admit it's remarkable, how she had the woman convinced." He chuckled, recalling another woman's face when he showed up after Kina had told the same tale, pretending she was traveling alone.

"How can you *allow* her to tell such macabre stories? It's hardly the way to raise a child."

"I should have thought," he said slowly, "that I'm the best judge of how to raise my own child?"

Gail stood her ground. "You're teaching her the wrong things, though."

"That's your opinion. I don't think making up a clever story is bad."

At that, Gail lost her temper. "But it's a lie!"

He glared. "Please Gail, is it necessary to shout? *You're* the one behaving like a child."

"How dare you! After everything I've done?"

Xavier did not respond. He went to Kina's door, knocked on it and said, loudly. "Come, *chérie,* we must go out."

Nervously, Gail said, "But where … you can't just …?"

He looked at her coldly. "I'm sorry to have given you so much trouble." He handed her a spare key. "In case you need to go out. We'll see you later."

Kina said, "*Zaijian,* Auntie Gail. Thank you very much for bringing me home."

Together, they left.

The shut door confounded Gail. How had she gotten everything so wrong? Her first instinct was to leave, to escape from the apartment, Shanghai, even Hong Kong, to get as far away from Xavier as possible.

She took in the apartment. It was a woman's space, that much was obvious. Another "roommate," perhaps? For the first time, since Xavier came into her life, Gail became truly worried about who he was and what kind of life he led.

Their relationship was all wrong.

Gordie's silence, the morning she returned from Xavier's, had been deafening.

What Xavier and Kina were, what they represented, was a return to the world of her childhood, where truth was slippery and life changed daily, depending on who was paying her mother that night.

She couldn't go back to all that.

Daijeih *had a good life, a long life. A-Yi's* words, from the funeral, echoed.

Number One *A-Yi,* the girl had asked, *Is my mother a smart woman?* Gail had been only a couple of years older than Kina at the time.

Her mother had looked especially nice that night. Her *cheongsam* smelled of fresh air and soap, having dried that afternoon out on the clothesline. Number One *A-Yi* had ironed the dress. The *A-Yi's* were always around, playing *mahjeuk,* sipping tea, gossiping. Mom lent all the women her clothes. Stockings and shoes littered their living room. They told *Gay-lo,* one day she'd go to America and find a rich Chinese to marry, perhaps a business owner, of a restaurant or laundry, although Mom scoffed at these. Oh no, my *Gay-lo* will marry a high class man, from a respectable family, because she's the smartest girl in the world. Then the *A-Yis* laughed their agreement until one or other of them, usually the youngest *A-Yis,* became sentimental, wishing they had clever daughters too, wishing their lives were as full as that of *Daijeih's.*

Number One *A-Yi* had exclaimed, *Silly melon niece!* What a question. Your mother is the most popular dancer. Do you know, every night, many men want her as a partner. Our bosses like that, and give her extra tea money. You're lucky to have such a clever mother.

But she can't read, can she? She says she's dumber than me.

You listen to me. Your mother hustles. She says, my *Gay-lo* has an American father so she must attend Maryknoll. How do you think you got in? One of her good customers is a police inspector who knows a priest who arranged it with the nuns. He made a big donation to the church—police inspectors have plenty of extra income of course—and even gave your mother money for your school uniforms and books, don't you know? No second-hand books for my *Gay-lo,* she says, only brand new ones. Remember the day we went to Swindon, the bookstore in Tsimshatsui, to buy them?

Yes! Mom took us to *yum-cha* at Highball.

That's right, and afterwards, we wrapped the books in chicken skin paper while your mother was working, remember? She insists your books will look as good as all the other pupils'.

She never has time for me, though. Even you have more, *A-Yi.*

Your mother works all the time *for* you, so don't you dare complain.

But she doesn't rest. She gets all tired and grumpy. Sometimes, she cries in the bathroom.

Don't worry, *Gay-lo,* she has a good life.

Then, *A-Yi,* when I grow up I'm going to dance like Mom and be the best one too, don't you know?

What! Don't you dare let your mother hear you say that! She'll think I gave you ideas and get angry at your *A-Yi.* You don't want her to be mad at me, do you?

Why should that upset her?

Oh, *neuih-neuih,* you're still too young to understand.

But I want a good life, like hers.

You'll have a good life, *Gay-lo.* You will. Better than all her dreams.

An hour later, Xavier and Kina returned. Gail was about to apologize, offering the excuse of fatigue compounded by a desire to do the right thing, but she stopped at the sight they presented.

Xavier looked awful and Kina was crying.

Kina said, "Please help me, Auntie Gail, something's wrong with Papa."

Xavier waved at his daughter to be quiet. "Don't pay any attention. It's just a toothache. Minor problem." But he was holding his hand to his mouth, cradling his left cheek, and was obviously in great pain.

Gail asked. "How long a problem?"

"I don't know, two months or so, maybe longer."

She wanted to exclaim, *two months!* but instead switched on her cell phone and called Barbara Chu to ask for the number of her cousin—*an American trained dentist if you ever have an emergency in Shanghai*—and Gail called him, mentioned Barbara and explained the situation. She was told to send her friend over right away. Telling Kina to wait, Gail brought Xavier down the lift and put him in a taxi. Before the taxi drove off, Xavier mumbled, "Thank you Gail, I don't know what I'd do without you right now."

Kina was in her room coloring pictures when Gail came up. Gail left her alone, feeling strangely like an intruder. At one point, Gail went to Kina's room to try to talk to her, but the child put a finger to her lips and wouldn't say a word.

The afternoon dragged.

By six that evening, Xavier had not returned. Kina emerged from her room, holding a picture.

Gail said, "Would you like something to eat?"

She replied. "No thank you. I want Papa to come home. Where is he?"

"He'll be home soon. I can make you something here. We don't have to go out."

"No. I don't want anything until Papa comes home."

Gail was about to insist—the child must be hungry—but afraid, suddenly, of upsetting her, kept quiet.

Kina came over and handed her a picture of a floral bouquet. Every blossom was half filled with a different color.

Gail looked at it. "You haven't finished."

"But Auntie Gail," she replied in a puzzled voice. "What more needs to be done?" She picked up Gail's bag, which was on the coffee table, and took out a pair of sunglasses. Giggling, she put it on, danced around, and said, "Look Auntie, I'm blind."

Gail smiled, pleased that Kina was being communicative. She hesitated, not sure whether or not to ask what was on her mind. Then, deciding she had to know, took advantage of the moment. "Sweetie, do you remember your mother?"

The girl didn't reply.

Gail glanced at the silent face buried under the sunglasses. "Kina, didn't you hear me?"

"I don't have a mother, Auntie Gail."

"Of course you do. She's just … away right now."

"You're wrong. Papa's my mother." Her voice held a fierce conviction.

The girl removed the glasses and handed the pair to Gail. "Here, Auntie, put them on. That way, you can be blind again."

At seven-fifteen, Xavier returned, exhausted. He fed Kina a bowl of soup. A little after eight, he put her to bed. She asked, again, if Auntie Gail was his girlfriend now. He smoothed her hair gently and replied, "Go to sleep."

Xavier was glad to be able to pay some attention to Gail at last. Handing her a glass of shiraz, he said. "You're a savior."

She examined his cheek. It was slightly swollen. "I'm just glad you're feeling better."

He tried to kiss her, and winced.

"Don't," she said. "You need to rest your mouth. Come, let's go to the bedroom so you can lie down." She led him by the hand.

Xavier lay on the bed. Gail sat beside him.

He said, "This has been a lousy visit. Hardly a romantic weekend."

She shrugged. "It's just life."

There was something refreshing, he thought, about a woman who didn't flinch from reality. He stared at the ceiling, choosing his words carefully. "Gail, I don't want to give you the wrong impression. About us, I mean."

She tasted the shiraz. It was rounded and pleasant, with a lingering hint of berries. "*Us*" did not have a melodic ring.

"Are you going to tell me something unpleasant?"

He reached for her waist. "I wouldn't do that. It's just that, well, you know my situation."

"Do you love your wife?"

"That's a difficult question to answer. All we have by now is longevity."

"That's honest." She was grateful he hadn't said yes, which was what she had expected. Her mother's pathetic refrain—*Of course your father loves his wife. They've been together so long, how can he help it? So I have to suffer*—had always struck Gail as sad and a little frightening.

He decided to level with her. "There's a possibility Shelley might be released soon."

"What do you intend to do?"

"I don't know yet." He widened his eyes, trying to fight the drowsiness brought on by the painkillers. "It's still only a possibility." His eyes drifted shut.

Gail put down her glass. It was still full. She slipped on her shoes and prepared to go out. "Get some sleep. It'll help."

He opened his eyes half way. "Don't leave me. Not yet. Wait till morning, please?" and reached for her hand.

Leaning over, she kissed his forehead. "Xavier, I'm starving. I have to get something to eat."

Standing at the entrance of the building, Gail considered the possible directions.

If she went straight ahead, there was a series of lively cafes and restaurants along the stone-paved street. A pattern of small squares dominated the street, as if it were meant only for pedestrians, even though cars drove over it. There was a modernity about the area unlike anything in Hong Kong. Past and present made friendly neighbors, a landscape where pre-war structures fitted easily with the new, the contemporary, the future.

If she turned left, the history of this former French Concession would assert itself. Red tiled roofs and brick faced structures lined the road. A beautiful building, full of dark wood and pillars, stood in the middle of that block.

To her right was the way to a main thoroughfare with its noisy traffic.

The sound of an overhead plane made Gail look up. The red glow of evening had already disappeared into darkness.

Connie's plaintive voice sang in her head. *I worry and wonder.* The rest of the melody and lyrics eluded Gail and she envied her brother's ear for music. *One two three*—something, something *may be near*—and then it vanished again.

Instead, *a lousy visit.* Xavier's voice drifted like a refrain, faintly heard—except that this song had no memory, no past, no history. Only the present, improvised clumsily, like a jazz soloist lost amid the changes of an unfamiliar piece. With nothing to cling to or point the way, there was no harmonic path leading towards the right chord, to musical resolution, to what musicians—if they're able to play their way back—call *home.*

There were ten thousand questions Gail had wanted to ask, but at this moment, under a Shanghai night sky, the need for answers seemed irrelevant.

Part Four

Hong Kong to New York

but sort of via Shanghai Paris

(or HKG–JFK OW OJ SHA CDG)

26

Gail left for Hong Kong Sunday evening, promising to fly back the next weekend. Their day went well, but circumstances made it impossible for any private time with Xavier. She returned home feeling slightly cheated, though she understood, and accepted, things as they were. The trouble with this lover was that investment did not yield enough return, and Gail's problem was that she did anticipate, remember and need his lovemaking.

On Monday morning, the temp did not show up. Only then did Gail realize she could have stayed on in Shanghai because it was Easter Monday, a local public holiday. She took it in stride at first, since the only holidays that mattered to Northeast Trust were when the New York Stock Exchange closed. But then, annoyance crept in. As long as she were the last local staff of the Asia division, why *shouldn't* she have the time off due to her?

She was in this mood of ambivalence when Kwok Po called.

He said, "Come with me for a swim. My wife's off somewhere in Thailand, Koh Samui, I think, and the weather's too nice to stay in the office. We can have lunch afterwards."

So, at eleven, Gail and Kwok Po were lounging by the pool at the American Club.

Kwok Po said, "What's all this talk about you moving to

New York? Everyone says you are. Are you?"

"I suppose I am." She sipped her lime soda. The bubbles made her burp.

"'Suppose' meaning what?"

"I am because my boss thinks I am, because I haven't said I'm not, but …"

He finished her sentence. "You don't need the money."

"No, it's not that. I'll *give* all my salary away if I must but the point is, I can't imagine what else to do if I don't work."

"You …" he paused. Rarely did he make comments on her personal life. "You could think about getting married again."

Gail was sipping her drink when he said this and burst out laughing, which made her choke. "Sorry," she said when she recovered. "That's just too funny."

He was piqued. Marriage did not strike him as a laughing matter. "Why?"

"Why on earth would I need to get married again?"

"People do, more than just a second time these days. Companionship. Love, maybe?"

"I don't make the same mistake twice. Besides, I already have a lover," and she told him about Xavier.

Later, when Gail was doing laps, Kwok Po reflected that he had never, ever imagined her with a European, especially a *married* man, although he wasn't sure what kind of man would be best for her. Her ex, a boy, really, more like a kid brother than a husband. What he *really* didn't understand, however, was why she seemed uninterested in working in Shanghai, given the opportunities, timing, who she was.

They were lunching by the pool when Jim Fieldman sighted her.

Jim said, "Hey there. I'll tell on you to Josh." He was also in swimming trunks.

"Not if I tell on you first." She made introductions.

The two men shook hands, sizing each other up.

Jim recognized him. "Not, by chance, Leyland-Tang, Colleen's husband?" When Kwok Po said yes, they chatted a bit more, and Jim made a mental note to send a business card, puzzling again over Gail, *She wasn't related to* that *Tang family, on the mother's side maybe, the Shanghai connection?* since he knew she was Shanghainese, but what preoccupied him, what was foremost in his psyche—not so anyone would notice—was his checking out the rest of her *really great body.*

After Jim walked away Gail said, "He was 'Psycho on Call,' when we were in Boston," but Kwok Po had no idea what she was talking about.

Before they parted company that day, Kwok Po did say, point blank, that she ought to be careful of *intimate strangers*—not that he was suggesting anything about Xavier—but a woman, correction, a *powerful* woman with money was definitely a target.

Men with money, Gail decided as she drove back home, worried too much about the money itself.

If Xavier wanted her money, as Kwok Po and Gordie thought—and even Perry had hinted—what *would* they all say if she simply gave it to him? Wouldn't that be funny? Besides, Xavier was not even remotely a problem. The conversations she had with everyone about the money, like the old girls, only left her more uncertain about its intrinsic value. A charity or foundation, a scholarship fund perhaps, all that was easy. But she personally wanted for nothing.

But Xavier *didn't* know about the size of the inheritance, because Gail hadn't told him.

The pressing question, the one she avoided even more than how she felt about Xavier, and Kina, was New York.

She pulled into her car park space underneath the building. Stepping into the flat that had been home these past six, almost seven, years, she asked herself, how much did remaining in Hong Kong matter now? A three-bedroom plus servant's quarters, high floor, partial sea view, paid for by a mortgage readily obtained on the strength of her then new job at Northeast Trust, Asia division. A salary in the top five percentile in Hong Kong; now the top three since her promotion.

In New York, what percentile sliver would her total net worth represent in America? The Ashberry connection opened doors. Even on her own, she could climb further up, move to a larger firm, go from there to any place on the planet. Shanghai would roll out a welcome greater than Hong Kong had; all she needed to do was seize her day. For the first time in her life, nothing stood in the way of ambition. Her responsibilities were only to herself.

Earlier, Kwok Po had told her. *Gail, you can afford time to do what you want, including nothing. Why settle for a relationship with no future? You have all the time in the world to fall in love. Isn't that what every woman wants? My wife always says so.*

No, it wasn't, Kwok Po was wrong. Perhaps he had never understood her at all. Work, with all its challenges, chaos, conflicts, compromises and comedies was what she wanted. Discipline created a rhythm for stress. Life at present was okay. Grief was abating. Sometimes, she even had fun.

Love? Well.

Gordie, singing, *We'll have Manhattan,* hit the speed dial.

As one deal unraveled, so did another come together. A yen contract reaped an unexpectedly large profit. The owner of the 1967 XKE, who wouldn't sell for the longest time, caved, and the mint condition Jaguar now sat in his garage. The gods were relenting.

When Gail answered, he was still singing. *The zoo.*

He said, "I'm coming to Hong Kong this weekend. Got to go to Shanghai. You around?"

It was Tuesday. Shanghai Industrial's CFO had just confirmed dinner with their Hong Kong operation Friday and a meeting Saturday morning. Gail knew her weekend with Xavier was already shot. She replied, "I'll be here. Come stay with me." It was the first time she had ever offered.

"Whoa," he said, "Steady there. That's a lot of Ashberry to take in all at once."

"Must be spring. These days, I even find *you* bearable. But seriously, why pay for a hotel? I've plenty of room."

"I never say no to a deal."

In Manhattan, the sun shone. Gordie decided it was a good day to go shopping. Perhaps he would actually get Gail that present. Firsts for everything. There was something he wanted to give her, an idea that had been ticking for awhile, but held off, afraid it was too much too soon. Right now, however, nothing seemed impossible.

It didn't dawn on him till much later that he'd forgotten to ask after Xavier.

Xavier was disappointed. "But Gail, can't you change your meeting?"

"It's difficult." She had told him it was a client, which was half true, since a suitor—which Shanghai Industrial was in this not entirely equal merger—got treated not unlike a client.

"Well then perhaps you could come Saturday afternoon and stay Monday?"

"I would have suggested that myself if it were possible. Besides, it's impossible now, because Gordie will be here and he's staying with me."

"Ah well, family comes first, I suppose," he said, but the sarcasm in his tone was unmistakable.

Gail became impatient. "Xavier, what's the problem? I'll be there next weekend."

"If something doesn't come up."

"Honestly. After all, it's not as if..." She stopped, mid- sentence.

"What?"

"Nothing. I have to go. Give my love to Kina."

Now, Xavier was pissed. Why was Gail always in such a hurry, and worse, so willing to drop him for work? Everything about her was intense and melodramatic. And why this attachment to her brother all of a sudden? Having claimed that she limited contact and even disliked Gordie, she seemed peculiarly intimate, spending the weekend together on Block Island, staying with him in New York and now having him as a guest in her place. Surely ... the hate-love pattern was suggestive, and it *was* only half blood ... Xavier quickly dismissed the idea. Gail was too strong-willed and moral to give into anything illicit.

The problem was, the problem continued to be, he wanted and didn't want Gail.

Good sex, yes, but that wasn't enough to cause this compulsion he felt to continue the pursuit. That was the reason, wasn't it, for *Ma'mselle C'est Moi* and the *étudiante?* He did not want to feel trapped into the relationship. Gail could be difficult, uncompromising, even selfish and demanding. It was her way or not at all, a little like it had been with Shelley.

He had to admit, though, that she could be tolerant when she wanted to be, and kind. Unlike Shelley, Gail liked sex, and children. But he didn't want to encourage too much of an attachment to his daughter. Yet sometimes, when he considered how little Shelley was a mother, he wondered, why not?

Still holding his cell phone, Xavier stood by the littered table top, contemplating, and did not see Kina creeping up behind him.

She grabbed his waist with both hands. "Tag, Papa, you're it!" she said.

Xavier jumped. "Kina," he shouted. "How many times do I have to tell you *not* to sneak around like that? You gave me a terrible fright."

His daughter tugged at his arm, turning her cheek towards him for a kiss. "Papa," she giggled. "I like it when you're scared."

On Gail's computer screen, Dick's email did not mince words.

Quit stalling, Gail. You're not playing fair.

She moved it to her action file and opened the next email which came from Perry's personal account.

Hey lady, my new ship wants to set up an Asian office in Hong Kong. Interested? Btw, Peter's making REAL LOUD noises about getting together again. Persey so misses him. Think I should do it? I'm starved (not food ;) How's the X man? Or is the other one getting into more than your head? Sorry, mine's in the gutter. Later.

Gail smiled. Perry would be a bonus in New York, even after she moved to Greenwich.

It was Wednesday, shortly after ten at night. In a few minutes, the phone would ring and Josh would blurt out his latest query. Neurotic and a pain, he did at least say exactly what he meant. Predictability in a boss was a good trait.

The empty apartment was restful. Conchita's departure left a strange void, but for the first time in years, Gail found solace in solitude.

Kina's overnight visit had been a revelation.

Her presence reminded Gail of everything she missed about

being a mother, and it was, at times, painful being around the girl. Playing the role, even temporarily, resuscitated grief, electrifying the tendons of a heart that perhaps would never heal. This child, however, was obviously spoilt—Gu Kwun had been an *angel* by comparison—but Gail's greater surprise was to discover how *little* she wanted to mother Kina, or possibly, any child ever again. No one, nothing, could ever replace who her son had been or the love she had to give him. Also, Kina was all about Xavier. The trouble with Xavier was his messy life, and she wasn't sure she wanted to look after it, cleaning up after his trail of chaos.

Josh rang, interrupting her thoughts.

He said, without preliminaries. "Would you live in Shanghai?"

"Why are you asking?"

"Come on, yes or no."

"Maybe."

"Gail …"

"Did Shanghai Industrial ask?"

"Fieldman did. He seems to think that would make the most sense for the merger."

And that was how and why Gail decided her immediate fate.

What she did *not* want, what she had never wanted, was *anyone* dictating her life's direction. Shanghai she could do anytime. She was a rare Chinese, without family ties or obligations either to hinder or help, with all the right visas—a Harvard MBA, a contact network for international finance, professional experience in America and Asia—and a greater bi-cultural and bi-lingual fluency than most Chinese, even those born to advantage, could ever acquire. Hadn't she earned, *through her own efforts,* the right to be a privileged Chinese? But to return to America, privileged, having paid more than the usual dues for the rights of citizenship, *was* the new experience. Her American face still felt foreign, despite her ability to negotiate the spacious skies.

Ngaahnggeng.

The split second for these thoughts sped past.

Gail said, "So does Fieldman want to make *me* your boss? Shanghai Industrial might like that. It's their long term game plan, you know. They've more or less told me."

There was an eternal, five-second silence. "Okay," he said,

"Scratch that one."

"Josh, in future, ask me, not Jim. He can't possibly know China the way I can. Besides," and here, she quickly improvised, "I was planning to move to Manhattan before the end of this month, since I have to be there last week of April anyway, for the announcement. To get a jump on things."

"You've *already* found a place to live? In New York?"

"My brother has a place, in Gramercy Park. I'll stay there till I've settled in."

"Gramercy? Really? Good gi-… good going. Thanks for the vote of confidence."

"Josh, I know when to play ball." Gail was tempted to add that she knew she could stand working at Northeast Trust, at least for the moment, whereas Shanghai Industrial was yet another typically dubious Chinese bank. But she didn't think her boss had either the patience, or temperament, for the joke.

Afterwards, Josh rubbed it in to Dick, saying, *I told you, she* is *one of us.* Dick was a little taken aback, but didn't really care. It was always easier to keep Josh happy, which he was as long as he could be right. What Dick puzzled over briefly afterwards was the brother. Nothing in Gail Szeto's personnel records indicated any relatives whatsoever, in New York or anywhere, certainly not after the deaths. But families were complicated these days, neither happy nor unhappy, and as unpredictable and mercurial as human resources.

27

Jim stopped by to see Gail at eight the next morning. "Hope this isn't too early," he said, knowing it wasn't. "I'm on my way to the airport. Got to be in Shanghai for the next two days. But I've got something for you, about investigating mystery Bermuda accounts."

"You do?"

"All my man said he'd likely come up with, assuming it's in the name of a business, which such accounts mostly are, would be maybe the country of registration."

"Oh thank you, you really shouldn't have. I didn't mean to put you to such trouble."

He smiled. "Anything to oblige."

She blushed. "Oh, I ..."

He found her embarrassment cute. "Mind me asking what this Bermuda account's about?"

"It's to do with my mother. Probate."

"Oh yeah?"

"Her financial affairs were a bit ... complicated."

"I think I understand," he said, which he felt he did, even though his discreet inquiries concerning Gail's background hadn't yielded much beyond her professional résumé. "Well, I best be going."

"One moment," she said, "What's this about moving me to Shanghai?"

"Oh, I …" It was his turn to blush. Josh had said, *No way, we want her in New York,* without further explanation, and Jim didn't think Gail knew. He laughed. "I guess that makes us even," he said.

"How so?"

"We can stop making each other uncomfortable. Deal?"

Now it was her turn to smile. "Deal."

Losing control, Jim decided, sometimes yielded unexpected results. From his standpoint, it seemed Gail would prefer working in Shanghai, which was the *only* reason for his suggestion. Well, perhaps not the only one. Handling Northeast Trust was easier the further from Josh he was. A problem, mixing business and friendship.

Josh, however, had unintentionally brought Gail closer to home for him.

In this mood, he arrived at Xavier's place in Shanghai.

Xavier had just fed Kina lunch, and sent her to her room when Jim arrived.

Jim took in the apartment. "Nice place." Then, as Kina's room door closed. "That's your daughter, I take it. What's she doing here?"

"Long story," and he explained.

It *was* long, as all his partner's explanations were, and convoluted. Jim half listened.

Xavier was saying, "… luckily, a lady friend was coming to Shanghai and brought her. I don't know what I'd have done otherwise."

It was amazing, Jim thought, how Xavier got women the world over to do his bidding. He said, "But the Monkey International report's okay, right? I've called them twice since Monday but they're not returning calls."

"It's all set." But that was a signal, Xavier knew, *This was it, Jim's out* and privately, he exulted. "But about this apartment, with Kina here, it's impossible for you to crash, I'm afraid."

"Oh, that." He had already forgotten. His only interest would have been if Gail had relocated. "Don't worry about it. But listen," and he told him about the merger, naming Northeast Trust, because, as he told Josh, he couldn't *not* tell at least his senior associate, since the Shanghai Industrial work couldn't be done properly without Xavier knowing.

Xavier listened. Watts clicked brightly; dominoes fell in rapid succession. He was mildly incredulous. "A merger. With Northeast Trust?"

"Why not? It's in the bag."

"I would have thought Shanghai Industrial would be acquiring, not merging."

"You don't know Northeast Trust. But listen, to change the subject, mind if I ask some advice?" He hesitated. "It's about this woman."

Xavier suppressed a smile. "The high priest falls?"

"Cut that out," he said, sharply. "Sorry, it's sensitive," and he proceeded to talk about finally meeting the thwarted blind date, without naming Gail specifically, but from Xavier's standpoint, there was no mistaking whom Jim meant. "So, my question is, how do you ask a client out? I mean, she's not really my contact, her boss is. But …"

Xavier said, as nonchalantly as possible, "The lady's interested, is she?"

"That's the other problem. She's already seeing someone, but it's a recent thing so I figure I have a shot."

"Ah," he said, "Double jeopardy. Jim, take your own advice. You don't mix business with pleasure, right?" And then he changed the subject.

Afterwards, Jim regretted saying anything about Gail—not that he was worried about indiscretion, his partner was good about keeping his mouth shut—but he didn't like having to admit to feeling vulnerable. His buddy Vince wasn't much help, offering only, *I just have this feeling about you guys.* However, Jim firmly believed that when in doubt, ask the expert. On the subject of women, Xavier was the best one he knew. Besides, he could *hardly* ask Josh.

Xavier did not have long to ponder this unexpected turn of events because right after Jim left, Monkey International's CEO called to say they *loved* his report, his strategic insights were exactly what they needed to help them get to the next level, and how would he like to come on as a long-term consultant, *provided,* he emphasized, *you get rid of that* gwailo *partner of yours, and,* he added, *an exclusive relationship, of course, no competitors or related industries.*

"Of course," Xavier said. They discussed money, a contract start date for September, so that he could clear through existing jobs with Jim—by June at the latest, he reckoned—and set himself up with a place in Shanghai.

His daughter, peeking through the crack of door she kept open, watched to see when her father would be done with his grown up concerns. As soon as she heard the click—*call over*—out she ran. "Camel ride, Papa. You *promised.*"

Xavier would not pick her up. "Aren't you getting too old for this? You're almost eight."

She pouted. "But you promised."

He led her to the dining table. "Now, sit Kina. We're going to have a grown up conversation."

Kina sat, unwillingly. Papa sounded really serious and she knew there was no getting around her father when he had that voice and look.

He sat next to her. "How would you like to go back to Paris?"

Her eyes widened with pleasure. "Do I get my room back?"

"Whenever I'm there." Seeing the start of tears, he rubbed her cheek with the back of a finger. "Boarding school, Kina. Your grandmother's arranged it."

Her voice trembled. "But *why* can't I stay with you?"

"Because I have to remain in Shanghai to work, because Auntie Ursula's left, because Kina, I simply *cannot* look after you all the time."

"Why can't I stay with Auntie Dahlia then?"

"Because you can't."

She frowned. "Auntie Gail?"

"Absolutely not."

Now, she burst into tears. Xavier watched, his heart hurting. He did not relent, allowing the tantrum to run its course.

Eventually, Kina stopped, and wiped her eyes with her hand. "Will you come to see me?"

"Better than that, we'll go to the beach with grandfather and grandmother this summer, like we did when you were five. Remember the villa we stayed at? You liked it."

She nodded. "The *whole* summer?"

"The whole summer," he promised.

Kina considered this a moment. Then. "Will Auntie Gail have to come?"

"Only if we invite her," he said and, opening his arms, scooped her into a hug. This was one promise, he knew, he wouldn't have to break.

Xavier made a call to the secretary he knew at Shanghai Industrial and found an excuse to drop Northeast Trust and Gail's name. *Yes, Ms. Szeto was one of the Americans they dealt with,* she confirmed, figuring he must be in the know. *Did he want an introduction, she'd be happy to arrange that either in Shanghai or Hong Kong?* He smiled to himself, remembering how emphatic Jim had been that Shanghai Industrial did not want him to have any contact with Northeast until after the announcement in two weeks. *A merger of equals.* How little Jim understood the ways of the Chinese and what made them tick. When it came to doing business with the new China, there would *only* be unequal treaties with the West for the foreseeable future.

Before the end of the day, Monkey International had sent a letter as promised, by messenger, confirming their understanding. Xavier was still euphoric. It was a large contract, the biggest he had landed on his own in several years.

The best part was that he could finally begin the break away from Jim.

That evening, he called Gail.

He said, "I've got some news."

"Must be infectious. Me too."

"Ladies first."

"Things have been accelerated at work. I'm moving to New York right after next weekend. When do you get back there?"

"Ah," he said. This was the day for change, apparently. "I won't be. I'm giving up the flats in New York and Hong Kong," and he explained about Shanghai, adding, "But the good news is, the board wants me to accompany them on regular trips to New York, as an interpreter and observer. They are eventually looking to list on one of the exchanges."

Silence followed.

Xavier wondered if this was the beginning of the end. The logistics daunted her, perhaps. The distance was not impossible but neither was it easy. He almost wanted to let things take their natural course, but then, the idea of *Jim* and Gail ... he said, quickly, "Have you ever been to the beaches on the south of France, my love?" Before the end of their conversation, Gail was already planning a vacation for the summer—she had a huge amount of unused vacation days—together with Xavier and Kina, a vacation, she assured him, that wouldn't cause any problem whatsoever, not with *this* boss, guaranteed.

After their meeting the next day with Shanghai Industrial, Xavier suggested it might not be a good thing for Jim to attend the Hong Kong meetings. "You should give the two companies a little time alone," he said, "They're still getting to know each other."

"Good point," Jim agreed.

Unable to resist, Xavier continued. "Besides, you're needed here, to lead their training sessions. From what some of the staff have said to me, they'd like it if you'd stay longer. You're the key person on this one. In fact, to make it easier on scheduling, you should think of spending, say, about two months here in Shanghai? June and July would be ideal."

Jim groaned. "It'll be sweltering," but he knew his partner was right, because Xavier's presence was helpful, but not critical. "By the way, thanks for letting me bend your ear yesterday, about the woman thing, I mean."

"Always glad to be of service," he said.

Walking home afterwards, Xavier was bemused. Sooner or later, Jim would have to know, both about the "someone" Gail was seeing and the Monkey International contract. Jim would be, firstly, upset, and then, raring for a fight. Not about the job though, beyond the few predictably snide remarks; Jim could take or leave that client, and Xavier could see perfectly well that Tony Dong was there to edge him out. Gail was another story. That was territory Xavier feared to tread, except as lightly as possible, out of the line of fire. Perhaps he ought to say something. As much as he liked besting Jim, this was below the belt in more ways than one.

The city rushed past him, its frenzy a blur of modernity. Everything changed, given time, but at this moment, Xavier felt in control. About Gail, he didn't mind seeing where things might go. A call from Shelley's lawyer this morning raised the possibility of divorce for the first time. Only a possibility, but the prospect of freedom was hopeful.

Whether or not Jim would ultimately win Gail away from him was not something about which Xavier bothered to speculate. He was sure of a couple of things however. When it came to people, Jim was altogether too enamored of pedigree. He imagined Jim trying to figure out Gail's background! Also, how *anyone* who could possibly refer to Gail as "cute," as Jim had … well, enough said.

But his real trump card was simple. Gail, he knew, was loyal, a one-man woman, and right now, *he* was the man. In matters of the heart, it was all a question of opportunity and timing.

Flying, Jim mused, was about keeping the mind airborne. Altitude sharpened vision, and in-flight time was one for regeneration. He made a note of this. Might be useful for a training module someday.

A productive trip. Tony Dong was working out, and Xavier seemed exceptionally on the ball. He did not relish the thought of spending that much time in Shanghai. Perhaps he could make a case for his continued stay in Hong Kong, which he preferred, on the grounds of cost. The free apartment at his disposal there meant the client didn't have to shell out for a hotel. But then he thought of Josh—Mr. *Why-can't-you-do-it-today what-do-you-mean-no-flights,* a statement, not a question—and knew that argument wouldn't stand.

His flight landed in Hong Kong. Outside Customs, he rang Josh, who would probably be frowning at the Nikkei and Hang Seng closes, now that dawn was breaking over New York.

"… so I won't take those meetings with Gail this weekend," Jim finished.

"Fine." Then, "How are things working out with you and Gail?"

Jim said, cautiously, "Sorry?"

"Working together okay?"

"Oh that, yeah."

Perhaps because of the long and short of cattle and corn, which Josh had called correctly that week, or his wife's face watching their son getting ready for his very first date last night, or the fact that he missed the squash games and chats with Jim, or because spring was more or less in the air … but Josh, for a change, was in the mood to talk.

Josh asked, "So what do you think of her now?"

Jim did not like the direction of this conversation. "Okay. Smart, like you said."

"I like her," Josh said, "She's a straight shooter. Can be really funny at times too," but his thoughts swung to her recent personal tragedies. *And divorced. So alone. Sad.*

"Yeah," Jim agreed, trying to sound casual. "She is kinda cute."

Josh paused, mind ticking. He had known Jim too long and too well to be easily fooled. Then, "Oh, so about the training this summer, what say I get Gail to go to Shanghai and sit in on a few sessions? She'll be good presence for us on their home turf. Takes a Chinese, you know. You'd be okay with that, right?"

Jim smiled. "Sounds good to me."

As morning unveiled daylight over Manhattan, Josh Rabinowitz scrolled through his market reports. Fieldman and Szeto. Szeto-Fieldman. *Cute.* Potential there. He made a mental note to have his wife seat those two together at their next dinner. In his universe, divorce was tiresome, and more importantly, messy, which got in the way of life. Not a good thing among the people he liked. If *he* ran the world, people would *stay* married to one person, like he did, or at least re-marry and get it right the second time, because at heart, Josh Rabinowitz was a family and marrying kind of man.

28

It was Saturday night, after dinner, and Gail and Gordie were hanging out in Gail's living room. She had taken him to a first-rate Chiu Chow restaurant, and ordered cold crab, salt water goose, crisp pea leaves with chicken, the dishes he loved, but had little opportunity to eat.

Gail said, "We could use each other's homes. That way, I wouldn't have to do anything with my apartment just yet." It was the very least she felt she could do. On arrival, her brother had presented her a gold lady Rolex as a gift, saying, *I think you need this.* The band was just the right size and fit perfectly on her wrist.

Gordie said, "You'd let me do that?"

"You're letting me live in the Gramercy townhouse."

He glanced around her flat. Sterile. No paintings, no music library, a handful of business books. Austere, functional furniture. Not the most convenient location without a car. Still, gift horse. He said, "It would make things easier for me."

That made her happy. There was something natural about Gordie being here, with her, as if they had always belonged together. It still caused havoc inside, but how could she properly know about matters of the heart? She had no map, no guide; she was only now beginning to understand what family might mean for her.

The radio, which had been on low, began playing "In the Mood", the classic Glenn Miller version. Gail turned up the volume. "Hey," she said, "Know how to jitterbug?"

"*You* dance?"

"I *am* my mother's daughter," and pulled him up off the sofa. "Come on."

He protested, "I don't dance much."

"Anyone can dance," and she swung her brother into motion. He was good, although not as good as Jason, who was exceptional. The familiar movements raced up Gail's feet into all of her—exhilarating, *fun*—a return to seasons past when she and Jason were happy together, before the cracks had appeared.

When the song was over, they both collapsed, laughing.

Gail said, "Hey, you dance pretty well."

"And you're brilliant. You wait. This fall, I'm taking you to all the functions, the ones for Mother's one hundred and one charities. There's dancing at some. I'll introduce you as the Chinese Ashberry. They'll *love* you. It'll be utterly scandalous."

"Sounds fun," she said, although she felt some trepidation. Around Gordie, though, life always felt like that and she was beginning to get used to it.

"Where do you get so much energy?" His breaths were sharp and short. Gail was breathing normally.

She laughed. "Good habits, discipline, no vices." Then. "Did *your* parents dance?"

"Sometimes. Dad liked to."

"I know." She became reflective. "My mother used to try learn the lyrics of songs she danced to, to improve her English. One time, I guess I must have been twelve or thirteen maybe, just old enough to think I knew everything about sex, when Mom asked in English, '*Gay-lo,* what means *in the mood?*' I laughed my head off at her. She got mad and snapped at me for making fun of her. Our father came by late that night, which was unusual. He generally took her out to eat and they went … well wherever it was they went. They quarreled—they did, you know, quite a lot, used to say the most *awful* things to each other—and then, just before he left, I heard him shout at her *You're a goddamned cock teaser, you're* never *in the mood except for everyone else* and slammed the door. It was possibly the only time I heard Mom cry, I mean truly *weep*, not just complain, over Dad."

Gordie said softly. "Ouch."

Love, *well.*

Gail did not sleep soundly that night. In the half-life of a fitful slumber, another song played, one her mother had tried to learn English from before giving it up as impossible to understand.

Whenever we kiss

I worry and wonder

From behind the closed door of her room, Gail heard her father laughing when Mom tried to sing it for him. *Doll, you're beautiful but you can't sing.*

Connie Francis crooned across Gail's memory, taking the piece of plaintive pop to its bridge.

It's a sad thing to realize
That you've a heart that never melts.
When we kiss do you close your eyes
Pretending that I'm someone else?

She woke up abruptly, and remembered. The last time she'd heard that song was because of the painter, her mother's friend.

A few months before Gail left for the States, the painter and Mom had an argument, a loud one, that woke her. It was late, around two or three in the morning. Her mother left. Gail lay in bed, listening. The man turned on the phonograph and played the song twice.

You must break the spell
This spell that I'm under
Your lips may be near
But—where—is—your— heart?

Then, he left. She didn't hear him in their home again after that.

Before Gordie took off for the airport on Sunday afternoon, Gail made them tea.

She handed him his cup. Gordie sipped the steaming *loong jeang*. Then, gazing at the delicate whiteness his face turned as green as the tea. Stunned, horrified, he held up the cup to the light. "What on earth … it *is* …" He leaned forward and picked up its mate, which was still empty. "Damn, these *are* the ones. But they were stolen, or lost, or something, I thought." He poured the tea back into the pot. "Gail, have you any idea what these are worth?"

"Mom gave …" She stopped. Her thirty-ninth birthday, the night she cursed out her mother. The present she had received indifferently, because she thought it was just an excuse for Mom to tell on Jason. *Have you ever seen anything like them before?*

"Didn't you know? Dad found them for her. They're wine cups, a couple of hundred years old, maybe older." He wiped the cup dry with his handkerchief, taking care not to soil the monogram, and held it against the light. "See the figure of the Buddha? It's engraved into the biscuit before the glaze goes on. Each one's hand potted."

Gail knelt next to Gordie, who was seated in the armchair, to take a closer look. He held up the other cup to a similar scrutiny, pointing at its see-through crane pattern.

He said, "Aren't they exquisite? *Blanc de Chine.* Eighteenth-century most likely, possibly earlier. You might have heard of this referred to as *foo yao* or *qian chi?* From Fujian province. They first appeared around the thirteenth or fourteenth centuries, as ceremonial vessels. This Buddha one is the much rarer of the two."

"I had no idea." She handled them delicately, gazing at their milky translucence. "And all this time, I thought that Mom could at least have gotten me a matching set of teacups!"

Gordie sat back and refolded his handkerchief. "They loved each other, you know," he said, abruptly, "Did she keep his letters?"

"You know about …?"

He rolled his eyes. "Who do you think *read* them to her?"

"But you couldn't possibly, I mean, you weren't around when she got them."

"Doll, of *course* not." It made him impatient that his sister could be so fucking literal. "Dad didn't know she couldn't read. She said she was too ashamed to tell him. But she kept the letters. After his death, when I started visiting, she asked me to read them to her. I'd read one each visit, in the order they were written, and she'd tell me what was going on between her and Dad around that time. Her memory was amazing. It was enough to make a grown man cry."

Like a son.

Gail sat back on her haunches and looked up at her brother. She clutched his hand to help herself up. "I think," she began, and then leaning forward, gave him a hug instead.

"Don't," he said, "Or I *am* going to start bawling again."

Flying, Gordie thought, was an escape from earth. From his window seat, he stared out at the city as the plane ascended off the strip of runway at Kai Tak. Hong Kong wouldn't feel the same taking off from the new airport after this one finally shut down in another couple of months.

As the plane found its cruising altitude, he leaned back. Leaving was always an advantage. There were simply too many memories down there.

After twenty-five years, what did it mean to have a sister at last? Everything about Gail regurgitated the past, making his heart shudder, crackle and snap at all the wrong moments. Did a man *need* this? Perhaps it was the fate of all people at middle age, that the past should be forced open for examination, or else.

Or else, what?

He still hadn't told Gail about her mother's loan.

In fairness, he had put his foot down and refused Gail's money. It wasn't like he needed it. His assets were worth easily seven times her inheritance, if not more. It wasn't like he ever *really* needed money, not even Fa-Loong's, which she called *My investment in your business*. But it was paying off. This venture, unlike the one that almost landed him on the wrong side of the law, might really have a future, enough so that he dared to tell Gail about his deals, even if he couldn't bring himself to say what he ought about the money.

And what about love, Gail had asked last night, and then slipped in, slyly, *Jimmy Kho's daughter, for instance?*

He evaded reply and she had said *and you think* I'm *secretive?*

The last time he had seen Jimmy, they talked about Dad.

Gordie could tell Jimmy was not a well man by then, and probably shouldn't have drunk scotch with him. It was, however, their ritual.

"We had good times together, Mark and I," Jimmy said, "When we were both Flying Tigers, we used to chase each other around in the sky. At night, we drank lots of whiskey, looked for girls. That kind of thing."

"What did you talk about mostly?"

"You." Jimmy held up his hand to prevent Gordie's interruption. "I know, I know, I always say that and you never believe me. Your father loved you, Gordie. He just wasn't good at showing it."

"You weren't like Dad, were you Jimmy? He chased women all his life."

Jimmy shrugged. "I gamble, Mark screwed around. We all have our vices."

Gordie said, "I guess." Then. "Did he love Mother?"

Jimmy didn't say anything for awhile and simply gazed at his dead friend's son. Finally, adopting an exaggerated American accent, he said, in a voice like Mark's. "Gordon *boy,* now just what kinda question is that for a son to ask?"

The flight attendant's voice interrupted. "Something to drink, sir?"

Gordie glanced up at the Chinese woman. "Scotch."

"On the rocks?"

He replied, "Is there any other way?" and watched her walk off. She was petite, like Rose, Jimmy's daughter. He stretched out his legs. All these Chinese women in his life were a mass of complications, Gail being the penultimate. *I've told you, she's married,* he had replied to Gail's query about Rose.

His sister's response had surprised him. *I know that, but does she know you like her? Have you ever told her?*

He changed the subject, unwilling to delve further with Gail. He wasn't ready. Also, he didn't want to admit she had something there, that he had been hopeful once, so hopeful when she had agreed to come to New York, ostensibly to work for him but really because of that Australian partner of his, her former boss. But he had believed in that hope, seeing her day after day, she far apart from her husband defying her unhappy marriage, and willing enough to party with him till dawn, a little wild and out of control, sexy and inviting ... and yet, nothing, at least not with him. *Of course* he hadn't told Rose, which was why she was still married to that excuse of a husband, while *still* having affairs with everyone except him.

What, indeed, about love?

Women, well.

Gail approached the next week, refreshed. She finally threw out the report left by the analyst, conceding it probably wasn't worth untangling, half finished as it was.

Her brother cheered her up, and she liked that as she told Xavier. What she didn't tell him was that she'd heard through the grapevine some news about Jason, that his wife had given birth to a baby, their first, a girl.

Send a gift, she told herself, to congratulate them. It might be a way to make amends. Being around Gordie made her remember why she'd fallen in love with Jason in the first place. The early days with her ex were different from these with Xavier. Jason had been the promise of a future she could count on, of family, the way Gordie was now.

In the end, Gail did not send anything. Jason's wife probably wouldn't appreciate it. Besides, you couldn't change the past. There were some things that were "sins so bad," as Conchita used to say of any badly done work, whether domestic or secretarial, that "not even the Lord in heaven should dare to forgive them."

29

It was just past noon on Friday. In Shanghai, Xavier and Kina entered the building and returned to their apartment. He was unnerved. They had run into the *étudiante* who had emerged from a neighborhood café just as they passed by. *You didn't tell me you had a daughter,* she said, and tried to prolong the conversation, but he brushed her off.

Kina asked. "Papa, who was that Auntie? Is she your Shanghai girlfriend?"

"No!" And then, seeing he had scared her, softened. "I'm sorry *chérie,* but you mustn't say things like that, especially around Auntie Gail. That was my ..." he groped for an explanation to satisfy her. "Student."

"*Ah oui, je comprends, Papa,*" and she went to her room. Papa knew an awful lot of Aunties, so perhaps some of them weren't his friends, but she wondered how exactly she was supposed to know.

Around five, Xavier said, "Kina, I need to go out for about half an hour and buy something for dinner. Can you be a good girl and stay here by yourself?"

"*Oui*, Papa."

"And what must you do?"

"I must let Auntie Gail in when she arrives, but no one else."

He planted his fingertips on her cheek in a pretend kiss and left.

Fifteen minutes later, the doorbell sounded. Kina opened the door on the chain. The *étudiante* asked, in Chinese. "Is your mother home? I brought a present for her," and held out a bag of oranges.

To the shock and horror of the *étudiante,* Kina burst into tears and said that her mother had been murdered in the bath tub and Papa was gone and would Auntie please, please help her. She unhooked the chain, reached for the woman's skirt, pulling at it with such force she caused a tiny rip. *The police,* Kina said in Chinese. *They promised to come but they're not here yet.* The woman wrenched Kina's hand off her and fled. She did not leave the oranges.

When Xavier got back, Kina said nothing. Gail arrived shortly after his return.

Later, Kina insisted that Auntie Gail come in and put her to bed along with Papa, refusing to go to sleep otherwise.

Xavier stepped out into the living room and asked Gail, adding, "Do you mind?"

"Not at all, I'd love to."

They went into Kina's room together where she was sitting up in bed.

Kina said in English. "First, Papa must kiss me, and then Auntie Gail, and then I have to tell Papa my story."

The adults complied. When Gail sat down to kiss her, Kina put her arms around her neck and said, "Are you Papa's special girlfriend?"

Gail laughed. "I think so."

"Then," the child continued, ignoring her father now that she had another ally, "you must come visit us often, and teach me many more new dances." Kissing Gail on the lips, she said, "I think I love you even more than Papa does."

Xavier exclaimed, "Kina!" and shook his head.

"Goodnight," Gail told her.

Kina said, "Now, you must go outside and close the door so I can tell Papa the story."

From the living room, Gail heard a burst of laughter from

Xavier, and then hushed voices.

In the bedroom, Xavier whispered, "But Kina, *why* did you do that?"

"I didn't like that Auntie, Papa. Besides, she's only your student, not a friend."

When he emerged minutes later, Xavier said, "My daughter can be a strangely honest child." He went to pour Gail another glass of wine, but she shook her head.

"I've had enough," she said, "What story did she tell you?"

"That's our secret." He poured himself a glass and led her to the bedroom.

Afterwards, Gail smoothed and rearranged the sheets. She sat up. "Xavier, why won't you tell me about yourself?"

He propped an arm under his head and was tempted to say, *Because you insist on fixing the sheets.* Instead, "But I do. You know about my family, all the drama about Shelley and Ursula. These things are intimate. I don't share them with everyone." He waited. Having told Gail earlier that Shelley might want a divorce, he thought that would avoid the kind of discussion he disliked.

"You have other secrets, don't you?"

"Doesn't everyone? Come, Gail, you've had more than most."

She studied her hands.

He saw that the nails looked improved. Taking hold of both her hands, he said, "Gail, my love, sometimes you're such an innocent. You're as bad as Kina."

"Why, because I've only had one lover before you, while you've had several? How many other women …?"

He interrupted, "That's every man's secret." He kissed her hands, feeling their shape—*exquisite*—imagining his father's sculptor's eyes lusting over such perfect specimens.

She said, "Jason used to tell me everything. That's how I knew he loved me. That is, until, well, you know."

"And you love him still?"

"Sometimes."

Xavier sat up and put an arm around her. Her shoulders curled, adjusting to his reach. Gently running his teeth and tongue around her neck, he whispered. "Here's *our* story, you have me to love now, for as long as necessary."

His tongue raised goose bumps on her skin. He moved his hand under the sheet, his fingers reaching for the crease at the top of her thigh, searching for *that* point. Pressing down, he felt the involuntary shudder, recognized the curl of her upper lip against her teeth. He kissed her before she could protest. She closed her eyes. He slid her down. As he edged himself over her, she whispered. "I love the cologne you use," forgetting for the moment that Xavier never used scent. Xavier heard her but what she said did not register.

On Saturday morning, Xavier took Gail and Kina to the interior garden. For a weekend, it was not extremely crowded. The air was remarkably clear for Shanghai.

Xavier said, "I've come here before just to sit. Shanghai modern is too much sometimes. Come, I want to show you my spot," and led them to a pagoda, constructed in the traditional style, the way everything in this tourist paradise had been reconstructed. "You have to take peace where you can before our globe shrinks away entirely."

Gail and Xavier sat on the stone bench with Kina between them.

Xavier said, "Kina, Auntie Gail will come with us to the beach this summer."

Kina frowned, then looked puzzled, and Xavier was afraid a tantrum might follow. He should have waited and told her alone, but to his surprise his daughter said, "Can she come the whole summer?"

Gail said, "I'll come for two weeks."

"No, Papa." Kina said, not looking at Gail. "You *must* let Auntie Gail stay the whole summer."

He said, "But she has to work. Auntie Gail has a very important job."

"*You* don't," the girl countered.

Gail smiled.

He said, "That's not the point."

"But *Papa*," and her voice became almost angry, "she's *not* your student."

"Kina! *Assez*."

The child pouted, and her features threatened to erupt. Gail smoothed her hair, and adjusted the pink ribbon barrette which was crooked. Kina turned to her. "Auntie Gail, when we're in France, will you dance with me so I can show *Grandpère* and *Grandmère* what I learned?" Then, folding her arms in exasperation, she added. "Papa doesn't dance properly, does he?"

Gail laughed. "If you like." It was true that Xavier had two left feet.

The girl pulled Gail down to her level. "I want to tell you a secret, but Papa can't listen. She frowned at Xavier and waved him away, then whispered in Gail's ear. "You mustn't speak to *Grandmère* in English. She doesn't like it. I think she doesn't always understand."

Xavier, meanwhile, hoped Kina wasn't saying anything more about the *étudiante*.

The day passed rapidly. The weather remained beautiful. Xavier was delighted at how well Kina seemed to take to Gail. Having invited Gail to the south of France, he had had a panic attack at the idea of her with all his family. Yet now, everything seemed fine.

When they exited the garden, Kina wanted to climb onto one of the stone lions, the matching guardian pair at the entrance. Gail lifted her up, and Xavier stepped back to watch. That was when he realized the lions were not identical. The one on the left was completely inclined in the same direction, its body and head turned left towards the other and its eyes downcast, its expression almost coy, but a lion nonetheless, fierce, prideful, capable of unconscionable savagery. The one on the right, however, was poised in an arrogant stance, its paws and body facing left, *away* from its partner as if readied to run if necessary. Only its head turned right, over its shoulder, the eyes staring at the other, a look of presumption rather than confidence.

On Sunday afternoon, Gail prepared to leave. Her airport car waited below.

Kina said goodbye, and then went to her room without being

asked. Papa would want to see Auntie Gail off alone, she knew, but she kept a tiny crack open to watch them.

Xavier said, "I won't need to go to New York, I'm afraid. May will take care of things."

"I suspected as much."

"I will have to go back to Hong Kong, though, to take care of the flat. Sometime in May," but he knew he was simply prolonging the time before her actual departure.

"I'll be gone," she said.

"I know." He could tell she was getting impatient. "When do we see each other next?"

Gail glanced at her new watch. Except for the brand and the cost, it could almost be her old Seiko. "Hard to say yet, but we'll work something out. One of us is bound to have to travel."

"Come, let me bring your bags down."

"I'd rather say goodbye here. It's more private." She leaned forward and kissed him, her body closing into his.

He clutched her, trying to will desire out of himself. A fear, that he might never feel her again, even as he told himself this was ridiculous. Her rangy, lanky body, that toned slenderness, left so little imprint. What her absence meant was a memory of order—*touch her here like this, there like that and eventually would come her bite on his shoulder or arm to stop the* cri de coeur, *Scream, he told her, but she wouldn't or couldn't*—an order that translated into life for him in a new way, that he should, that he *must* do this, or that, because these were *precisely* the right, the proper paths out of chaos. These paths required decisions, like Monkey International demanded, and if he dared to make the choice, he could go where he wanted instead of being forced to take the only road available. Gail's presence was a reminder that satisfaction, and even pleasure, could be derived from order.

Then she was gone, the front door closed, and all that remained was empty air. Xavier stood with his hand on the handle and did not move for several minutes.

Kina, from behind her door, pulled it shut as quietly as she could. This was not a good time, she suspected, to frighten Papa.

Flying, Xavier decided, was not the way to travel, and he was glad for his current reprieve. In particular, he was pleased not to have to return to New York in the near future. It meant more money to go to Europe, which was where he knew he belonged.

Once, when he was a boy, his parents had taken him by ship to Greece. It was the only time Xavier had ever traveled by sea. He could still recall the languor, the salt lingering on his tongue and skin, the rocking undulation that was so seductive.

Making love to Gail was like taking an ocean voyage. Impatient about everything else, she slowed down in one place, the bedroom, and never got bored. Even during the breaks, when her mind kick started, it was easy to distract her back into the next round, and the next. Xavier had never been with a woman who so luxuriated in the act itself. This was the one thing, whether or not he was willing to admit it, that possibly *might*—if he were to be so incautious—make him fall in love with the likes of Gail Szeto.

That, and the idea of Jim Fieldman, horny, hovering and *still* in the dark. It was almost enough to make a man delirious.

In Hong Kong, the sky slowly settled into darkness as night fell over Sunday.

Gail sat in her tub, enjoying a long, hot soak. Stretching out her hands, she inspected her nails. They were beginning to look respectable again, less intimidating in their ugliness. It was a relief to be home, to be away from Shanghai and Xavier's chaotic life. Even when things went well, an uncertain rhythm prevailed.

In the stillness of privacy, she finally felt clear about her future path, at least for the immediate future.

Her mother's voice broke through the silence. *Find a man who loves sex and food to keep you happy, but marry the one with money.*

Gail closed her eyes, slid underwater to wet her hair and sat back up. *I married my job, Mom.* Her eyes remained shut.

A job is not a man.

I can't do both. I'm not you.

But you're still a woman.

There're many ways to be a woman now.

Her mother did not respond. Gail glanced at the letter on

the shelf beside the tub. Surely Xavier proved she wasn't always *ngaam,* that she could occasionally surrender to another way of being, even if she must retreat to the sanctuary of self. Surely it was too much to give in entirely or pretend to the way her mother did.

The way her mother must.

Startled, she opened her eyes. Who was that? A cigarette voice coughed, rasped. The way your mother must. *"Silly melon," your mother loves you don't you know? Don't you know? Listen to your Number One* A-Yi, *she knows more than you think.*

Gail shook her head, sending a spray of water around the bathroom. A few drops splashed on the letter. She dried her hands on a towel, and, taking care not to get it any wetter, she slit open the envelope.

Mark Ashberry had written on one side of a single sheet of lined white paper. It was folded in half and inserted into a square blue envelope, the airmail variety, as if he meant to mail it but changed his mind. Christmas, 1956. He would have just turned forty-seven, only a year older than she was now.

She unfolded the sheet and read.

"I'm not very good at writing letters. You will probably have lived a whole lifetime before you read this, if you ever even see this letter. Someday, I might give this to your mother to pass along at an appropriate time.

"We met this past May. You wouldn't kiss me. I couldn't believe how cute you were, such a serious little four-year old. You have your mother's eyes. I wonder if you'll dance as well as she docs when you grow up?

"It's taken me all this time to accept your existence. Don't be mad at me about that. We, none of us, deliberately make the mistakes we've made, not that your mother is one. But there are other people in my life as well. Maybe you'll meet your brother one day. He's a boy who laughs and knows how to make folks happy.

"This is Christmas though. They call it a time for joy. These past seven months have been a worse torture for me than all the combat I saw at war. Your mother asks for something I am unable to give, but what rips me apart is how wrong what I will not do is to you. Know this, though, that if there had been no others to hurt, I would do the right thing, would have done it from the moment of your birth. But you are my daughter and I cannot deny you anymore, at least not in my heart.

"Today, it's snowing in Connecticut. Gordon (your brother) is all excited about his new model aircraft. I have no other present for you except this letter.

Love, Dad."

Gail refolded the letter and replaced it in the envelope. *Dad.* There was a peace in knowing, if not him, then at least the part of him that counted. The part of him that loved her mother enough to eventually accept his bastard child. Being right was less important than being able to love. If she could continue to believe in love in its myriad manifestations—for her own lost boy and the memory of her difficult mother, for Gordie, Jason, perhaps even for Xavier—the way Dad had in this brief note, she might find her way to another plane, one where pain was absent and not merely numbed.

She stood up in the tub. The water that dripped off her was still warm. Carefully, she placed the letter on a shelf, away from the damp. A fragrance seemed to waft past. *Old Spice,* Dad's scent. Recently, more than once, where? Xavier? But he didn't use either cologne or aftershave, or did he? Then, the memory byte vanished and she could not recall.

30

Flying, Gail knew, was the safest way to travel. Statistics do not lie about mortality rates of other forms of transport. Midway between Hong Kong and New York, she gazed at the cumulus skyscape from her aisle seat. On this flight, no one sat beside her and her view was unobstructed. Altitude could at times be more restful than sleep.

What means "in the mood?"

Xavier, every time, without fail. Yet how was it that she never minded leaving him behind, without worrying when they would meet again? What made her feel she knew him less the longer they were together? Why did she find herself not caring, or at least not worrying about who he was, what he really did, how his life would or would not fit with hers? With Jason she had been possessive, couldn't get enough of him, until she had swallowed and digested him completely. It was not a process that she wanted to repeat.

Gay-lo, what means?

Her mother, a true innocent, like Kina. The idea made Gail slightly sad, because there was no such thing as innocence, not really, only the absence of guilt.

Time to silence Mom's voice. Gordie was showing her how.

The week prior to her departure had flown by.

Late Sunday night, Gordie emailed. *Sis, I know this is asking a lot, but could I have the letters?* At first she wanted to say she needed to think about it, but decided, what's the difference now, and so replied right off *I'll bring them to New York for you.*

Dead voices spoke in their own tongues and her brother was clearly the better interpreter.

Gordie, meanwhile, fedexed her a spare key to the Gramercy townhouse on a ring with an inscribed silver label that read "Ashberry & Szeto, Unlimited."

Monday morning, Josh called at seven-thirty. *Private dinner, our place, a week Saturday, 8 p.m., to celebrate the merger.* Gail noted this on her calendar. That evening Dick's email said she must be doing something right. In twenty-five years with Northeast, *he* had never received an invite to Josh's home.

What baffled Gail though was her boss's directive: *Wear something nice, no suits,* since this was still business, not pleasure, as far as she was concerned. However, as long as she chose to work for Northeast Trust, she wouldn't bother questioning the ways of management over such a trivial detail.

What Josh had also said was, *My wife likes ladies in dresses at our parties,* because, he knew, a woman would go out of her way to impress another woman. To his wife he said, *Don't forget, tell Jim to take her home. He'll do it if you ask.*

Tuesday evening, over drinks at the American Club, Jim told Gail about his move to Shanghai. "It's temporary. I'll catch up with you properly when I get back to New York at the end of July. You must come to one of my summer parties up at the Cape in August," adding that of course, he would be there next week for the announcement as well as at Josh's dinner and around for most of the month of May. He was headed back to New York in the morning.

Gail liked her growing friendship with Jim, pleased that their awkward start—the whole thing still embarrassed her slightly—wasn't getting in the way, and most of all, that he seemed unconcerned. Sitting opposite him, relaxed, in contrast to their hurried coffees, breakfasts, lunches, calls and emails, she couldn't help thinking how good looking he was. How he was comfortably taller than her. How she always felt sexy around him, wanting to flirt a little, the way she had with Jason. How her hips deliberately shifted as she crossed and re-crossed her legs.

He offered dinner. She declined, feeling the pressure of closing down her life in Hong Kong, even if the move might only be temporary. He looked disappointed, which pleased her, so she was quick to say, *Rain check?* which went over well. But in bed that night, she was surprised to find that the teasing flirtation between them did not leave a strong, physical imprint, and she thought, Jim would not be as exciting, as sensual, or as generous a lover as Xavier. Why she couldn't say, other than to trust the way her body felt, but filed this thought away to take up with Perry, in person.

Jim also asked, that same evening, *So how's your friend, he's based in New York, right?* and was extremely pleased to learn of the upcoming distance between Gail and his mystery rival—not likely that journalist, he reckoned, having identified Rick Hammond—although the vacation planned for summer had a dangerous ring. *Meeting the parents in June,* he told his friend Vince once he was back in New York. *Pal,* Vince responded, *you'd better make your move quick or you're history.*

Late Tuesday night Xavier called, ecstatic, to say that Shelley confirmed she wanted a divorce. More importantly, she was making no claims on Kina. His parents, he added, were looking forward to meeting Gail. Flowers appeared the next morning. Gail's temp was impressed by the arrangement.

But in the midst of their phone conversation Gail suddenly panicked, and felt like backing out of France, except that she didn't know how to tell him since she couldn't really say why. Instead, she wondered aloud what she would say to his mother, who didn't like speaking English.

Xavier, sensing a problem—*her voice a dead giveaway*—ignored Jim's irritation over his trumped up excuse, left Kina with Dahlia's favorite lover in Shanghai, a responsible Auntie, and jumped on a flight to Hong Kong the very next afternoon. *Only for the night,* he told Gail apologetically, but by the time he left her Thursday morning, she was less guarded and more romantically inclined. It had been the right thing to do.

Over their farewell lunch at the Jockey Club Thursday, Kwok Po wondered aloud to Gail *Would you consider adopting?* His wife's latest charity project was an orphanage in China—*girls, naturally, what else?*—and in Gail's case, even as a single woman, adoption might not be a problem, given her background and position. Gail gave him a large check as a donation. The idea struck her as potentially of merit.

When they were ready to part, Kwok Po pecked her on the cheek, something he never did. *Not goodbye,* he said. *We'll get you back here, and to Shanghai, you wait and see. China needs Wonder Woman too, you know.*

Friday night, Barbara Chu gathered the old girls for dinner to send her off. Twenty showed up. Their raucous behavior drove all the other patrons out of their chosen venue, and Gail privately slipped the captain a large tip afterwards as compensation.

Barbara told her *we're starting a scholarship fund for our old school, so that's what you can do with some of your money.* Gail replied, *Better yet, I'll donate* and *serve on the board,* and Barbara was so very pleased that her old friend seemed to be finally recovering from the terrible experiences of these past few years, although what puzzled her was Gail mentioning her brother. In their—*good heavens, forty!*—years of knowing each other, Barbara had never heard mention of a *brother,* but then, *life's a thousand surprises, one after another, non-stop.*

On Saturday morning when she was scheduled to depart, the flat was clean.

Xavier called just before she left for the airport to wish her *bon voyage.* He said, “Gail, I know we’ve only known each other three months or so …”

“Not quite three,” she interrupted. “You didn’t ask me out till late February. Today’s only May 2.”

“Yes, yes, of course. You’re right.” He smiled. “Well, I know I haven’t been willing to talk about us, but things are different now, with Shelley I mean.”

“That they are.”

“Then let’s talk this summer.”

“I like the sound of that.” She paused. “Our summer’s lease.”

“*That* sounds almost romantic,” he said, but did not recognize the phrase.

“It does, doesn’t it,” she replied, then thought, *who said that* and recalled Jim, yesterday, when he called with an offer to help her look at apartments in New York, and she replied immediately *Yes please that’d be great,* adding that her brother Gordie, who was going to help, had to leave suddenly for Hong Kong and wouldn’t be around. It wasn’t quite true, the part about Gordie helping her, but she knew it was the right reason to give. She then asked if *summer’s lease* was a quotation from somewhere, but all he said was *Oh, just something about the month of May,* and smiled. Later, Gail had emailed Perry to say she wouldn’t need her help apartment hunting after all, adding, *Blind date’s a Prince Charming,* which only made Perry more sure than ever that she *must* talk Gail into dumping that Kevin character since clearly the right man was ready, waiting and available.

Gail took a final walk through the flat, making sure everything was turned off. On the wall of the bathroom was a black streak she hadn’t seen before. Wetting her finger, she wiped it. It smeared. An irritant, but she let it go.

Her bags stood by the front door. *Wallet, passport, keys.* Gordie was picking her up at JFK in his new Jag. It was the least he could do, he said, for family.

She bent to pick her bags up and stopped. All the room doors were open. She was about to go close them but changed her mind, leaving them the way they were. Air, she decided, would circulate better this way.

Acknowledgements

These "foreign skies" gave sanctuary to the writing:

The **Vermont Studio Center** of Johnson, Vermont, the **Anderson Center** of Red Wing, Minnesota and the **Jack Kerouac Project** of Orlando, Florida all showed faith in the early manuscript and gave me time and space as a resident writer.

Kulturhuset USF of Bergen, Norway, provided an artist's retreat, soundproofed solitude and the long light of summer, all of which were conducive to completing the first, real draft.

New Zealand, the country at the top of time, whose inhabitants graciously welcomed a stranger to their coast, allowed this book to end.

Meanwhile, ***South Park,*** that American thing flying around the world over cable lines and satellite beams, kept me strangely sane.

Thanks also to **Tom Jenks,** navigator-editor *par excellence,* who rescued and guided this solo flight safely on its path back to that landing strip sometimes known as home.

Excerpts of an earlier version have been published as follows: Chapter One in ***American Letters & Commentary,*** New York, Issue 17, 2005; Chapters Two & Three in ***International Literary Quarterly,*** London, Issue No. 4, August, 2008; Chapters One & Two in ***Biblio,*** New Delhi, October, 2008. Also, an earlier version of the novel-in-manuscript was shortlisted for the inaugural **Man Asian Literary Prize 2007.**

About the Author

XU XI (www.xuxiwriter.com) is author of seven books of fiction and essays, including *Evanescent Isles*, *Overleaf Hong Kong* and *The Unwalled City*. She is also editor of *Fifty-Fifty* and two other anthologies of Hong Kong writing in English.

Of reluctant fixed abode, she inhabits the flight path connecting New York, Hong Kong and the South Island of New Zealand. Lately, she has returned to her birth city, Hong Kong, to haunt the district of Tsimshatsui. For eighteen years, the author had a parallel career in international marketing until she surrendered to the writing life.

Xu Xi currently teaches at Vermont College of Fine Arts and is Writer-in-Residence at City University of Hong Kong, where she founded the first international MFA program that specializes in Asian writing in English.